GUARDIAN

Book One

By

A.L. Crouch

Dedicated to my warm and loving family: to my children who breathe inspiration into my life, to my mother who always gave me a soft place to land, and to my husband who makes me feel as though I can do anything. You all are my angels and my proof of heaven on earth.

Angel of God,
my guardian dear,
to whom God's love commits me here,
ever this day,
be at my side
to light and guard,
to rule and guide.

One

When I was ten, I thought I would live forever. It was a child's way of thinking, full of innocence and naïve optimism. Even as our car plummeted down the mountainside and came to a crunching halt, I didn't know it was over. Hope is a hard thing to kill.

There was no pain at first, only intense pressure that pinned me down and made it impossible to escape this new, twisted reality. The pelting of the rain roused me back to consciousness. I strained to see through the dust, smoke, and shadow. The night was starless and black.

When lightning flashed, I saw that the floor of the car was now above me. The vacant seat belts dangled to my right. The left side of the back seat came apart from the frame and now had me trapped under its immense weight. I could barely move my head. My arms and legs were pinned.

Screaming for my mom, I struggled to look up to where the front seats should be. Among the twisted and mangled metal, I spotted what was left of the passenger seat. It was now pulverized, entwined around the enormous pine tree that broke our fall. My throat tightened with panic as my eyes darted around the wreckage in search of movement.

The white-hot suddenness of the lightning ripped a cry from my throat. The answering thunder echoed off the tops of the blackened mountains around us. That's when I saw it. My mother's bloodied arm was spread across her seat. I followed the line of it to the outside of the car where I caught a glimpse of her blond hair, now soaked with crimson.

I screamed to her. No movement.

"Gary!" I cried, straining to see the driver's side of the car. "Gary, wake up. Please wake up. Mom needs help. Wake up!"

With the next flash, I saw that Gary's seat was still intact, though now suspended in the front of the car. His arms dangled from his seat above. I screamed to him again, a hoarse cry, and winced at the pounding in my head. A slight movement from Gary's hand gave me the motivation to scream louder, the hope to keep trying.

I stopped when I heard the footsteps. They sloshed against the sodden earth behind me as they approached our car. Relief washed over me. I struggled to take a deep breath.

"Help us, please!" I cried to our rescuer. "My mom isn't moving. She fell out of the car. I'm stuck. Help!"

I listened as the footsteps approached the right side of the car where my mother lay motionless. The shattered window on that side made it almost impossible to see. Another flash, a glimpse of denim. A hand, covered with a brown leather glove, stroked what I could see of my mother's blood drenched hair. There was so much blood. My mind refused to register its significance.

"Please. Is she alive? Help her . . . please!" I cried.

There was no answer, only footsteps. They slowly, purposely, retreated to the rear of the car and came up beside me on the left.

"Hello? Please, call the police! Get help," I panted, the reality of the situation setting in. I could see Mom in the background, still motionless and red.

As the footsteps approached my door and slowed, Gary moaned and brought his dangling hand to his head.

"Gary, wake up. Help is here!"

"Alex?" I heard him mumble.

Twisting my head as much as I could, I tried get a look at Gary's face. Before I could, the driver side door tore open with abrupt force. *Thank God*, I thought, *Gary is going to get out. He's going to get me out so we can help Mom.*

With the next flash of lightning, a gloved hand reached into the car for Gary. Before the brightness faded, light glistened off of a shiny object in its grasp. With the ensuing darkness came an eruption of thunder. Over the rolling clap I heard Gary shriek into the night. Frozen in confusion, I held my breath and waited for the next bolt of lightning to illuminate the scene.

When the next flash came, my eyes darted to the front of the car. I watched the gloved hand pull away from the driver's seat and struggled with my blurred vision to make out the shiny object clutched in its fist. The hand held a slender knife. The handle, crafted in the shape of a snake, curved around the palm. The blade now trickled with fresh blood. Gary's hands fell, lifeless, back to a dangle. They too were splattered with crimson. Then darkness.

Panic pulsed through me like a static charge. *Why was this happening? Was this real?* The footsteps came again. They moved to the door beside my head. The handle lifted.

I threw myself against the seat that trapped me until I could wiggle my left leg. Concentrating every bit of strength I had, I struggled to free it from the seat as the leather-covered hands worked the handle beside me. I thrashed about as much as I could, but it was no use.

The hands beat and tugged at my door, but it wouldn't open. Then footsteps again. They stalked back to the driver side of the car. I held my breath and tried to decipher their next move in the blackness, but all I could hear was the hammering of the rain against my upholstered prison.

When the world lit up again, I strained to take in my surroundings as fast as I could. Before I could focus, the blade flew at my face from the front seat. With a scream I turned my head away from the strike. The leathered hand jerked to a sudden halt, the console and rubble stopping the blade just short of my cheek. Then darkness again.

Struggling to breathe, I beat on the seat above me as the gloved hands struggled to get to me. It was all I could do, yet even at my young age, I knew it was useless.

It was then, amidst the panic, that I heard his velvet whisper against my ear. A familiar voice, separate from the horror surrounding me, called to me. With his words came the steady, strumming rhythm that always calmed my soul.

"I am with you, Alexandra. It will be okay," the whisper said. "I need you to sink further into your seat for me, okay? Quickly, as far inside as you can. That's good, Alexandra, just like that. It's almost over."

When the gloved hands reared back, instead of thrashing to get free, I sucked in all the breath in my body and squeezed further into the depths of the fallen seat. I wasn't able to get more than an inch further in when the hands came at me again, shoving harder against the wreckage to get at me. Sinking further and further into the crevice, I listened in stark terror as my attacker struggled and heaved against the remains of the front of the car. The blade scraped against the metal above me.

When I couldn't go any further, I closed my eyes and focused on the steady strumming that I had come to know so well. The sound of it always signaled his presence. I knew I wasn't alone. He was with me, and that thought comforted me even as the thrashing hands above came closer with each forward thrust.

In the distance, the sound of screaming jolted me from my focus. *No, not screams. Sirens!* The scraping and grunting stopped abruptly. My attacker heard them too. For a moment all I could hear was the gentle strumming and the wails of the sirens steadily approaching. They rose in pitch to match the screams I realized were coming from my own throat.

Another flash and the knife-wielding hand made a final, desperate attempt to reach me. It thrust forward with acute force. The biting sting on my forehead tore the remaining breath from my lungs and choked my screams. As I was once again plunged into darkness, the hands pulled back. I had no energy left to keep fighting, so I braced myself for the next jab. The world around me was fading in and out. I listened for the strumming . . . for him.

"It's over now, Alexandra. You're safe," the voice whispered.

The footsteps retreated. They moved quickly back the way they came. *Running. They were running away.* I was in too much shock to be relieved. My head burned and throbbed. The pain made it even harder to catch my breath. When the next flash of lightning came, the world appeared red and thick. Blinking back the moisture, I watched as blue and white flashing lights enveloped me.

Then I saw him.

His familiar face smiled reassuringly to me from the front of the car. I stared into his deep blue eyes. With the next soggy blink he was gone. The strumming was replaced with dozens of new footsteps, all running towards me. The fog in my head thickened, and I struggled to call out for help.

"Help me," I cried before the world was plunged into darkness one last time. "I think they're dead."

Two

"We're just descending. Nothing to worry about." The voice behind me startled me awake.

I rubbed my eyes as the past dissolved into a forgotten dream. The middle-aged man behind me gave my shoulder a pat and leaned back into his seat.

"Sorry," I said between the cracks in the seats. "I'm not a fan of flying. I try to remain unconscious for as much of it as possible."

Straightening my blouse, I wiped the sweat from my temple with the back of my sleeve. I must have called out in my sleep again. Looking out the window, I saw that we were maneuvering through an expanse of wispy cloud. It was impossible to gauge our distance from the ground.

"Well, your plan paid off. You missed one hell of a storm about 30 minutes ago. It shook me up a bit, and I fly all the time," the man behind me chuckled. "Mind if I join you?"

"Sure," I said, welcoming the distraction.

The man was pleasant looking enough, with the perfect splattering of gray in his sandy-blonde hair to categorize him as distinguished. It was his smile that stood out. It was brilliant, flashy, practiced.

"Thanks." He winked. "The kid behind me was practicing to be the next *Lord of the Dance* on the back of my chair."

"No problem."

When the captain announced our final descent into the Asheville Regional airport, I fumbled for my purse. I yanked a brush through my long, sleep disheveled hair and worked on calming the nerves. Within minutes we would be safe on the ground in Asheville, North Carolina. That realization panicked me more than the entire tumultuous flight.

"Is this your first time in Asheville?" the man asked. "Make sure you see the Biltmore."

Though I'd never been one for small talk, I was desperate for things to feel mundane and normal and less like the cataclysmic event my mind built this trip up to be. I needed to keep talking.

"Actually, I'm visiting family up in Saluda, about thirty-five miles away," I said.

"You're kidding." He chuckled and offered another practiced smile. "Believe it or not, that's exactly where I'm headed in the morning. I'm just meeting with a client here in Asheville today. Isn't that funny?"

"You must have family in Saluda then," I said, chancing another look out my window. "That's the only reason anyone ever goes there."

The plane descended below the blanket of downy cotton. Mountains, dappled with autumn color, peaked just beneath it. I'd forgotten how glorious they were, the enormity and majesty of them stimulating some childlike admiration buried deep within my core.

"Actually, I'm contracted out from Raleigh to do some renovations up there," the man answered. "Maybe we'll run into one another."

"Oh, I don't plan to stay long. Just taking care of some family business, and then I'm headed back to Chicago," I answered, turning to him.

The plane teetered to the right, throwing the view of the ground below and the airport into the windows across the aisle before straightening out again. We were going to be on the ground within minutes. Anxiety gripped my shoulders and threatened to hold me captive in my seat.

"So you're a contractor?" I asked shakily, giving the man my own forged smile. "What buildings are you renovating?"

"Let's see." He rubbed the scruff on his chin. "They want to add on to the gazebo on the main street, and the elementary school in Flat Rock wants us to expand their auditorium."

"Upward Elementary?" I asked, my pulse quickening.

"That's the one."

I'd thought about visiting my old school while I was in town, but now I doubted I would have the courage. It wasn't part of the itinerary that would get me back to Chicago in a hurry anyway.

When the plane touched down, the man offered me a rough hand and another flawless smile. "My name's Rick Brightman. I hope to see you around, even if your stay is brief."

"Alex Nolan," I said, taking his hand. "Saluda is a small town. It'll be hard to miss one another."

It was a struggle to keep my thoughts positive as I blew through the terminal to retrieve my single suitcase from the baggage claim. *The faster this was over with, the faster I was on a flight back,* I told myself over and over. Taking a moment to steady my nerves, I strolled out into the cool mountain air. The scent of crisp pines and wet earth filled my nostrils as I took in the emerald landscape that rolled in waves around me in all directions.

I scanned the curb for my ride. Instead of the standard police cruiser I was expecting, I spotted a sizeable Ford Explorer boasting the blue and white "Saluda Police Department" insignia. I ran my finger along the glossy finish, admiring the 17-inch chrome wheels and tan leather seats inside.

"You're going to have to sit in the back seat just like all the other criminals."

I spun around at the sound of the deep, booming voice.

"Uncle Sully!" I smiled, taking in the features of the man who for a short time had been my uncle, but whom I'd loved as a father for as long as I could remember.

A man I hadn't laid eyes on in fifteen years.

Six feet tall and heavy-set, he was broader than I remembered. His once medium-brown hair was now kissed with a tinge of white at his temples, making him look as authoritative as the silver badge he wore pinned to his crisply pressed uniform. His brooding, puppy dog eyes were the same though, save for a few delicate wrinkles around their edges. Those eyes now burned through me with shock and amazement. His stout jaw hung agape.

"My God in heaven, you look just like her," he whispered. "I mean . . . your hair is darker, but it's uncanny. You look just like she did before . . ."

I'd been told how much I resembled my mother. We had the same small stature, high cheek bones, and hazel eyes. My head, however, was adorned with a multitude of mousy brown hair, much unlike my mother's golden tresses. I could only assume I inherited that from my father, though I'd never cared enough to ask anyone who had met him. It was just now dawning on me how my resemblance to my mother might affect the people of Saluda. The people I left behind.

The tension wafted like a lingering odor, so I did what I always do in uncomfortable situations. I made a joke.

"Well, it's easy to look like her when you have her same eyes." I smiled sheepishly.

Sully let my words register a moment before breaking out into raucous laughter. Grabbing me up in a bear hug that threatened to crush my lungs, he rocked me back and forth. I clung to him a moment and allowed myself to feel genuinely happy to see him again after all these years.

"Ah, but that's all Alex wit for sure." He held me away from him, all smiles. "That was a terrible joke."

"I know, but it's all I had at the moment." I sighed. "It's great to see you, Sully."

"And it's great to finally see you too. It's been too long. Not that I haven't enjoyed the phone calls every now and then," he said, tossing my suitcase in the back seat. "It's great to finally have you back. Now, let's get you home."

I climbed into the passenger seat and marveled at the wood-grained dashboard and internal navigation system. I missed my car, a modest Accord, which was not as high tech as Sully's new ride. It was easier to fly than to drive from Chicago, but not having the means to escape at any given moment made me feel trapped.

"This is quite the upgrade from the squad car," I said.

Sully positioned himself behind the wheel.

"Yeah, well spend a decade and a half on the force, and they give you the good car," he winked. "Radio works pretty well up here too, which is an upgrade in itself, but all that's on the thing right now are those damned reports from that Fort Bragg shooting. Had to stop listening. It gets me all fired up."

The shooting was plastered on every television set in the airport as well. Something about a soldier turning on his own, but I didn't have the heart to listen.

"Once a grunt, always a grunt, huh?" I teased.

"Hooah!" Sully smirked, putting the truck into drive, and navigated us onto the highway.

We spent most of the trip to Saluda in comfortable silence, neither of us feeling pressured to make small talk. Sully was a brooder, and even though we weren't blood related, we shared that personality trait. He must have sensed that I needed to be alone with my thoughts.

Staring out the window, I was mesmerized by the kaleidoscope of fall colors that shifted in shade with every leaf. I'd forgotten just how many trees there were. Cascading from the hills and mountaintops, they formed an intricate patchwork quilt, which flanked the truck at every curve of the road.

The afternoon sun cast a golden hue upon the tips of the pines from where it lay nestled in the crevice of two tall peaks. Bright reds and purples adorned the oaks in a gown of the deepest velvet. The constant breeze that floated between each branch created a delicate sway. The dance was breathtaking.

My emotions waltzed too, bouncing from angst and dread to warm nostalgia. I spent most of my life trying to forget this place: the trees, the smells . . . the people. Yet, seeing it all again made it feel as though I'd never left. Maybe it never left me.

When the curves in the road tightened and the truck swayed right and left intermittently, I knew we were close to town.

Breathing in and out became my sole focus. Sully, who had been sneaking curious glances at me throughout the drive, offered a reassuring smile.

"So how are Dan and Maggie?" he asked, breaking the silence.

I ripped my eyes away from the window to look at him.

"Aunt Maggie is loving life now that Uncle Dan retired. They travel all over the place. I barely ever see them anymore."

"You still have that teaching job? I still can't believe you teach social studies of all things. You should be teaching music, like your mom did."

"I like teaching social studies, and I've got some good kids this semester. Music was Mom's thing . . ." I lowered my head, my thoughts darkening.

"You sure you don't want to stay with me and Gram tonight? We've got plenty of room. I'm sure she'd be awful glad to see you . . . in her way," Sully said, sensing my change in mood.

"I'm sure. The sooner I can deal with the house the better," I said, shaking my head. "And I don't know if I'm ready to see Gram just yet. It's been a long day. I think I'd rather take the night to get settled in first."

It was hard to explain the way I was feeling when I couldn't even figure it out for myself. I was desperate to keep the past in the past, yet some things I wished could be the same. Gram was one of those things.

"I understand. Just know the offer's open," Sully said.

"What if she doesn't know who I am?" I asked, a lump forming in my throat.

Sully sighed and patted my hand. "I know this is difficult for you, coming back here after all these years. I get it. I do. Take all the time you need. As far as Gram goes, she has her good days and bad. Hell, on a bad day she doesn't even know who I am any more. She called me Baxter the other day."

"Baxter?" I asked, brightening. "Who is that?"

Sully raised an eyebrow. "Baxter was the family beagle."

I covered my mouth to keep from laughing. One look at Sully, and I failed. "That's terrible!"

"Yeah, well, good days and bad. You never know what to expect with her disease. Things could be much worse, I'm just glad she's still with us. Even if she doesn't recognize you, Alex, a part of her knows. A part of her will always know."

"I know, and I've missed her so much," I said. "I promise I'll come over tomorrow."

"I'll hold you to that." Sully grinned, and I knew he would.

It wasn't that I didn't want to see the woman who'd been a grandmother to me even before she was legally so. Far from it. I was afraid that seeing her as she was now, her mind warped by Huntington's disease, would scar my memory of her.

Many childhood nights were spent at Sully's house where Gram taught me to make her famous oatmeal cookies. Tying on one of her aprons and helping to gather ingredients made up the fondest of my memories. My favorite part was always when Gram handed me the spatula to lick clean as we waited for the cookies to bake.

The whole town savored her cookies, but I was the only one privy to the secret ingredient. Keeping it to ourselves had been our little pact. I thought of those days often and wondered if Gram even remembered them, or if she ever thought about me at all.

Just miles from town, the road began to weave tighter along the narrow highway. The trees whipped past the window. In the spaces between their long trunks was a vast expanse of nothing, the ground below unseen. Holding onto Sully's hand, I sucked in a breath. He gave me a reassuring squeeze.

"Sorry," I said, trying to keep my voice cheerful. "I guess I'm not used to these mountain roads anymore."

"There's nothing to worry about. We're almost into town, and then it's smooth sailing from there," he said. Then a devilish grin twisted the corners of his mouth. "We could always sing the road trip song to get your mind off the road."

"Oh wow, I remember that song as clear as day. One Hundred Bottles of Pop on the Wall. Imagine my surprise when I found out what the real lyrics are," I said.

"Yeah, we censored it a bit. Had to come up with something to keep you happy on the way to the beach that one time. You were driving me and your mother nuts," Sully teased.

"I was six years old on a six-hour drive. And as I remember it, we had a pretty good time," I said.

"You lost your shorts in the ocean. One big wave and your butt was hanging out for all the world to see. Hysterical!"

"Whatever." I snorted. "You gave me your shirt to wear so it all worked out fine."

Sulley laughed and wiped his brow. "Your mother tied it around you at least 5 times and you were still drowning in it."

"You two laughed at me the rest of the day," I said, indignant. "You're still laughing."

"Hey, better us laughing at you than you being bare-assed and having strangers laughing at you all day."

"Har, har." I slugged him in the shoulder and turned my attention back to the window.

Sully's truck took to the curves of the road like a bobsled on an icy track. The height of it made it feel as if we were hovering, weightless, over the pavement. When we rounded the next curve, I noticed something large and white hovering just above the road. No, it wasn't hovering. It rested atop a jutting rock in the mountainside along the road. As we got closer, I stared at the cement statue of an angel, one like you would see in an elaborate garden or cemetery.

I leaned forward, taking in the ivory features and imperial face. Graceful arms cradled a dove as the angel's wings rose outstretched toward the heavens. Mesmerized by its beauty, I tried to remember if it had always been there. I was sure I would have remembered it. *How did it even get up there?*

When the truck passed by, my thoughts about the statue vaporized. The road straightened out, and the small town of Saluda, North Carolina, unfolded before us. Consisting of one main street adjacent to the Norfolk Southern Railway, the town's once colorful buildings had aged like prized antiques. The main street was surrounded by neighborhoods that weaved in and out of the narrow mountains around it.

Long forgotten memories flooded back as I shifted my gaze from building to building. The old bookstore, the general store, even the dilapidated diner was still there, untouched by the fingers of time. What had been a lifetime to me seemed but a midday slumber to this quiet mountain town.

Sully slowed the truck to a purr as we passed the town library and its large bay windows. Every season the town council recruited the talents of their citizens to create magical displays in those windows. The décor exhibited now consisted of an assortment of stunning fall colors. Leaves and gourds lay scattered about tables topped with cornucopias, which were filled to the brim with Indian corn and pine cones. Framing the window were hundreds of twinkling white lights. The council had outdone themselves. The Christmas display had always been my favorite. I caught myself looking forward to seeing it, but stopped. *Take care of business and get the hell out*, I remembered.

Sully pulled up to the Saluda police station, which was small and plain in contrast to the buildings surrounding it. Painted a bland eggshell white, the station's only color came from its forest green trim. Crooked vinyl blinds masked its large windows, adding to the nondescript aura. Were it not for the two blue and black squad cars parked across the street, the station might be missed altogether.

"Stay here. I've just got to run inside real quick," Sully said, hopping out of the truck.

I saluted him. "You got it, Chief."

As Sully walked in, I rolled down the window and stuck my head out. Filling my nostrils with the invigorating autumn breeze again, I let the vague sent of chimney smoke and wet grass stir some part of me that lay dormant somewhere deep within. When I opened my eyes, I spotted a man staring at me through the slats in the blinds of the station.

He was turned from his desk where he glared at me through the glass. The intensity of his stare made me uncomfortable. I grinned and gave the man a slight nod. He immediately turned away, no smile or nod in return. *Rude*, I thought as Sully emerged from the station toting a slender paper sack. He handed it to me through the window.

"Almost forgot my welcome back present," he said.

I pulled the sleek bottle of expensive Merlot from the paper bag.

"You are old enough to drink that, right? Figured you may need it to help you relax tonight and all." He positioned himself behind the wheel and brought the truck back to life with a roar.

"I love you, Uncle Sully," I said with a smile.

The drive to the house was a short one. The winding side road off of the main street was as unchanged as the rest of the town. A-framed roofs blended into the tree-tops exactly as I remembered them. I wondered if all the same owners still lived inside. Did their lives remain constant and undisturbed while my own had fractured and shattered into a thousand shards of glass? Those shards stabbed deeper into my heart as we pulled onto my old street.

"Does Mrs. Middleton still live next door? I wonder if she would mind if I ran through her flower bed once for old time's sake," I said, finding safety behind a shield of sarcasm and humor.

"Hell, you could probably get away with it. The woman's near eighty years old. She won't be chasing you with her hose now for sure." Sully winked at me, not buying my humor front. "It's not too late to change your mind about coming home with me you know. You don't have to stay here."

It was tempting. Now that we were here, I wanted nothing more than to run away. I wasn't sure I could face the memories inside my childhood home, but I knew that the sooner I dealt with business, the sooner I could escape back to the safety of denial and sublimation in Chicago.

"No, I'm okay. I want to do this. I have to," I finally answered.

After passing a row of tall hedges, the house came into view beneath the setting sun. The small, white, two-story home sat oddly cheerful atop the inclined drive. Time slowed as the truck climbed the driveway. The windshield framed my view, making it seem as though I were watching a home movie filmed a lifetime ago.

The first scene to play through my mind was of the hand-painted mailbox at the foot of the drive. I saw my mother laboring over each pink flower on its white-washed surface. She smiled down at me as I held up the tray of paints. I stared at her handiwork with admiration. The purple hand print that she let me contribute was still there, captured forever beside the flag. My mother's was next to it. I stared, unblinking, at it until it we passed by.

At the top of the drive, a glimpse of the porch brought on a new scene. I saw the two of us rocking in the porch swing on a humid summer night as we watched the fireflies dance to the sway of the warm breeze humming through the trees. I could see the "For Sale" sign leaning up against the railing, the big red letters across the top announcing the house had been sold. Mom kept it there for months, just so we could admire it.

When we came to a stop at the top of the drive, I saw that last overcast morning. The morning when I was escorted by Sully and all of our neighbors, their heads downcast, into my aunt and uncle's car. They waved to me from the porch as the car pulled away from the house that I would not see again in my childhood. The house that stood before me now, more than a decade and a half later.

"Just remember that whatever you decide to do with the house, I will support you. Now that you're twenty-five it's all yours. It's for you to decide. Take your time. The mortgage is paid up for the next few months. Just don't rush into a decision is all I ask. Now that you're back, I'd hate to lose you again," Sully said. "Just think about it."

I blinked back to the present and looked into Sully's beckoning face. I gave his hand a squeeze and feigned a smile. "Thanks Uncle Sully. I promise I'll take time to really think about it."

"Good." He smiled back. "Then let's get you settled in."

I took a deep breath and exhaled slowly. "Okay, I'm ready."

Sully retrieved my things from the back seat. I stood at the foot of the steps willing myself to go up them. My mother loved this house more than anything we ever owned. To her, it had represented our independence. It was the culmination of the many struggles she'd overcome. More importantly, it was the home that she always wanted for me. Now it was mine to decide what to do with.

I followed Sully up the steps as he fumbled with the keys. When he swung the door open I took in as much as I could at once. The warm beige carpet, the mahogany railing on the stairs, and the vaulted ceiling in the living room were exactly as I remembered. Sully set my stuff down at the foot of the stairs and opened all the vertical blinds, allowing the waning sunlight to fill the house.

"Now, I was able to furnish most of the house with what tenants have left behind over the years. You've got a bed in the master bedroom and a dresser. There's the couch here and some end tables. Kitchen's got a table as well. I'm working on getting a T.V.; though, you'd need a dish to get regular channels. I've got an extra DVD player at the house you could use for movies as least," Sully rambled, straightening the lampshades on each end table.

I heard only pieces of what he said. My gaze was fixed on the corner of the room where a glossy baby grand piano sat.

"Is that . . . ?" I asked pointing to it.

Sully stopped and gave a quick glance to the corner before he came to where I was standing.

"Yeah, it is. I brought it out of storage for you. I thought you might want to play some. It's just as much yours as the rest of the house. It belongs here as much as you do." He patted my shoulder and moved past me toward the kitchen.

I stared at the glossy, wood-grained instrument a moment more. My mother's piano was a part of her. Seeing it again was like seeing her ghost. Shaking the thought, I followed Sully into the kitchen where he was opening cupboards.

"I got you some basics to get you through a few days or until you get to the shop. I just put the wine in the fridge. You've got eggs, milk and bread in there too. Cups and plates are here in the cupboard, and there's forks and things in the drawers. I brought a radio over from my place. It's nothing fancy, but it works," he shrugged.

Looking around the kitchen, I remembered quiet breakfasts and playful lessons in the art of mac and cheese making. I recalled homework sessions and late night games of *Go Fish* with Gary after he and Mom got back from their honeymoon. The table was different, but the white cabinets and French toile back splash remained untouched by time.

"Thank you, Uncle Sully, you've done so much. I really can't thank you enough."

Sully smiled down at me. "It was the least I could do."

"I meant with you keeping up the house all these years. I know Mom would have appreciated it a lot."

"Yeah, well, we're family. Even before your mom married my little bro. Don't you ever forget that, Kiddo."

"I won't," I grinned back.

Sully closed the cabinets and went to the door.

"Well, I've got to get back to the station and check on some permits I've been waiting on. I can run into the diner on my way home and grab you a burger if you'd like."

I held the door for him, but I didn't want him to leave.

"No, I'm fine," I lied. "I've got plenty to eat here if I get hungry. Don't worry about me."

Sully hesitated. "You sure you're going to be alright? I mean, without a T.V. or anything?"

"Oh, I have better things than T.V. in mind for tonight. Big plans," I said. "I'm going to take an extra-long shower and then curl into bed with my book."

"Party animal." Sully winked, then gave me a quick kiss on the top of my head before walking to his truck.

"You have my number if you change your mind. I mean it. Call me if you need anything. I'll be by to pick you up around noon.

You can come back to the station with me and let me show you off some before we go back to my place to see Gram."

"Sounds great. Seriously, don't worry about me." I waved. "Thanks again for everything."

Sully started the truck and pulled back down the driveway.

"Family, remember?" He called out his window. "Call me if you need me. I'll see you tomorrow."

I watched as he pulled onto the street and waited until I could no longer hear the roar the truck's engine before I turned to face the empty house. With a sudden ache in my chest, I accepted that I was alone. I didn't want to go back inside, didn't want to face the onslaught of emotion waiting for me at every glance around each room. Then I remembered the wine, and I let out the breath I didn't realize I was holding. A new plan formed for the evening.

Back in the kitchen, I filled half my glass and shakily threw it back in one swallow. It went down smooth. I started to refill the glass, but thought of a better idea.

"Why bother?" I said, setting the glass in the sink.

Taking a swig from the bottle, I savored the cool liquid as it slid down my throat. The first waves of numbness hit while I was preparing a box of mac and cheese with a pot and spoon I found in one of the cupboards. I welcomed the wine-induced fog with open arms and let it carry away some of the tension. *This was a much better plan*, I told myself, making a mental note to pick up more wine while I was in town tomorrow.

As I waited for the noodles to cook, I fiddled with the radio. I craved music, any kind, but all I could find within the static were news broadcasts and fuzz. Sully was right. There was nothing much on the radio besides the story from Fort Bragg.

I hated all things violent. Which meant I avoided the news. It served as nothing but a constant reminder of how broken and decayed the world around me was becoming. I knew that well enough from my own experience.

However, I needed a distraction, and the voices coming across the station were all I had. So I let it play and sat down to eat.

More wine made it into my mouth than food, and soon the fuzzy radio's words ran together in my mind.

". . . early in the morning Thursday when the shooter opened fire on his own regiment as they gathered for morning PT," the newscaster said, "killing an officer and two soldiers. A dozen others are reported wounded. Many more lives may have been lost if it were not for the heroic efforts of one of the regiment's soldiers, whose name has yet to be released. The soldier threw himself at the shooter pinning him to the ground with his body. Though severely wounded, the soldier held the shooter until Special Forces arrived to disarm him. Due to the seriousness of the soldier's injuries, it is doubtful that he . . ."

I switched the radio off. Even in my inebriated state, I didn't want to hear anything more about meaningless death and tragic endings. The sudden silence was oppressive. Taking another swig of my wine, I wandered into the living room and caught the last rays of sunlight fighting against the darkness that steadily consumed the room. I closed the blinds one by one, forcing the remaining light to seep through the cracks between them. My eyes landed on my mother's piano, and as I stared at it numbly, reality melted away to reverie.

Time was again suspended. My home movie resumed in slow, inaudible motion in front of me. My mom sat at the piano, bathed in morning sunlight. A younger me sat beside her smiling and singing along with the tune. As I watched, I wished more than anything that I could hear the cheerful song we both sang and laughed along to. With my eyes closed, it was almost possible to hear our voices joined as one. When I opened my eyes again, though, we were gone.

With a desperate cry, I forced myself behind the piano. My trembling knees rested on the bench. Lost to reverie and wine, I raised the lid to expose the keys. I positioned my fingers above the keys; though, I hadn't played in years. Not since the night of the accident. The recital we were driving home from had been my last.

Picturing the sunny scene with my mother at the piano, my fingers began to play the familiar tune. I smiled as the notes reverberated throughout the room. This time I could hear the music. In my delirium I could again see myself beside my mother as her fingers danced over the keys with unequalled grace. She taught me everything I knew. My mother's rich brown eyes illuminated with the music, and her golden hair flowed with the breeze from the open window.

I wanted to tell her how much I loved her and missed her. I wanted to tell her how much I wanted to be with them, wherever she and Gary were. Why did they leave me behind? I wanted to tell her how much I needed her- that more than anything, I wanted her here with me.

Aching to hear our voices together again, I sang the melody. I needed to hear my mother's soft honeyed voice joined with mine just one more time. My heart withered into dust when my voice was the only one I could hear. My mother's voice was lost to me forever.

Tears slid onto my cheek when I opened my eyes to an empty room, to the reality of a decade and a half passed by. My fingers persisted on the keys as the last bit of restraint broke away inside me and I began to weep.

The piano belted out a cacophony of bitter chords as I collapsed onto the keys and cried uncontrollably. All the emotions awakened in my soul by coming back to this place came screaming to the surface with violent vindication. I waited to be swept away by the waves of anguish that slammed into me now that I finally unleashed the pain.

Happy, sunlit memories tarnished under the dark remembrance of blood-stained hair and closed caskets. The longing and hopelessness, pushed away for too long, swirled and ebbed in my head.

Then, as if calling to me from the shores of my rational mind, I heard a faint strumming. Like the rhythm of a muted drum, or of feathered wings beating together in a steady rhythm, the noise was calming. I focused on it as the storm of my released emotions raged on.

As I clung to the sound, it became louder, closer. Following it through the bitter torrent, my body relaxed and the heaving in my chest slowed to shaky breaths. I could feel the strumming then, vibrating against me in a blanket of pulsing warmth. My weeping stopped, and the debilitating grief withered like smoke from an ember.

I forced myself to open my heavy eyes. The room swayed when I tried. As everything steadied, I thought I heard a soft voice call to me.

"Alexandra."

A glimpse of something reflected in the glossy finish of the piano caught my eye. The reflection showed a man standing behind me at the foot of the stairs. He was dressed in black, his ebony hair falling over piercing blue eyes. They beckoned to me as he held out his hand.

My first reaction was to scream, but I didn't. Maybe it was the wine or the gentle strumming that caused me to hesitate. Or maybe it was something else that made me stare, transfixed, on the reflection before me. Those eyes, that voice, were both so familiar.

I heard my name again.

"Alexandra."

It was then that reality took hold of me. I gasped and whipped around to face him. There was no one there. The room lay quiet and empty. I turned back to the piano, fatigue taking a swift hold of me. I saw nothing in the reflection.

I must be losing it, I thought. Too much wine and too many memories. I rested my head in my crossed arms atop my mother's piano and let exhaustion take me over.

"I miss you," I whispered and then let the wine carry me off to sleep.

Three

Morning daylight assaulted my eyes and woke me with a start. The throbbing in my temples made it hard to focus. I didn't know where I was, though the muted yellow paint and high ceiling looked familiar. The events of the previous night rushed back to me, and I sat up from under soft flannel linens. I was in the master bedroom, my mother's room.

My shoes were on the floor beside my suitcase, but I was otherwise still dressed. I couldn't remember how I got there. I certainly didn't remember lugging my bag up the stairs. Searching my bruised memory, it was clear I drank too much wine. Playing my mother's piano and the bitterness that had consumed me was a fuzzy memory at best. After that, the night was a blur.

I attempted to stand only to be knocked back down by the heaving in my stomach. Staying down, I waited for it to pass and tried to put the pieces of last night together to where they made sense.

How had I gotten upstairs and into bed? I vaguely remembered someone helping me up the stairs and coaxing me into bed with a gentle word. That was impossible though. Unless . . . maybe Sully came back to check on me? That must be what happened. Shrugging it off, I made a note to never consume that much wine again.

Staggering toward the bathroom, I shielded my eyes from the sunlight spilling in through the open blinds. I was stunned when I came face to face with my own reflection in an antique mirror which hung from the wall exactly as it had years ago. I remembered the day my mom and I found it in an antique shop in downtown Asheville. To me it had been ugly, the then dull brown frame and scratched, cloudy glass hadn't impressed me in the least. Mom saw only its possibilities. She always saw the potential in even the ugliest of things. It was one of the things I admired about her most.

Sure enough, after Mom had wiped, polished, and buffed the mirror for over an hour, it was a beautiful sight. The wear on the glass in some spots showed its age, but gave it a rustic appeal when set against the gleaming yellow brass. Mom would be happy that the tenants throughout the years had left it hanging. I admired it a second longer, then headed into the bathroom.

Eight hundred milligrams of ibuprofen and a hot shower later, I felt like myself again. I emerged from the bathroom wrapped in a fluffy white towel followed by a trail of steam that billowed into the room behind me. Nothing beat a steamy shower, nothing. I was guilty of using every bit of hot water in the house on more than one occasion. I took a deep, relaxing breath and noted how cheerful the room looked now that the explosives in my head had been disarmed. It was funny how things felt so much more positive in the light of day, when the darkness of night was vanquished.

Once dressed, I stopped to peek into my old room. It was barren. The once plum-purple walls were now painted a standard eggshell white. The only remnants of my juvenile decorating abilities were the dozen or so glow-in-the-dark stars adhered to the ceiling. I was glad that Sully chose to put me up in Mom's room. It felt more familiar.

Downstairs, I paused at the piano to lower the lid back over the keys. I glanced in its glossy finish again. When there was nothing there, I shook my head, chiding myself for being such a lightweight when it came to wine.

I opened all of the blinds and let a flood of golden rays permeate the shadows. *Yes, everything felt better in the light of a new day,* I decided and continued into the kitchen.

While forcing a scrambled egg and some toast into my queasy stomach, I realized that I'd forgotten to call Aunt Maggie last night. She'd begin to worry if I didn't call soon. Excavating my phone from my less-than-organized purse, I scowled at the lack of battery and even worse, lack of reception. There were no bars whatsoever. *Great.*

It was half past ten. Sully wouldn't be here for over an hour, so I decided to save him a trip and walk to the station. I could use the phone there. It looked like a nice day for a walk, and it would be good to get some fresh air, to get a feel for the old neighborhood, and more importantly, to put some emotional distance between me and the house.

The walk to the police station wasn't a long one, and the air was brisk and refreshing. I didn't have a key to the house, which almost stopped me. Then I remembered how rarely the people of Saluda locked their doors, and I decided to risk it.

I couldn't help but to stop at the mailbox on my way to the street and run my fingers over the hand-painted roses. Following the same compulsion, I placed my palm against the hand print I had left as a child. My hand now dwarfed the purple print. I felt a strange connection to my childhood self and an intense longing to protect that child from a future she couldn't see coming. I ran my fingers over my mother's hand print and sighed.

The sound of a gunning engine made me jump. Down the street, a white Chevy pickup truck sped away, its screeching tires wailing into the distance. I barely had time to note the rental plate before it disappeared down the street.

"Someone must be late for work," I mumbled, continuing on my way.

Vivid leaves swirled about my ankles as I walked, and the air smelled of sweet cedar and chimney smoke. I occupied my mind with thoughts of the house and what I might do with it. It had been my intention to sell it to the first taker, but now I wasn't so sure. There was a stirring inside of me that I couldn't settle. I longed for the cool indifference that I'd felt less than twenty-four hours ago.

My mother would want me to keep the house. She would also want me to be happy. How could I be happy here without her? I knew what she would say. She would tell me to pray about it. That was always her answer to everything. Should I take up the flute or aspire to be as brilliant on the piano as she was? Pray about it. Getting picked on at school? Pray about it. Princess pajamas or butterflies? Pray about it. And we did. It always seemed to help back then.

I couldn't remember the last time I had prayed. Well, aside from the occasional, "*Please, God, don't let me fail this exam*" or "*Thank you, God*" when the light stayed green when I was late for work. But an actual sit-down, tell-him-what's-on-your-mind prayer? I hadn't prayed like that since I kneeled beside my bed at night as a kid. Truth was, after Mom and Gary died, I couldn't find the use in it. It wasn't that I didn't believe in God. I did. I just couldn't wrap my mind around how he could let such evil things happen to good people.

My mother took me to church every Sunday. She made sure I said my prayers before I went to sleep each night, and I couldn't count the number of times I climbed into bed with her during a storm to find her propped up reading from her Bible. Gary had been a believer as well, and a good man. In the little time we'd had together as a family, he loved me like I was his own daughter.

How could God allow them to be murdered, butchered on the side of that road? What did Mom or Gary do to deserve that? Where was God that night? How could he let their killer go free for all of these years? Why did he leave me alive to suffer their loss?

I never understood it. It's not that I didn't want to pray. Sometimes I did. I just couldn't think of anything to say to a God that I had once thought of as loving and kind, but who turned out to be so cold and cruel.

By the time I made it to Main Street, the wind had died down and the air was warmer. I looked at my watch, pleased. It only took half an hour to walk into town. Not bad. I crossed the railroad tracks towards the station and was glad to see Sully's truck still parked in the side lot.

The smell of stale coffee and yesterday's cigarettes assaulted me when I opened the flimsy, glass door. I'd never been inside the station before, I realized. It was less impressive than I imagined even. The main room, which was the color of a dirty dishrag, was scattered with wooden desks littered with papers and disposable coffee cups. In the corner of the room sat a small office with one lonely window.

Sully exited the office and began to rummage through a pile of hand-written messages on a nearby desk before he caught sight of me. He smiled and gave a wave as I removed my coat and tossed it over the nearest chair.

"Well, there's a sight for sore eyes," he said. "Thought I was picking you up here shortly. Have a rough night?"

"I got through it well enough thanks to your housewarming gift." I shrugged. "Just felt like taking a walk. Clear my head a little."

I took another glance around the room.

"Where is everyone?"

Sully shrugged. "Eh, well, there aren't many of us to begin with. Just me, my deputy, and a few officers. Oh, and Evelyn. Today should be pretty slow, so I sent everyone home except for Will."

"It isn't just today that's slow around here," an officer said as he exited the office behind Sully.

"Ah, speak of the devil, and the devil appears," Sully scoffed.

The officer was a handsome man, older than me but not by much, with sandy brown hair and commanding dark eyes. He gave me the once-over as he approached. I countered with a smile and a nod, which he did not return. *This must be the jerk from the window yesterday*, I thought. Apparently he was not big on returning friendly gestures.

"This is my deputy, Will Galia. Will, this is my niece of sorts, Alex Nolan," Sully said.

"Nice to meet you." I caught myself glaring into his intimidating gaze, wondering why I felt nervous.

Will just glared back as if he were scrutinizing my every feature. He made me uncomfortable, and yet there was something very familiar in that sullen expression. And his name . . .

"Galia. That name sounds familiar," I pondered. "Wait, I think I know you. Billy Galia, right? You used to take piano lessons with my mom."

When his expression didn't change, I knew he'd already made the connection. He nodded and looked away. I remembered him vividly now. Billy, now Will evidently, had been the high school bad-boy when I was still in grade school. He was never pleasant to me when he came over to the house for lessons, always making fun of my pigtails. I remembered retreating to my room when he was over. He didn't smile much back then either, but he had been extremely popular as the "too cool for school" types usually are.

"That's right. I was real sorry to hear about what happened to her. I hated piano lessons, but I did really like your mom. She made it suck less," he said.

"Thank you, I think. She was an incredible woman," I said, watching as Will walked past me to grab an empty cup from a desk.

"Would you like some coffee?" he offered.

"Sure. That would be great."

"Chief, what about you? Coffee?"

"Thanks, but I've got to return a couple of these calls before we go grab some lunch. I'll just be a minute," Sully said, then vanished into his office with the stack of messages.

Being alone with Will felt awkward. I tried to figure out what it was about him that made me so uneasy. Was it his rugged look or the intensity in his expression? It was hard to say. I never knew him well, but always wondered what the hype surrounding him was about. There had to be some redeeming quality about him to have been so popular back then and for Sully to have hired him on as his deputy. I hated that I was so intrigued by him.

"You look exactly like what I remember of your mom, by the way," he said handing me my coffee. "Glad you got rid of those pony-tail thingies though. The loose look is much better."

"Thank you. You never were a fan of the pig tails. Always gave me hell," I said blowing the steam from my cup. "Had I known

I would run into you today, I would have thrown on a couple of hair bands for old time's sake."

Will finally showed a glimpse of a smile. I wished he would keep it up. It helped to smooth his rough edges.

"Well, I'm sure I would have appreciated the gesture," he said coolly.

There was an awkward silence after that as we both searched for something to say. At a loss, I sipped my coffee. The hot liquid was thick and bitter going down.

"So, how long are you planning to hang out with us in the sticks?" Will finally asked and walked to his desk by the front window.

"I'm not really sure," I sighed. "There are a few things I need to take care of. I have to decide what to do about the house, and I'd like to go visit Mom and Gary at the church. It's been too long."

"That's understandable, but how are you planning to get around? The church is too far of a walk from here."

"I thought about renting a car, but I really hadn't planned on staying long enough to need one. I'll probably just ride with Sully. If not, I don't mind the trek."

Will sat behind his desk and put his hands behind his head as he leaned back in his chair. He squinted his bronze eyes at me, warring with some decision in his head.

"Sully will be here at the station a lot. I swear that man never takes a break. There's no way you're walking these highways either," he sighed, scratching his head. "You know, I've got the old Mustang just sitting here. I've been driving the squad car to and from work these days. The old gal needs to be driven. What do you think? You want to borrow her? You'd be doing us both a favor."

"You still have the Mustang?" I gawked. "Wow. Now that was an amazing car. I couldn't possibly . . ."

"She's STILL an amazing car," Will said, "and she deserves to be driven more than I've been able to lately. Seriously, you'd be doing me a solid."

I contained my excitement before I embarrassed myself with a huge grin. No need to play into his practiced arrogance, even if it was justified. He wasn't just the hot, older guy anymore. We were both adults, which evened the playing field. *Just play it cool,* I told myself, *and consider the offer.*

The Mustang was quite a beauty and also part of Will's whole bad-boy façade. It was his sidekick. Now after all these years I had the chance to drive it. Who could say no to that?

"Okay, then. I guess . . . if it would help us both out," I said, coolly.

"Then it's settled," Will nodded, just as Sully emerged from the office.

"What's settled?" he asked.

I motioned to Will. "Your deputy here was kind enough to offer to let me borrow his car while I'm in town."

Will coughed and readjusted himself in his seat. "That's right. It's just been sitting out back all day. Might as well be driven by someone. I'll dig up the keys and introduce you when you get back from lunch."

Sully scratched his head while Will and I awaited his response.

"Actually, I think that's a great idea," he said. "Keeps you from having to come to the station with me every day and waiting around."

"Well, then, you see? I am good for something around here." Will winked at me and sipped his coffee.

"I wouldn't go that far," Sully scoffed, then turned to me. "Ready to grab some lunch? I know it's early, but I'm starving."

"Yep," I said, starting for the door. "Thanks again, Will."

"Not a problem," he said before turning back to the papers on his desk.

I pushed the door open and smashed into someone coming in. As I regained my balance, I came face to face with the man from the plane. He smiled that flashy smile, and I knew he recognized me too.

"Well, I knew we'd bump into one another. I just didn't think it would be literally," he said with a chuckle.

"It was bound to happen either way, I guess." I said. "Mr. Brightman, right?"

"Please, call me Rick."

Sully opened the door wide and offered Brightman a hand. "Good morning, Mr. Brightman. I see you've met my niece."

"Your niece?" he asked, taking Sully's hand. "It is a small world then. She and I were on the same flight yesterday."

"That explains the acquaintance. I assume you're here to pick up your permits? I finished signing them this morning. They're on my desk. Let me get them for you. Alex, why don't you go on and get us a seat. I'll be there in 5 minutes."

"Not a problem. Can I borrow your cell phone? I have no bars, and I need to call Aunt Maggie and let her know I'm in one piece."

"Sure thing." Sully tossed me his Motorola.

"It was nice to see you again, Rick," I said with a wave.

"Until next time."

I jogged across the street and had a seat on an empty bench beside the gazebo, then dialed the familiar Chicago number. When no one answered, I figured my aunt and uncle had gone to the park. It was their new Friday ritual now that Uncle Dan was retired. I left a message letting them know that I had arrived in one piece and informed them of the bad cell phone reception. I'd call them before I left for home . . . whenever that was.

I was glad I got their voice mail, which surprised me. I'd anticipated being homesick by now, but I wasn't. Maybe that's because I'd never come to think of Uncle Dan and Aunt Maggie's as home.

It wasn't for their lack of trying. They'd raised me as their own until I was old enough to move out. They even helped pay for college. Aunt Maggie was the one who helped me land the interview for my first teaching job, but they'd never felt like home. Neither did my humble apartment in the city, I realized as I jogged back across the street in time to meet Sully coming out of the station.

After lunch, Sully and I walked back to the station still laughing from our conversation. Will followed behind, a to-go cup dangling from his fingers.

"How was lunch?" he asked, returning to his desk.

"Well, Alex here reacquainted herself with the old soda fountain," Sully teased. "You'd think she was nine again."

I rolled my eyes. "Who doesn't like a strawberry Coke?"

"Grape Seven-Up is my personal favorite." Will winked.

I motioned to him. "See there? A man with taste."

"Yeah, well he drives twenty minutes to get a Big Mac for lunch every day, so his culinary opinion doesn't count." Sully glanced at the two of us and frowned.

"Anyway, I promised you a set of keys and an introduction," he said as he rummaged through the drawer. Perplexed, he emptied the contents onto the top of his desk, piling up papers and notepads as he scoured.

"That's strange. I always keep them in this drawer." He opened the other drawers and looked around before shrugging. "I guess it's possible that I grabbed them and took them home on accident. I'm sorry. Rain check till tomorrow?"

"Don't even worry about it. Tomorrow's Saturday. I don't want you to come all the way to work." I waved him off.

"Oh, I'll be here. So will the chief. Weekends are when all the fun happens. I'll have them tomorrow, promise."

"Well, I guess that works then," I said with a shrug.

"You want me to drop you back off at the house? Before I leave, I've got to plan out how I'm going to close off this side of the street when they come to renovate. I can pick you back up in an hour or so," Sully offered.

"No, that's okay. I'm just going to go into the grocery, maybe grab a new book," I said, opening the door to go back out. "I'll be back soon."

I didn't want to tell him that I wasn't ready to go back to the house. Not yet. So instead I browsed the shops I used to shop in as a kid. By the time I returned to the station, Sully was locking up the front door. He waved and nodded to the shopping bags I carried with a smile.

"I see you've had a productive time," he said.

"Yep. I got another bottle of wine, some chocolate, and a couple of used books. You know, everything one needs to survive," I said as we walked to the truck.

"I must say, you have excellent survival instincts," Sully laughed.

Every curve of the road to Sully's house was a key that unlocked some distant memory of the many visits with he and Gram. I thought of the hilarious family stories at the dinner table and the baking lessons too numerous to count. I could almost feel the thousands of warm hugs and cuddles that always made me feel like the most loved little girl on the planet. The excitement of seeing Gram again was overwhelming, but so was my sense of dread.

"Do you think she'll remember me?" I asked Sully.

Gram was the only grandmother I'd ever known. My mother lost her mom before I was born, and I'd never known my father, let alone the rest of his family. If she didn't remember me, it would be like losing her all over again.

"Well, you just never know from day to day. She was doing well this morning, so maybe today will be a good day," Sully sighed. "Just remember, if she says something that doesn't make any sense, just shrug it off. There's just no telling where her mind is."

Sully's street had always been quiet, the houses set back into the pines and only accessible through long, private driveways. As we turned into the last driveway on the left, I stared up at the quaint but aging log cabin where so many of my childhood memories were created. I didn't want to be nervous, but I was. If Gram didn't remember me now in her deteriorated state, how would I end up remembering her?

"Well, here we are. Home sweet home." Sully put the truck into park and hopped out.

I followed him to the front door where an attractive, middle-aged black woman smiled warmly as she greeted us.

"Oh, good, you guys made it home early. Gram just finished putting dinner in the oven," she said. "It needs to cook a while yet, but she'll be happy you're here."

Sully went straight into the living room while the woman looked me over in the entryway.

"My name is Nadine. I watch after your grandmother. You, my dear, must be Alexandra," the woman said, clasping my hand. "I have heard so much about you. You're even lovelier than I imagined."

I shook her hand. "It's very nice to meet you."

Nadine waved off the handshake and giggling, leaned in to give me a firm hug. She smelled of sweet lavender and vanilla, which instantly put me at ease. I found myself hugging the stranger back.

"She talks about you all the time, you know. Whatever condition she is in tonight, I know that she has missed you very much. No matter what happens, just remember that everything is going to be alright," Nadine said, then released me to grab her coat from the rack. I found it hard to take my eyes off the lovely woman.

"Thank you for taking care of her," I said.

Nadine put her coat on and turned at the door.

"Now, you don't ever have to thank me. It's a blessing and an honor to be the one to look after your grandmother. It was nice to finally meet you, Alexandra. I am so glad that you are back," she said, cupping my face in her hands. "You must remember to have an open mind and heart, dear. Only then will you see."

Then she patted my cheek and walked out the door.

I stared after her for a minute trying to make sense of Nadine's words when I was distracted by a soft, familiar voice that called to me from the living room.

"Well, now, come on in here, young lady. Supper will be ready in a little while, and I haven't gotten my hug yet."

I turned slowly, my heart racing in my chest, and followed the sound of Gram's familiar voice. In the living room, I found Sully bent down as he embraced the old woman. I watched as delicate, pale arms reached around him and gave his back a pat. Then Sully stood up and glanced over his shoulder at me.

"Looks like it's a good day." He grinned.

When he stepped aside, she was real and in front of me. No longer a memory, she smiled and outstretched her arms. She had the same warmth about her that could melt even the coldest heart or pretense. Her hair, once a steel grey, had faded into a white cloud surrounding slender shoulders. A few more wrinkles had settled into what was an otherwise timeless face.

As I walked up to embrace her, I looked deep into her eyes and was saddened. Something about them was different. Those eyes, which were once so bright and expectant, now seemed dark and tormented, as if the life reflected through them was weighed down by an unseen burden.

"Now you give Gram a big ole hug, missy. It's been far too long since you've come round here," Gram said as she patted me on my back and gave me a peck on the cheek. Tears welled in my eyes as I embraced the small woman and clung to her.

"How are you feeling today, Mom?" Sully asked from the corner. I straightened and wiped my eyes.

"Oh, now, don't you worry about me one bit, Sullivan. We have a guest. Why don't you set the table for dinner? As for you, young lady, why don't you come on in here and let me get you something to drink. We can catch up on life." Gram motioned me towards the kitchen. "Sullivan, could you turn that television off? I can't stand to hear one more thing about that shooting or that poor young man. After all he did to save those people . . ." she said as she disappeared into the kitchen, her voice trailing off.

Sully sighed and rolled his eyes at me before walking over to the television. I followed Gram into the kitchen giggling. Despite what I'd seen in her eyes earlier, she was the same old Gram.

In the kitchen, Gram poured me a glass of her sweet tea and motioned for me to have a seat at the white-tiled kitchen table. I admired the whole scene, down to the last faded daisy on the yellowing wallpaper. Gram checked on the roast and carefully chopped vegetables for the salad. I smiled each time she stepped on the creaky floorboard by the sink. Gram was oblivious to its squeak, and I decided that the floorboard matched Gram: old and unsteady, but still full of spunk.

We talked about everyday things, like the turning of the leaves and the council's display in the library window. I was glad for the light conversation. It made me feel as though I'd never really left, and for a moment I was that happy little girl again spending time in her happiest of places.

Dinner conversation turned to stories about Sully and Gary and their brotherly exploits. Although Gram's stories made me miss Gary all the more, the mortified look on Sully's face made me laugh. He turned beet red when Gram recounted a dare that he and Gary had once, on who could urinate the farthest. It was all fun and games until Sully inadvertently watered an electrical socket and was given the jolt of his life.

"He always won. No matter what the game, he always won," Sully snickered, "but always by default. The universe just seemed to always be on his side."

Sully's expression changed then, and I knew his thoughts had shifted into darker territory, to the night when the universe was not on Gary's side. The night that changed everything.

I refused to let go of the light-hearted mood though. I wanted more than anything to cling to this fleeting moment of real family time. I rose from the table and gave Sully an encouraging pat on the back and began to gather up plates to take to the sink.

"And what do you think you are doing, young lady?" Gram asked.

"Clearing the table," I answered on my way to the sink.

Gram rose from her chair and grabbed a few plates shakily. "Nonsense, you are the guest. You have yourself a seat. I'll get these out of the way."

"I am hardly a guest. Besides, we have to get these out of the way so you can show me how to bake your famous cookies, remember?"

Sully got up from his chair to gather the remaining dishes and set them in the sink. Unlike Gram, he was skilled at avoiding the squeaky floorboard.

"That's my cue to leave you two ladies alone. I don't want to get in the way of cookie time," he said, excusing himself from the kitchen. He looked back and gave me a smile on his way out. "Just like old times."

I smiled at him, and he gave me a wink as he left Gram and I alone.

"Cookies, huh? Why, I could make those in my sleep," Gram said as she began to gather all the ingredients.

I paid close attention as she assembled the flour, sugar, baking powder and oatmeal into one large mixing bowl. I stirred them with a wooden spoon. After adding the dry ingredients to the wet ingredients, she dipped a spoon in the bowl and gave the dough a taste. She pondered for a moment and then sighed, looking puzzled and distraught.

"What is it, Gram?" I asked.

"It's not right. It's missing something." Gram looked back at the counter full of ingredients. "But I can't seem to remember what else . . ."

I studied her face for a moment and then walked to the spice rack and pulled out the nutmeg and brought it to Gram. "Is this what's missing?"

Gram's eyes grew wide. "Why, yes, that's it exactly! How could I have forgotten my secret ingredient? Thank you, dear." She sprinkled some in. "The trick is to add just a pinch. Too much will overpower the cinnamon."

My heart threatened to break. I'd missed so much time with Gram, and I learned the hard way to cherish the ones you have while you still have them. How could I have stayed away so long?

When Gram pulled the cookies from the oven, I waited until they cooled just enough to pluck one off the rack to taste. They were better than my memory had served. Each bite was sweet and spicy heaven laced with love. Gram oozed with delight at my obvious satisfaction as Sully wandered back into the kitchen, following his nose.

"Best damned smell in the world," he said, grabbing a cookie off the cooling rack.

"How about some milk?" Gram offered.

"Actually Mom, it's getting pretty late. I should really get our guest home so you can rest. I'm sure it's been a long day for you both."

I glanced at the clock above the stove. Time had flown so fast. I didn't want to leave. I didn't want this familiar feeling to end, the feeling of belonging. The thought of facing my empty house made me want to stay even more, but I knew that Gram needed her rest, and I remembered the wine waiting for me in the truck. That offered some comfort, anyway.

"Sully is right. I should be going. I'll be back soon, though," I promised.

"Well, you're not going anywhere without taking some of these cookies with you," Gram said, dropping a dozen into a small paper sack. She walked us to the door.

"I'll be back in a bit, Mom. Call me on my cell if you need anything. Remember, the number is by the phone," Sully said. He left us alone to go start the truck.

Gram handed me the bag of cookies and wrapped me in a hug. She gave me her usual pat on the back and leaned in close.

"It was so nice to have you over again, Tina," she said against my ear.

I shot upright and looked into Gram's smiling face, puzzled.

"Tina?"

"Now you make sure and come back and help me bake some more cookies," she said with an oblivious smile.

I stood there stunned, unable to speak. She let go of me and leaned in close a second time.

"He loves you, you know," she whispered. "That's why he did it."

I could only stare at her, dumbfounded. I opened my mouth to correct her, to tell her that I wasn't Tina. I was Tina's daughter. Then I remembered what Sully said and decided not to argue. I didn't want to upset Gram by telling her she was confused, so instead I kissed her on the cheek and got into the truck beside Sully. Gram waved goodbye as we pulled out of the driveway. I waved back, contemplating what she said.

"She called me Tina," I told him. "She thought I was Mom the whole time."

Sully nodded solemnly. "Yeah, I knew she was stuck in the past when she called me Sullivan. She hasn't called me by my full name since before the accident."

"It was still a wonderful time, I just . . . I really thought she remembered me."

"I'm sure that somewhere in that marvelous mind of hers, she does. Somewhere inside there, she remembers everything," Sully said.

"I hope so." I was still shaken.

"Did she say anything else?"

"Yeah, it was weird. She said something like, 'He loves you, and that's why he did it.' What do you think that means? You think she was talking about Gary?" I asked.

Sully brooded for a minute and then shrugged. "Ah, who knows? Like I said before, sometimes it just doesn't make any sense. You just have to shrug it off. Besides all of that, today was a really good day. We should just hang onto that."

I sighed. "You're right. Tonight was perfect."

"Yes, it was. It's good to have you back," Sully said, smiling.

It was a six-minute drive from Sully's house to mine if you took a small gravel road that cut through the neighborhoods and surrounding forest. Mom had never been willing to take the shortcut at night when the road was dark as pitch and the dust from the gravel dimmed the headlights. Sully took the road without hesitation. He switched on his fog lights, and even though it did little to overcome the oppressive dark that surrounded us, I wasn't afraid with Sully there.

Soon the gravel dumped us onto a side road in my neighborhood, and street lights once again illuminated our way. When we pulled up to the house, I made a mental note to keep the porch lights on before going out from now on. The house looked macabre dressed in the shadows cast from the moonlight against the trees. I climbed out of the truck, and Sully hopped out behind me.

"Don't forget your survival kit," he joked, grabbing my bags from the back seat.

"I wouldn't dare," I said, taking them from him. "Also, I don't have a key to the house, not that I really need it around here. I'd guess I'd feel better if I had one though."

Sully unraveled a key from his ring. "Don't know why I didn't think of that. Take mine. I have a spare back at the station if you ever lock yourself out. You going to be okay tonight? Don't think I have to remind you that you're welcome back at our place."

I grinned and raised my bags. "I'll be fine. Got my survival kit, remember?"

I turned towards the house and then back to Sully when I remembered the night before.

"You didn't happen to come back by last night, did you?"

Sully hopped back into his truck and turned to me with concern. "No. Why? Did you hear something last night? Get spooked?"

"It was nothing. Must have been dreaming, that's all."

"I hope it was a good dream." He laughed. "I'll pick you up around nine on my way to the station. Call me if you need anything, okay?"

"You got it." I waved and went inside as the truck pulled out of the driveway with a roar.

The first thing I did was turn on all the lights in the living room and kitchen before taking my bags to the counter. I opened the bottle of wine immediately. This time I used a glass. Moderation was key, I reminded myself even as I downed half the glass in one gulp and topped it back off.

Grabbing a cookie from the paper sack, I leaned against the counter. Today had been a great day. I closed my eyes and savored each cinnamon-flavored memory. However, the sting of disappointment that Gram thought I was my mother lingered on my mind. What did she mean when she said, "That's why he did it?" *What had Gary done*? I shrugged it off. Sully was right. It could be anything.

I took another drag from my glass and topped it off once more before grabbing one of my new books and heading upstairs. Deciding to leave the lights on, I made sure not to glance at the piano as I passed through the living room. There was no way I was going to let my emotions get the best of me tonight.

With my hands full, I was unable to switch the light on the second floor hallway, so I took to speed walking to the master bedroom. I almost made it to the end of the hall when a loud creak followed by an even louder thud made me jump and stopped me with a squeal.

In the dark, I could see that something was now blocking the doorway to the master bedroom. My heart beat faster as I watched in silence for further movement. When there was none, I set the book on the floor and searched with my hand for the light at that end of the hall.

When I flipped it on, I found that the attic door overhead had opened. The pull-down ladder lay extended to the floor, blocking the entrance to the bedroom. I was relieved that was all it was, but how had it opened by itself? Maybe Sully or the last tenant hadn't shut it all the way and the movement in the house caused it to fall open? That had to be it. I took another swig of my wine and set it down on top of the book.

"What the hell," I said with a sigh and started up the ladder, the wine spurring my confidence.

I reached the top and found the chain for the light and pulled it, illuminating the mostly empty space surrounded by fluffy pink insulation. Pulling myself up, I took inventory. There was a medium sized box in the corner, an old vacuum cleaner, and a few

Christmas decorations scattered throughout. I made my way on my knees to the cardboard box.

I brushed the dust from the top and peeled away the faded brown tape. The first thing I saw was a framed picture of me posing with my mother, which I remembered used to hang in the upstairs hallway. With a gasp, I yanked it from the box, studying the picture as an archeologist would an ancient artifact.

I owned only a couple of pictures of my mom from the years right before she died. My aunt had shown me plenty from their childhood, but this photograph captured my mother not much older than I was now. Her long hair hung about her shoulders in golden waves, and her smile contained the hope for a future of possibilities laid out before her. I stared in amazement. I did look just like her. Even though my own hair was shorter and a deep chocolate brown, our light eyes matched exactly, both a bright shade of maple. Same sloping nose, same full mouth.

I tore my gaze away from the photo and reached into the box again, this time pulling out old school work and awards and a yearbook from third grade. Another from fourth. I set them aside and I felt around the bottom of the box where I found a small piece of folded paper. As I unfolded it, I recognized my baptism certificate. Printed on it was the church emblem, the date, and my own signature in purple crayon.

I flipped the certificate over. On the other side was a drawing of a man, also done in crayon. He was dressed in black and had a head of shaggy, black hair. It was his royal blue eyes, drawn bigger than any other features of his face, that made me gasp.

I brought my hands to my mouth and dropped the certificate, remembering the figure I'd seen in the piano. He had the same blue eyes, the same black locks.

Shaking my head, I almost laughed aloud. The wine. It messed with my head last night, and it was messing with me now. This is what I got for being such a lightweight.

I plucked the certificate off the floor and giving one final look, folded it and tucked in under my arm before gathering all the contents of the box and throwing them back in. Dropping the certificate on top, I pushed the box to the attic entrance and carefully carried it down, turning off the light and shutting up the attic. Setting the box next to my bed, I went back for my book and quickly downed the remaining wine. I washed my face and brushed my teeth in the bathroom, all the while thinking about those piercing blue eyes.

By the time I climbed into bed, the wine had done its job, and my mind was growing increasingly drowsy. Instead of starting my book, I found myself reaching into the box for the certificate. Laying back, I unfolded it and stared into those sapphire eyes.

For a second, while my mind began to drift somewhere between wake and sleep, I thought I heard the gentle strumming come again. Closing my eyes, I searched the expanse beyond my eyelids for the source of the soothing rhythm until I drifted off to sleep.

Four

I laughed, full of contentment, as my mother and Gary smiled to me from the front of the car. Gary called me the next Chopin. It was the first time he'd seen me play, and he was brimming with pride. I jumped when the first explosion of lightning lit up the sky. The answering thunder growled to life and echoed off the darkened mountaintops outside the car.

"It's just a thunderstorm, Alex, nothing to worry about," my mom reassured me.

As I peered timidly out the window at the oncoming storm, bolts of white light danced in the sky. I watched them until I was distracted by another set of lights that rushed up from below.

I was too confused to recognize the oncoming headlights. By the time I did, it was too late to scream. The vehicle slammed into us, sending our car over the embankment. My body twisted with each pounding tumble. I could hear the crunching of metal and my mother's screams.

But this time was different. Instead of slamming against the great oak below like I expected, I kept falling.

Free from the car, my body descended alone into darkness. The only screams I could hear now were my own, which echoed back from the black abyss surrounding me.

Then I hit water.

"In the name of the Father, the Son and the Holy Spirit," I heard as bubbles rose to the surface.

I saw the light above me and the tender hands of Pastor James as he dipped me into the baptismal pool. A gentle strumming caused me to turn my head in the water. He was there. He smiled to me from beyond the depths of the shallow pool, his blue eyes gleaming. I heard the music too. The sound of a thousand voices singing out in perfect harmony.

"Illumina, custody, rege et gube'rna."

And above the voices, he whispered to me.

"It's alright. I am with you, Alexandra. Just open your mind, and you will see."

Then those tender hands pulled me from the water.

I opened my eyes with a start. Was it morning already? A glance at the alarm clock on the nightstand told me that Sully would be here within the hour. I'd overslept, yet I lingered in bed clinging to the dream. When I finally pulled back the covers, I felt the crinkle of paper under my fingertips. I picked up the certificate and jumped out of bed, looking for something to write with. Settling for an eye liner pencil, I wrote down the words from my dream before they vanished from my mind.

"Custodi, rege et gube'rna"

I scribbled them beneath the picture and then folded it up. When I was dressed, I tucked it into the pocket of my jeans. I had to find out what those words meant. It was probably nothing, the product of a stress-induced dream. All of my memories were rushing back in a hailstorm of jumbled facts and torn remnants of a child's imagination, but I had to know.

I finished dressing and jogged downstairs remembering that I had purposely left the lights on. Snickering at myself, I turned them all off except for the front porch light. I had just enough time to fry an egg and down a glass of orange juice before I heard Sully's truck towering up the driveway.

"How was your night?" Sully asked as I climbed into the passenger seat.

"I survived," I said with a grin.

"I see that." He laughed as he backed out of the driveway.

When we arrived at the station, I gawked at the middle-aged woman chatting away on the phone behind the front desk. Her bleached-blonde hair was gathered in a tall bun atop her head. It seemed to serve as a pencil holder as there were at least three eraser ends poking out in various places. Her bright red lips smiled at us as she jotted down a message.

The rest of the station was empty with no sign of any of the officers. I wondered why I was both relieved and disappointed that Will wasn't there.

"Why, you must be the lovely Alexandra I've heard so much about," the woman squealed as she traipsed around her desk.

Sully took my coat in time for me to shake her hand. "Evelyn, this is Alex. Alex, this is Evelyn, my secretary," he said.

"It's nice to meet you," I said, noting the long, hot pink nails on Evelyn's hand.

"It's nice to finally meet you, sugar. My, you are a beauty, aren't you?" Evelyn drawled in a heavy southern accent.

Again, I didn't know what to say. I'd never thought I was much to look at. Sure, I had guys interested in me back in Chicago, and I'd had a few boyfriends in college, but to hear the people around here, you would think I was beating the men off with a stick.

"Just like her mother," Sully interjected. "Don't know about you two, but I could use a cup of coffee."

Sully walked to the coffee pot and lit up with delight to see that it was already full of fresh brew.

"Have I ever told you how much I love you, Evelyn?" he teased.

"Oh, Chief, always getting a girl's hopes up." She winked at me.

"Can I get coffee for either of you lovely ladies?"

"I would love some," I answered as the front door opened and Will entered.

He looked tired as he hung his coat and turned with a smirk.

"Did I hear someone say coffee and lovely ladies? I'll take both," he said.

My heart sped at the sight of him. He nodded at me as Sully handed me a small Styrofoam cup filled with black silk. Then he poured another for Will.

"Hope you like it black. We don't believe in creamers or sugar around here," Sully said, taking a small sip of his.

"Leaves more room for the caffeine," Will agreed taking a long swig from his and wincing as the hot liquid hit his throat.

"Long night?" Sully asked Will.

"You know me." He shrugged, walking to the coffee pot to top off his cup. "I spent half the night looking for my damned car keys."

"Still no luck, huh?" Sully asked.

I sipped my coffee and watched Will over the rim of my cup. He walked back to his desk, puzzled. "I just drove her a couple of weeks ago. I could have sworn I put the keys back in the drawer."

He pulled his desk drawer out and rummaged around, his hand disappearing into the back of the drawer. When it emerged, he held a small key ring. A gold Mustang logo dangled from his fingers.

"Well, I'll be damned, here they are. They were in the back of the drawer. I must not have pulled it out far enough." Will tossed them to me.

I almost spilled my coffee on my sweater, but I caught them before they hit me in the face.

"Thank you, if you're sure . . ."

Will walked to the door and motioned me over. "You're helping me out, remember? Come on out, and I'll introduce you."

I waved to Sully on my way out. "Guess I'll come by later?"

"Sure. Don't have too much fun with that thing now. I know you love your muscle cars." Sully topped off his coffee. "Where you headed?"

"Up to the church. I want to visit Mom and Gary." I searched Sully's face for whatever emotion my answer elicited.

He only nodded in approval. "I'd say that's very fitting. Take your time. I've got a lot to do around here today."

"Okay," I said, grabbing my coat. "It was nice to meet you, Evelyn. I'll see you both in a bit."

"Don't let that boy give you too much grief over that car, now. As much as he messes with it, it's still older than dirt." Evelyn laughed.

"I'll keep that in mind." I smiled and followed after Will.

The sky was a pale shade of grey, and the air smelled of rain. I hoped a storm wasn't on the way. Walking around to the back of the building, I found Will behind the wheel of the bright yellow 1979 Cobra. The sight of him in that car brought up feelings of excitement and danger. Though, I didn't know what was exciting me more, the boy or the car.

Sully was right, my uncle instilled in me a great respect for muscle cars, and Will's Mustang was a beauty. Then again, Will was quite a specimen himself, oozing just enough darkness and mystery to make someone want to see what was under his hood.

When I reached him, I cleared my throat and chided myself for acting like a swooning school girl at a boy band concert. "She's still a beauty."

"Come on over so I can show you some of her quirks," Will said.

When I got to the driver's side, I casually leaned against the door and gave him my undivided attention.

"Okay, now when you start her, you've got to pump the gas twice like this . . ." Will turned the ignition and tapped the gas pedal until the reluctant engine turned over and purred to life, sending puffs of smoke from its elongated tailpipe.

"Any more than twice and . . ." he started.

". . . You'll get too much gas in the intake manifold and flood the engine," I finished with a flourish, loving the sound of the turbo engine.

Will nodded in approval. "So you know what you're getting yourself into. That's good. I assume then that you know how to drive a stick shift?"

"That's all I've ever driven. My uncle Dan and I spent summers fixing up old cars. It's always been a hobby of his."

"Well, then she's in the right hands. Just make sure you give her a couple of revs once the engine turns over, and you're good to go."

Will left the engine running and stepped out of the car. He motioned for me to have a seat behind the wheel. I tried to contain my excitement.

"She's got a lot of power now, and it's looking like rain. Don't let her get away from you on these mountain roads. I'd hate it if anything happened to her." He winked. "Or you."

"Trust me, I plan to take it nice and easy until I get to know the old gal. I'm just going up the highway to the church and back. Thanks again for letting me drive her. This would NEVER have happened back in the day."

Will shut the door and gave the hood a pat. "Yes, that's true. I'd like to think that I've matured some since then. Like I said, she deserves to be driven. Just promise me one thing?"

"What's that?" I asked.

"Don't call her old gal again. It hurts her feelings." Will smiled.

"You got it." I laughed, shifting into reverse.

"Now get out of here already. I've got work to pretend to do," Will said, jogging back to the front of the building.

I took a second to appreciate the butter-like leather interior and custom chrome dash before adjusting the mirrors and easing off the clutch. The car grumbled as it backed out into the main road. When I put it into first and hit the throttle, I caught a glimpse of Sully watching me through the station door. *Worry wart.* Waiting until I cleared the building, I leaned on the gas pedal and was thrown back into the seat as the engine roared and lurched forward.

"Woohoo!" I couldn't help but yell.

I smiled at the feel of the power at my control and fought the urge to gun it again on the straight-away, finding contentment in realizing just how awesome it was to be driving Billy Galia's "Stang."

He wasn't the jerk I'd always thought he was. Well, not as much of a jerk as he wanted people to think he was anyway. He just needed to smile more often. Then maybe he wouldn't be so damned intimidating. I felt a strong desire to make that happen.

Downshifting, the car moaned in defiance as I made my way towards the church. The wind was picking up, shaking ripened leaves from countless trees and sending them swirling down in a mass of fluttering color. The sky was morphing into an ominous shade of slate, my mood growing just as dark the closer I got to my destination. I hadn't been to visit the plot where my mother was buried since the day she was put to ground and I couldn't help but think of that day.

It was frigid out. I remembered the tears, which poured from my eyes, had stung my frostbitten cheeks. Gram held me tightly against her as they lowered my mom into her final resting place beside Gary. She whispered to me that my mother would want for me to move on and live a happy life. I hadn't been able to grasp the finality of it all. Happiness seemed like a distant memory.

It took a long time for me to stop expecting her to tuck me in at night, or pick me up from school, to accept that she was gone. Seeing her grave would be a harsh reminder of how gone she was. Still, I wanted to pay my respects and maybe even get a feel for what Mom would have me do with the house now.

Pulling into the parking lot, I was relieved that there were no other cars in sight. I parked in front of the A-framed church and sat for a moment to collect myself. The church was small compared to the chapels in Chicago, but it was large enough to fit a congregation who attended from the three closest surrounding towns. Painted a sterling grey, the church matched the intricate stonework that formed the entryway and sidewalk. The doors, a deep maroon, complimented the red and purple leaves of the large oak trees that surrounded the building.

I followed the stone walkway behind the main sanctuary. The cemetery, which stretched across an acre of flat meadow, was nestled between two rising mountain peaks behind the church. Mom and Gary were buried near the fence on the eastern side.

When I approached, I saw that my mother's grave was covered with a dozen fresh, white lilies. Someone else had visited recently. I wondered who as I moved the bouquet in order to see her name on the glossy marble gravestone.

"Tina Marie Nolan. Loving mother and wife. May the angels dance to your music for all of eternity," I read out loud.

The headstone next to hers looked empty to me, so I plucked a flower from the bouquet and laid it on the grave.

"Robert Gary Wiley. Loving son, brother, and husband. May you forever find comfort in the arms of your angel."

Gram had written both epitaphs at a time when words, for me, had lost all meaning. I admired those words now and, more so, Gram for having come up with such beauty in the midst of that kind of pain and loss.

I sat between the stones and stared at them a moment. There was so much I wanted to say, but the words would not form on my lips. It was too hard to think of them lying there in the cold earth, lifeless. Even after fifteen years it felt unreal. So I chose to think of them as they had been: full of life, joy and excitement about their future together. They weren't gone, just off together forever in a place that I could not yet go. Thinking of them that way helped me find the words. I turned to Gary first.

"Hey, Gary, it's me . . . Alex. I know it's been a long time." I lowered my head. "I'm sorry about that. I guess I was running away, you know? From what happened . . . from the memories. I guess I always thought that it would be better if I just forgot this place."

It sounded ridiculous once I said it out loud. I almost laughed.

"Pretty stupid, huh? The truth is, the more I tried to forget, the more lost I became. You were the only real father I ever had. How could I want to forget that?"

I stopped, realizing that I *had* been running, trying to forget the pain, getting far enough away so that it no longer seemed real. Since coming back to these mountains, to these memories, I realized that trying to forget my life here was denying Mom and

Gary who they were. I was losing the moments in life, good or bad, that made up who they'd been.

The joyful times that I let slip away, the times that filled my heart with love, shone even brighter against the memories of sadness and loss. They were intertwined, inseparably woven into the fabric of my being. To deny those memories was to deny myself, and to deny both Mom and Gary of their beautiful existence. To forget was to kill them all over again.

I turned to my mother's grave.

"I'm so sorry, Mom, for so many things. I'm sorry about what happened to you. I am sorry that I couldn't save you. I should have seen that car coming sooner. I should have warned you in time." I sighed. "I am so sorry that they never caught the bastard who did this to you. I'm so sorry that I tried to forget. But mostly, I'm sorry that I'm not with you."

My reflection in the polished marble headstone showed my tears, and I wiped them from my cheeks. I closed my eyes in an attempt to hold the rest back.

"I should have died with you guys that night. I should be with you right now. I wish I was," I admitted. "Instead, you left me here all alone, and I don't know what to do. After all these years, I still feel so lost."

It was then that I heard it again, the strumming, which sounded above the rustling of the wind through the surrounding trees. It grew louder, and I opened my eyes, releasing a stream of crystalline tears to flow down my cheeks. I looked back to my reflection, the moisture in my eyes making it hard to focus. I saw more than my own reflection staring back at me.

I blinked back the tears and wiped at my eyes in a panic. When I looked again, I saw his black hair and those blue eyes reflected next to me. They beckoned to me from the marble. Spinning around, I expected to see the man behind me, but there was no one there. When I turned back to the headstone, the image was gone. My own reflection was the only one visible.

Then I heard a whisper, as if someone were speaking low and hushed into my ear.

"You are not alone."

With a gasp, I jumped up. There was no one beside me. The strumming drifted away with the breeze. I stood there stunned until I heard a door open in the distance.

When I looked back toward the church, an elderly man exited the back door with a broom in hand. He obliviously swept the walkway, only looking up when he sensed me watching him. He stopped his chore and, setting down his broom, walked towards me.

Turning away, I blotted at the moisture from my eyes with the back of my sleeve just before he approached. I tried my best to smile. The man was in his late seventies and his face held a kind smile, his eyes the wisdom of ages. The closer he got, the more I recognized that smile.

"Why. . . Miss Nolan, is that you? I heard you were back in town."

I made one final swipe at my eyes. "Pastor James? I had no idea you were still the pastor here. How are you?"

Pastor James laughed. "Well, I suppose I should have retired ten years ago, but I just don't know what else I would do with myself. My gracious child, you've grown up into a beautiful young woman, haven't you?"

I smiled and took the hand that he offered. "It feels like it's been so long, and yet nothing around here seems to have changed that much. You included."

He patted my hand with his free one. "Well, you were forced to go through a lot of changes in a short amount of time. I suspect that it's been quite strange for you to come back here after all these years, given how you left."

The more he spoke, the more I realized how desperately I needed to talk to someone about all of the things I was wrestling with: being back in Saluda, Gram, the house, and the fact that I was hearing and seeing things that weren't there. Pastor James had a welcoming way about him that made it easy to confide in him.

"It's been very strange. I've been remembering all sorts of things that I'd forgotten. Things that I tried to forget."

Pastor James turned to my mother's grave, still holding my hand.

"Sometimes the good Lord works in ways we can't always understand. We still have to look for what he has planned for us even in the most difficult of circumstances. Coming back home was a good step. Give it some time."

"I guess I just can't accept that God would have planned this," I said motioning to the graves. "What good could possibly come from this?"

"This was not God's plan, but he can make good of this tragedy."

"How?" I asked.

He patted my hand again and his eyes met mine. "It's not for you to understand how, just for you to trust."

I was puzzled. "Trust what exactly?"

"That he will bring you through it, and maybe in the process, bring you closer to him."

I sighed and let his hand go, looking again to my mother's grave.

"I can't see how that's ever going to be possible. It's been fifteen years and I still can't find my way past it."

Pastor James met my eyes again. "That is because you are still lost, child. You've let the person who took your parents away from you rob you of your faith as well. You've got to let go of the anger. You've got to open your mind again so that you can see."

I stared at him in amazement. "That is the third time I've heard that said to me in one way or another since I've been back."

Pastor James chuckled. "Well, it seems someone is trying to tell you something."

"But what does it mean, to open your mind to see?"

"It means that sometimes you have to look past yourself, look past what is right in front of you, in order to see the bigger picture. All you see right now is the finality of your parent's death, but nothing is final if you believe. Open your mind to the impossible, and you just might see him." He pointed to the heavens.

"That he's been with you this whole time. All things are possible with him."

Reaching into my back pocket, I pulled out the certificate. I unfolded it and handed it to Pastor James. He studied the drawing with curiosity.

"Does this mean anything to you? This man I drew after my baptism?" I asked. "I found it in a box full of old things. I can barely remember drawing it."

He smiled at it. I could see he'd conjured the memory. "Why, I remember when you drew this picture. You were all lit up from inside after your baptism. You went on and on about the angel you saw in the water. You were only under for a second, but you came out of that pool with the biggest smile on your face. You drew this picture to show your mother what he looked like. Such a creative mind . . ."

I pointed to the words I scribbled that morning. "And what about this? Does this mean anything?"

"Illumina, custody, rege et gube'rna," he read aloud. "Well, it's Latin for sure. Let me see . . . to light and guard, to rule and guide. Why, it's an old Catholic prayer. It's part of the Guardian Angel prayer, I believe."

"The Guardian Angel prayer?"

"Yes, I remember it well now. I took a few classes on Catholicism in seminary. The prayers were my favorite, this one especially. Let me see if I can remember the whole thing . . ."

He thought for a minute before going on. "Angel of God, my guardian dear, to whom God's love commits me here. Ever this day be at my side, to light and guard . . ."

"To rule and guide," I finished.

"Amen."

My heart began to race. "Would you think I was crazy if I told you I've been seeing this man? The same man I saw as a kid? Well, not really *seeing* him, but more like glimpses of him? The strangest part is, I feel like I know him. Like he's . . ."

"Watching over you?"

"Yes. It's like that exactly!" I cried. "Am I going crazy?"

"There are many, especially in the Catholic church, who believe that we are each appointed a guardian angel upon baptism. I wouldn't say you are crazy, child. I would say you've been blessed with a gift. You should embrace it."

"A gift?" I asked, my hands trembling.

"The gift of sight." He smiled.

I shook my head. "That's not possible."

In the distance a car honked its horn twice, and Pastor James waved to where it parked in the lot.

"Open your mind," he whispered. "With him, anything is possible."

I looked up at him dazed. He gave an apologetic smile.

"Now I'm afraid I have to be getting along. My grandson is here to take me to lunch. Feel free to stay as long as you like, though it looks like a storm's brewing. It was such a blessing to see you again, Miss Nolan. Please don't be a stranger."

I smiled at him despite the turmoil churning inside of my mind.

"I won't. It was great to see you again. Thank you so much for talking with me. It meant more than I can say."

"That's what I'm here for." He patted my arm, then turned and walked back across the churchyard.

Turning, I stared blankly into my mother's headstone, searching for . . . what? Had there really been a man there? Maybe I was cracking under the pressure of being back home. His face had been so clear in my dream, in the water. Maybe it wasn't just a dream. Maybe it was a memory.

"To light and guard, rule and guide," I repeated.

Then I thought about my other dreams, the reoccurring ones that replayed the night Mom and Gary were killed. Had the man been there the night of the accident too?

It was all coming back to me now. I *had* seen him. He'd been beside me in the dark. I'd heard him that night. He told me to sink into the seat that I was trapped under, rather than try to get out. Doing that had saved my life. He had saved my life.

Impossible, I thought.

It was nothing more than a self-defense mechanism, a hallucination brought on by the traumatic event. That had to be it. The problem with that theory, though, was that I was starting to remember that he'd been with me long before that night.

Consumed in thought, I jogged back to the parking lot. I climbed into the Mustang and brought it growling to life as the first drops of rain began to fall. I knew if I hurried, I could make it home before the storm got too bad. Thankfully, the majority of the drive was downhill. I didn't want to chance punching the engine on the slick road until I was more comfortable with the car. Easing back onto the road, I began the descent into town.

I made it about halfway back when the skies opened up. Rain dumped in blinding sheets, which bounced off the road and the hood of the car. Backing off the gas pedal entirely, I let the Mustang coast, keeping my foot ready on the brake. I wiped at the fogging windshield, only to realize that the fog forming outside was just as thick. It became impossible to see the curves in the road ahead.

Deciding it would be best to just pull off to the side of the road until the storm passed, I looked for a place to stop. It wasn't worth making a wrong move and either slamming into the mountainside or worse, driving off the steep embankment on the other side of the road. Both thoughts made my stomach clench, and my palms sweat.

I hit the brake and heard a pop and a hiss. The car didn't slow. Instead, the pedal slammed all the way to the floor with no resistance. I stomped the pedal again and again, but the brakes were useless. Horror rose up into my throat as I downshifted, earning an angry snarl from the engine. It did little to slow the car.

I searched the console for the emergency brake and couldn't find the lever. *Foot brake*, I realized, pushing it down with all the strength in my left leg. The car slid across the wet pavement, the rear end fishtailing back and forth. The road was slick with the heavy rain, and the car was gaining in speed with the steep incline despite my efforts. I used both feet to push down on the foot brake, but it was a futile attempt against the forward momentum of the car.

Leaning as far forward as I could in order to see the curves in the road, I knew that I was going to crash or go over the side if I didn't do something fast. Helpless, I did the only thing I could think to do. For the first time in years, I prayed.

"Okay, God. Where is your guardian angel now? I need your help," I pleaded. "I know what I said before . . . but I don't want to die, not today. Not like this. Please help me, I need you."

I wiped the windshield again in a futile attempt to better my vision. The yellow lines of the road were disappearing beneath the rain and fog, and I could no longer see where the road was going. I cried out, a mix of unbridled panic and unleashed rage.

"Where are you? Did you ruin my life just to kill me off like this? Where are you now?"

The trunks of trees charged towards the windshield. Jerking the wheel to the right, I screamed as the tires squealed and clawed the edge of the tight curve. I fought to see some clue as to which way the road would curve next.

That's when I saw it.

A white blur suspended in the air in the distance. As the car soared forward, white, outstretched wings became visible.

"The statue!" I cried out.

It stood out against the rain and fog like a beacon ushering me to safety. I knew then what I had to do. Now that I had a clue as to where I was in relation to the road, I had to crash the car on purpose. That was my only chance. If I didn't stop the car right now, it would gain speed in the downhill turns coming into town, and I would run off the road. This was my only chance.

I steered the car towards the statue, remembering that it was resting on a jutting rock that protruded above the road. If I could aim the car to the right of the statue, I could scrape against the side of the mountain to slow the car to a stop. If my aim was off though, I could hit the mountain head on.

I wasn't sure I could survive a head-on collision at this speed, but I had no time to think about it. I focused on the statue, on the majestic face, and prayed as the car careened towards it.

"God, if you are really there, please get me through this."

When I saw mountain side fill the windshield, I turned the wheel and braced myself as the car jolted against the swiping impact. The wheel fought back, but I held it as still as I could as metal scraped against rock. The friction forced the car to the left. I had to keep it steady or else I would be bounced right over the edge on the other side.

Bracing my left foot against the driver side door, I pulled the wheel to the right, the leather burning welts into my hands. The passenger side windows shattered, and I ducked as shards of glass and sparks flew into the cabin. Hooking my arm through the steering wheel, I held it steady and mashed the emergency brake with my foot.

At last the car came to a crunching stop with one final jolting crash. The windshield shattered as my head was thrown into the steering wheel. For a second, the world around me spun out of control and then faded. The last thing I heard was a gentle strumming beside me before everything went black.

Five

When I came to, the world was a blur. A sharp pain in my temple made it hard to lift my head from where it rested against the steering wheel. The rain had stopped, and dust swirled in a thick, black cloud around me. I dared to move my head to the right. That side of the car was crushed inward like a stomped soda can, curving the interior into a gruesome frown. Shattered glass and dust covered the once supple leather seats. But I was alive.

Taking a shaky breath, I raised my head off the steering wheel and assessed the large lump forming above my eye with trembling fingers. A gust of wind sent the dust around me swirling away, and my eyes locked with the white eyes of the angel statue. It looked down on me from where it had landed, face down, on the hood of the car.

"Okay," I said between heavy breaths. "I believe."

Sirens wailed in the distance, growing louder as they approached. I stumbled out of the car and took in the damage with shock just as Sully's truck charged down the highway towards me, sirens flashing. He barely waited for the truck to come to a stop before jumping out and running to me. He gawked at the wreckage, then rushed to me and gave me a once over. He gripped my shoulders, shock evident on his face.

"You should be dead! What happened?" he asked, exasperated.

"I'm fine, I think. The brakes . . . they went out. I couldn't see the road . . . then I saw the statue. I knew I had to crash it. I'm so sorry . . . I had to crash it. It wouldn't stop," I rambled as another car, sirens blasting, pulled up and then another.

Sully pulled me into his arms and held me against him.

"Ssshhh. It's alright kiddo. I'm just glad you're okay. When I got the call, I thought . . ." he shuddered. "Are you hurt? Is anything broken?"

I stepped back to check myself over. Aside from a few scratches and a massive headache, I seemed to be unscathed.

"No, I'm fine. I hit my head, but . . ."

"What the HELL happened?" a shrill voice interrupted.

I knew it was Will before I turned around. He was staring, mouth agape, at his wrecked car. His fingers trembled at his temples. He walked around the car in disbelief, then he stomped over to me. He looked me up and down before surrendering to fury.

"What the hell did you do? She's totaled! You could have killed yourself!" he screamed.

I took a step back from him. "The brakes went out. I didn't know what else to do. I couldn't see, and I was losing control . . . I'm sorry . . . I–"

"You're sorry? Sorry doesn't fix this! What were you thinking?"

Will closed the gap between us, but Sully stepped in and forced him back.

"I'd say she was thinking about saving herself since your precious car almost got her killed!" Sully shouted. Then he took a deep breath and lowered his voice. "Now walk away, deputy, and make sure someone comes out to get this heap off the road."

Will stared straight into my eyes and let out a frustrated growl. Then he threw his hands up and walked back to his squad car. Sully turned back to me and swept the hair from my forehead in order to get a better look at the pulsating mass forming there.

"Okay, now I want to get you home and get some ice on that lump," he said, walking me to his truck.

I looked up at him, tears forming in my eyes. "He's right to be mad. He loved that car . . . but there was nothing else I could do."

"Yeah, well, he shouldn't have loaned it to you in the first place. I don't know what he hoped to gain . . ." Sully got into the truck next to me and pulled back onto the road, slowing down to talk to the tow truck driver as he pulled up.

"Hey, Hank. Just tow her on down to the shop. Looks like she's totaled. Do me a favor, though, get a good look at those brakes, will you? Seems they went out while she was driving. Give me a call directly on my cell once you do."

"Will do. Glad you're all right, ma'am." Hank nodded to me and I thanked him before we drove off toward the house.

After being fussed over all afternoon, I was finally able to pull up a seat at the kitchen table and relax. I hadn't had time to stop and think about the events of the day and what it all meant. Sully had insisted that the town physician come out to take a look at what was now a purple knot above my right eye. Sully threatened me with a trip to the Hendersonville ER if I protested.

Dr. Andrews concluded that I had a mild concussion and gave me a bottle of Percocet to ease the throbbing in my head. For that I was grateful, though the first pill made me sleepy. I fought the urge to crawl into bed and sleep the next few days away. There was too much to think about.

I wanted to be alone with my thoughts, but Sully doted after me like a concerned parent. He tried to insist that I come home with him, but I refused to be a burden to him or to Gram. He had enough to worry about there. He settled for making me dinner. The canned chicken soup was bubbling away next to a skillet filled with melting cheese sandwiches. Sully had not inherited his mother's cooking ability, I mused, but it would do. With all of the excitement, I'd skipped lunch. I was starving despite the drum solo performance behind my temples.

"You sure as hell gave me a scare today, you know," Sully said, flipping the sandwiches onto a plate.

I sipped my water. "I know. Gave myself one too."

"Smart what you did though," Sully chuckled. "I still can't believe you rammed Will's Mustang into the side of the mountain."

I gawked at him. "Oh, are we laughing about it already? He was seriously pissed!"

"I'm just amazed at your survival instinct is all. Not sure most people would have thought to do that." Sully dished up the soup and came to the table. "And don't you worry about Will. He is just as much to blame, if not more so, for that car getting smashed up. He should have kept up with those brakes."

I sipped my soup, considering. "Yeah, but he was being nice by letting me drive it in the first place, even if it did turn out to be a death trap."

"Yeah, well, I'm not sure he did it all out of the kindness of his heart to begin with."

I set my spoon down. "What do you mean by that?"

"I'm just saying . . . I noticed the way you two look at one another. I'm not so sure he wasn't just trying to win some favor with you."

"Are you suggesting that I'm interested in Will? That's ridiculous." I scoffed, embarrassed that my intrigue with Will had been so transparent.

"It IS ridiculous," Sully agreed. "He's much older, and not much of the dating type."

I thought about that for a minute and wondered why I felt so defensive. "Intrigued with" and "interested in dating" were two different things, first of all. And second, Will wasn't THAT much older than me.

"What do you mean, he's not the dating type?" I asked, crossing my arms. "Not that I would want to or anything."

Sully set down his sandwich and glared at me. When I didn't back down, he continued.

"Look, I love the guy like a brother, and you know that's hard for me to say. But the man's got a past. I don't want you to get mixed up with his baggage is all."

I didn't know what bothered me more, that Sully thought I wanted to date Will, or that he thought he had the right to forbid it. I cleared my throat and glared at him.

"I think you are forgetting that I am a grown woman, and if I wanted to date him, I would. Lucky for you, I have no interest in dating him or anyone else until I figure out what it is that I want to begin with. So this is really a moot point."

"Okay then." Sully chuckled and bit into his sandwich.

After finishing dinner in comfortable silence, Sully wiped at his chin with his napkin and sat back in his chair.

"So, have you thought any about what you are going to do? With this place, I mean?"

I tossed the last crust of sandwich onto my plate and sighed.

"I have, a little. To tell you the truth, when I first got here all I wanted to do was find a buyer and get back on a plane to Chicago." I stared out the kitchen window at the sun dipping below the tree line. "But now, I don't know any more. I'm sort of finding myself again . . . if that makes sense."

Sully nodded. "It does, and it's a good thing. Your mother would be happy that you're at least giving the place a chance."

"I only took the week off from work, but I guess I can find a long-term substitute if I need to. I might want to take some more time to really think about it, to figure out what's best," I said with a sigh.

Sully chuckled as he shook his head. "I don't want to push, but the elementary school here is looking for a good music teacher."

I waved him off and cleared the dishes. My head throbbed with the movement. "No, that was Mom's thing. Before a couple of nights ago, I hadn't played in years."

Sully stood, a smile spreading across his face.

"You played your mother's piano? I knew you would if I brought it down here." He turned me to face him. "Play something for me?"

"No. No, I can't," I said, shrugging away from him. I regretted saying anything.

Sully took the dishes from me and set them in the sink, then took me by the hand.

"Pretty please," he said, leading me into the living room and motioning me to sit at the piano. He sat on the couch with anticipation. "Please, just a little something. I know it will be wonderful."

Sighing, I lifted the lid and exposed the keys, then stared blankly at them. I imagined my mother's fingers dancing over them once again while I sat and watched in awe. I would never be able to play like her. Was it doing a disservice to her memory to even try? Unsure, I placed my fingers on the keys and met Sully's expectant eyes. *For Sully*, I decided.

I imagined my mother sitting at the piano and held the memory as I played the first movement of *Moonlight Sonata*. I fell into the music, my hands taken over by the echoes of a past performance. My first recital had earned me a standing ovation, and on the way home, admiring smiles from the front seat of the car. A tear slipped onto my cheek as my thoughts wandered from memories of twisted metal to lily-covered graves under a darkening sky. I saw heavy rain and fog, and the white outstretched wings floating above the road on a cloud of mist. I saw the stone-glazed eyes of a statue staring into my soul.

Above the music, a different beat sounded in my ear. Gentle at first. I couldn't identify it right away, only feel the gentle rocking of it as my fingers relaxed on the keys. Then I recognized the strumming. The realization threw off my rhythm and broke my focus.

I opened my eyes, and there he was. Reflected in the piano once again was the figure of the man I'd seen before. He stood behind me, glaring at me with those blue eyes. In the piano, I watched him turn and walk to the staircase. He motioned for me to follow.

Gasping, I jumped back from the piano, ending the piece on a harsh note. I looked to Sully who was gaping at me admiringly. He stood, eyes wide.

"Why'd you stop? That was beautiful . . ."

I glanced nervously behind me. No one was there.

"I just . . . my head hurts," I said, turning back to Sully. "I think I should go lie down now."

"Please, just a little more," Sully pleaded.

"I really can't . . ."

"Just one more minute? You play just like her . . ." Sully insisted, coming toward me.

I shot up from the piano, suddenly furious. A storm of emotions raged and pounded in my head, and I spoke before I could hold it back, not knowing what I was saying until I'd said it.

"I told you I can't! I'm not my mother. I'm not her. She was murdered a long time ago, and now we BOTH have to move on. You can't bring her back through me, Uncle Sully. Now please, just stop!"

Sully recoiled as if I had punched him in the gut. He lowered his head, wounded.

"You're right," he said. "I'm sorry. I shouldn't have pushed you. You've had a really long day, and I'm just making it worse."

"Please, I just want to be alone," I whispered, not looking him in the eyes, afraid to see the wounds my words had caused in them.

"Yeah sure, kiddo. You need to get some rest. I'm sorry." He nodded and turned for the door as I stood frozen in place, unable to react.

"I'll be by around eleven tomorrow," he continued in a soft voice. "I thought you'd like to come to church with me and Gram. Maybe come by the house for lunch after?"

I nodded to him, still overcome by emotion and afraid to speak again. Sully opened the door and turned back to me. This time I looked him in the eyes.

"I know you're not your mother. I know that. You just . . . you remind me so much of her. Having you back is like getting a little piece of her back," he said smiling. "I miss them too, and I know they've been gone a long time. There isn't a day that goes by that I don't think of them and wish that things could have been different. It's a hard thing to get over, Kiddo, but you being here is a major step . . . for both of us. Get some rest," he said and then shut the door behind him.

I stood there for a second not knowing what I felt more: pain, longing, or raw guilt. I sank to the floor and sobbed, unable to do anything else. I knew that Sully missed Mom as much as I did. They'd been best friends since childhood. And Gary. Gary was his baby brother, but I just couldn't play another note. It was too painful. Sitting at that piano connected me to a happier time, a time when life made sense and I wasn't afraid that I would fall into pieces at any moment. A time that was gone forever.

I let my head fall into my hands and continued to weep, the bitterness of loss bubbling up from neglected places within me. Then I heard it again. The gentle strumming which seemed to retrieve me from the darkest of places. I lifted my head to listen. The strumming was coming from upstairs.

I stood and wiped my face, and with head pounding, walked up the stairs and down the hall. My limbs trembled with anticipation, but this time I was not afraid. I was ready to face whatever I found waiting for me. When I reached the end of the hall and went into the master bedroom, the steady rhythm intensified. I flipped on the light, but there was nothing there. Not a thing was out of place.

I stood still and listened. The sound was coming from the bathroom. As I approached though, the strumming turned to a steady drip. I flipped on the light and saw that the shower faucet was leaking in a steady thud against the ceramic bathtub. With a sigh I turned the knob to quiet the leak, my heart rate returning to normal. Then on second thought, I turned the shower to hot and let the bathroom fill with steam. A hot shower was exactly what I needed.

Closing the door, I spotted the Percocet bottle on the counter and decided that it was time for another. Washing it down with a cup of water, I undressed and soaked in the hot spray until my muscles eased and my senses dulled. My head stopped throbbing, and the tension from the day ran with the soapy water down the drain.

When I pulled back the curtain, the bathroom was filled with steam. I inhaled it in long, deep drags as I dried off. Pulling on my bathrobe, I ran a brush through my hair and then opened the bathroom door. The steam rolled out behind me in billowing clouds that filled the bedroom with a misty haze. I glanced at the clock and noted it was late enough in the evening to justify climbing into bed. When something reflected in the antique mirror caught my eye, I dropped the brush to the floor.

Through the haze that had formed in a moist sheet upon the mirror, I saw the man standing beside me. Though his sudden appearance startled me, this time I held his gaze. Glancing behind me at the room, I saw that there was no one there and this time was not surprised.

I turned back to the mirror and watched the blurred reflection run a hand across my forehead. When the strumming came, I closed my eyes. Warmth, ever so slight, embraced the wound on my head. I opened my eyes, and his reflection was still there, beseeching me with those ocean blues.

"Who are you?" I whispered.

"Who do you think I am?" he answered in a deep, melodious voice as smooth as glass.

I groped for an answer. No matter how I worded it, it still felt unreal. "An angel."

The man in the mirror grinned at me as if amused by my hesitation. "I am a Guardian, your Guardian. You already knew that though, didn't you? Deep down you've always known."

I searched my memories. That voice, it was so familiar. I heard it whisper to me through the fleeting memories of my childhood, and I knew that he was right.

"Why can I only see you like this? In reflections?" I asked, motioning to the mirror.

"That is the only place your mind will allow me to exist to you," he said.

"I . . . don't understand," I groped.

"You won't let yourself believe that I am real, that I can exist in your world. So, I exist here," he motioned to the mirror around him, "in a reflection of your reality. The same, but separate."

I sat on the bed beside where the man stood according to the mirror's reflection. I looked across from me, stared at the spot where he should be, but could not make his image appear.

"I want to see you," I whispered.

"And you will, when you are ready. Right now you are half convinced that your concussion, mixed with that pain pill, is causing you to see things that aren't there." He sighed. "Only a part of you believes. That is why you can hear me and see me in reflections. You limit yourself."

He was right. I knew it. My rational side was telling me that this was not possible, and it was searching for a reasonable explanation. But I wanted it to be true. I wanted more than anything to lose myself in the fanciful side of me that had been lost for so long. So I started with questions.

"Are you from . . . heaven then?"

"Not exactly," he answered. "I exist in a place between here and there."

"What, like purgatory?"

He laughed, a melodious sound, warm and vibrant. "Not so drastic, no, but similar. I exist in the spiritual realm, while you exist here in the physical. I am there every bit as much as I am here with you right now."

"So you're in two places at once? I don't understand . . . that doesn't make any sense. None of this makes any sense," I reeled.

In the mirror, I watched him set his hand over mine. Again, I felt a tingling warmth where he touched me, slight and gentle.

"That's the biggest problem with humanity," he said. "You think that seeing is believing."

"So you're saying that believing is seeing then? Isn't that a bit cliché?" I asked a little more sarcastically than I'd intended.

"It's much more than that, more than just believing. It's accepting."

I shrugged at him through the mirror, not understanding. He smiled patiently at me.

"You only think a thing is real if you can comprehend it," he continued, "if you can make sense of it or understand how it works. You have to know how it's possible before you will believe that it is. Humanity misses out on so much beauty because it refuse to accept that things exist beyond the realm of reason or understanding. When in fact, that is what makes some things so glorious – not understanding how they can possibly exist, but just relishing in the fact that they do."

"Like you?" I asked.

"Or you."

For a long moment, we stared at one another through the mirror, like those taking in the changed features of a long-lost loved one. I followed him with my eyes, afraid to take them off of him for fear that he would be gone.

"You need your rest. I need to let you sleep. I know you have a lot of questions, but there's time. We can talk more tomorrow."

I didn't want him to go. I didn't want this moment to end. What if it wasn't real? Would I see him again? What if it WAS just the concussion or the pain medication making the impossible a reality?

"You'll be back tomorrow?"

He smiled. "I never really leave you, Alexandra. I am always with you."

I thought about that for a moment. My cheeks flushed when I looked to the bathroom, just now clearing of steam.

"Always?" I shrieked.

The man laughed and shook his head. "When you need me, that is."

I relaxed a bit. It was so much to take in, and he was right. I had so many more questions.

"What if I need you now? There's so much I don't understand . . ."

"I was sent here to look after you, Alexandra, and right now you need sleep. The answers will come. Give yourself time," he said. Through the mirror, I could see him motion for me to get into the bed.

I hesitated, still trying to make sense of it all. *He was sent here? By who, God? Could that be right?* I had so many questions, but I knew he was right. I was beginning to feel like I could fall over where I stood. The excitement of the day and the pain medication in my system were hitting me with full force now. I couldn't fight it any more.

Still, I didn't want to let go of this present reality. I was afraid that if I slept, the man would be gone and the calm that his presence gave me would vanish with him. Somehow, now that I had spoken with him and seen him more clearly, the familiar feeling of comfort and love that he emitted made me feel more like myself than I had felt in fifteen years.

"Please, Alexandra, you need sleep. You're going to need a clear mind," he pleaded.

I went to the bed and climbed inside. When I looked back to the mirror, I was relieved to see him smiling at me.

"It was you the other night. You helped me into bed after the wine . . . at the piano."

"Yes."

I laid my head on the pillow. "And it was you that night . . . the night of the accident, in the car. You told me to sink further into my seat."

"Yes," he said, a sadness washing over his features. Then lowering his head, his image began to fade.

I stared into the mirror, hoping he would return, but my eyes were weighted down by impending sleep. I closed them, focusing on the swaying rhythm of the strumming that seemed to vibrate against me.

"I know you're still here. I can hear you," I whispered.

Teetering on the brink of consciousness, I heard only the strumming reply.

"Did He send you? God?"

"Yes," came a soft whisper.

"What if you don't come back tomorrow? What if I don't believe that any of this actually happened in the morning?" I couldn't give in to the sleep that was overtaking me until I was sure.

"You will. You have to."

Yes, I had to. He had to come back to me.

"I . . . I don't even know your name," I mumbled, losing myself in the soothing darkness.

I heard his voice whisper to me from the edges of deep sleep.

"Donovan."

Then the strumming faded away and all consciousness with it.

Six

I shot up in bed as soon as I woke. Immediately, I looked into the mirror but saw nothing unusual. With a sigh and a freshly brewing headache, I laid back down. *What happened last night? Was it all a dream?* It couldn't have been real. And yet talking with him . . . with Donovan, felt more real and natural than anything else in my life.

Aside from the throbbing in my temples, I felt more rested than I had in months, maybe even years. A knock at the front door jarred me from this realization. I glanced at the clock. It was only 9 o'clock, too early for Sully to be here to pick me up.

Getting up from the bed, I glanced in the mirror before going to the window. I wanted to see Donovan. I needed to. I wanted to convince myself that last night was real. My reflection alone stared back at me.

Looking outside to the driveway below, I saw a squad car parked out front. Sully must have sent a car to come pick me up. When I remembered how I'd treated him the night before, I was filled with sudden regret. He must be upset with me if he sent someone else to get me. Lifting the window, I stuck my head out.

"I'll be right there!" I yelled, wincing at the ache in my skull.

Grabbing some clean clothes from my bag, I rushed into the bathroom. I paused when I saw the Percocet bottle on the counter. For a second I contemplated taking one, but pitched them into the waste basket beside the sink instead. I needed to have a clear mind.

Dressed in a floral skirt and a comfy blue sweater, I hurried down the steps and answered the door. Will nodded to me from the front stoop. I took a step back, my body tensing, and readied myself for another verbal assault. This time I wasn't going to take it in silence. He might be mad, but I was hurt. Though I still felt horrible about crashing the Mustang, the fact that I could have died hadn't seemed to bother him at all yesterday.

"What are you doing here?"

Will shifted from one foot to the other, his deputy hat held nervously in front of him.

"I . . . came to apologize," he scowled, "for my behavior yesterday."

I was speechless. An apology was the last thing I expected from him.

"Sully put you up to this, didn't he? Well, consider yourself off the hook," I said and then started to shut the door.

Will caught the door and pushed it back open. He stepped closer.

"No, I wanted to come," he said, staring at me with those intense eyes. "Can I come in?"

I hesitated. The thought of being alone in the house with him, especially after the way he had screamed at me yesterday, made me uncomfortable. It was only fair to hear him out, though, so I stepped aside to let him in. Will hung his hat on the coat rack and followed me into the kitchen. When he glanced into the living room, he paused mid-stride.

"Is that . . . your mom's piano?"

"It is," I nodded, continuing into the kitchen.

Will stared another moment then came in after me.

"I was just about to make some coffee," I said, going to the pot. "Would you like some?"

"That would be great." He had a seat at the table and unzipped his jacket. "Thank you."

I could feel Will burning a hole into my back as I filled the pot with water and measured out the grounds. Once I flipped the coffee pot on, I spun around.

"So, why don't you tell me why you are really here? Is it to make me feel even worse about wrecking your car?"

Will looked at his shoes. "I told you, I want to apologize. It's not the easiest thing in the world for me."

I had a seat across from him at the table and folded my arms.

"Well, you could say something like . . . ," I searched for the words. "Alex, I am sorry for my jerkishness yesterday when I yelled at you about crashing my broken heap into the side of a mountain."

"But I . . ." he started to protest.

"EVEN THOUGH," I cut him off. "I know you HAD to crash it in order to save yourself from my death trap of a car with crappy brakes."

Will stared at me blankly. "Are you done?"

"I think so, yes."

"First of all, *jerkishness* is not a word. And she was not a heap or a death trap . . . which is what I want to talk to you about."

I glared at him, undaunted. He sighed and continued.

"I AM sorry, more than you could know. I shouldn't have reacted like that. I guess I just . . . freaked out."

I sighed and sat back in my chair. "That car did mean a lot to you, so I get it. I'm really sorry I wrecked it, Will. I should never have borrowed it . . ."

"No," Will interrupted. "It's not about the damned car. I mean, yeah, I loved that car, but it's just a car. I freaked out because you could have been killed and it would have been my fault. I couldn't live with that," he said, then whispered under his breath. "Not again."

"What are you talking about?"

"Look," he leaned towards me, his intense eyes locking on mine. "I know the brakes were fine on that car. They were solid."

"Clearly," I scoffed.

"No, really. I just replaced all the brakes a couple of years ago when I rebuilt the engine. There's no reason they should've gone out like that."

I let his words sink in as I got two coffee cups down from the cupboard and filled them with fresh brew. "Maybe I hit something without knowing. Or maybe the rain . . ."

"That's crazy."

I sat a mug in front of him and sat back down, cradling mine in my hands. "Then you must have installed the brakes wrong to begin with."

Will sneered. "I know what I'm doing when it comes to that car. Even if I had installed faulty brakes, they would have gone out before yesterday."

"What exactly are you suggesting then?" I asked.

Will sighed, sitting back in his seat. "I don't know. I called the mechanic this morning, but he must not be open on Sundays. I'll try back tomorrow and see what he has to say."

"I think he'll tell you your brakes were crap," I said.

"Maybe, but maybe not." He took a sip of his coffee, and his face brightened. "Wow, this is a lot better than Evelyn's Black Death."

"Thanks, I think." I took my first sip and savored the feel of the hot liquid on my scratchy throat. "Maybe it will help this headache."

"Yeah, you don't look so good. That's a pretty nasty lump on your head."

"Always were the flatterer, weren't you?"

"I just mean that you got pretty banged up." Will cupped his hand over mine. "I am so sorry."

"Yeah, well . . . it could have been a lot worse."

Will leaned in close, making my heart beat faster. I thought I smelled a hint of whisky on his breath.

"I mean it, Alex. I am really sorry about yesterday. About everything."

I wondered if he was still talking about the wreck, but my thoughts were lost in the intensity of his deep, chocolate brown eyes. I saw pain and heartbreak in their depths and felt a compulsion to wipe it all away somehow. The thought startled me.

I cleared my throat and forced my eyes away. The heat of his stare was too much.

"Well, it's just too bad I wasn't here to borrow your car when I was in high school. Wrecking the infamous Billy Galia Stang would have made me the most popular girl in school," I smiled, watching his eyes soften as he laughed.

"And that is EXACTLY why I never would have lent her to you. I can't even imagine how bad of a driver you must have been back then."

I gawked, exasperated. "I happen to be a very good driver."

Will laughed and motioned to the lump on my head. "Clearly."

He met my eyes again, and this time we both burst into laughter. I was afraid that he was going to be mad at me for all of eternity, but here we were laughing about it already. The look of rage and disgust he'd given me at the accident scene had melted into a wide grin. Will was a totally different person when he laughed. I admired the way his smile softened his rugged exterior, making him look almost child-like.

We were still laughing when Sully walked into the kitchen. Jumping, both Will and I stopped laughing.

Sully held up an apologetic hand. "Sorry, didn't mean to startle you. I knocked on the door, but you didn't hear me."

Will stood and put his coffee cup in the sink. I watched Sully, trying to gauge his emotions. He looked more curious than anything, which I guessed was a good thing. He wasn't upset with me about last night, but I was sure to get another snide remark about Will.

"Not a problem, Chief. I was just heading to the station. I came by to apologize for my 'jerkishness' yesterday," Will said, shooting me a wink. "Thanks for the coffee."

Will grabbed his coat and went out the door.

"Jerkishness isn't a word," Sully hollered to him. Then he turned to me, questions in his eyes.

"You look as surprised as I was when I opened the door this morning." I retrieved another mug from the cabinet, then motioned for Sully to have a seat while I poured him a cup of coffee.

"Well, that was awfully nice of him."

"Yeah, but he's not the only one who needs to apologize for their behavior yesterday. I'm sorry I snapped at you. It was uncalled for. I love you, you know that."

Sully took a sip of his coffee and nodded. "Don't you worry about it, Kiddo. I know you're going through some stuff. I shouldn't have pushed you so hard."

I watched him shake the image of last night from his mind like an unwanted drawing from an Etch-A-Sketch. Then he offered me a smile.

"That bump on your head has you all mushy this morning," he said, snickering. "Or is it the visit from the deputy that has you all warm and fuzzy?"

I rolled my eyes at him. There it was. I stood to put my cup in the sink.

"Seriously? The man came over to apologize, not put the moves on me. I thought it was a nice gesture."

"Mmmhmm," Sully murmured.

"What's that supposed to mean?"

Sully threw up his hands and shrugged. "Hey, I'm not saying a word. You're a grown woman. Said so yourself. Moot point, remember?"

"That's right. Thank you." I smiled, satisfied with his answer. "You finish your coffee. I'm going to go grab my purse."

I jogged up the steps as quickly as I could with my fading headache. The coffee was helping, thank God. Though I longed for another pain pill, I was determined to keep a clear head. I needed last night to be real more than anything. I needed Donovan to be real. Last night was the first night I hadn't felt utterly alone in fifteen years. Before last night, I'd succumbed to the idea that I would always be alone. Donovan reminded me of how wrong I was.

When I got to my room, I looked straight to the mirror. Nothing. Standing in front of it, I closed my eyes. I took a deep breath and remembered what he said. I needed to believe. I focused on accepting the fact that I had a . . .

I opened my eyes and stared at myself. *Guardian.* Just thinking the word was too unreal. It felt insane.

"Let's go, Kiddo." Sully called from downstairs. "We've got to meet Gram at church. Evelyn took her to breakfast this morning. They'll be there any minute."

I looked into the mirror one final time. Frustrated with myself, I grabbed my purse and shut the bedroom door behind me.

The road to church felt different than it had just the day before. The sky was bright and clear without a single cloud. The sun was dazzling, casting down rays of light through the gaps in the trees. When we passed the spot where I wrecked the Mustang, I gawked at the skid marks, burned yellow and black, across the face of the mountain. Glass and bits of metal still lay scattered along the shoulder.

"What happened to the statue?' I asked. "They're not going to put it back up on the ledge?"

"No, thank goodness," Sully said. "I guess they hauled it off with the car. Good riddance. That thing was creepy as hell. Never did find out what nut job got it up there to begin with."

"That *thing* saved my life yesterday."

Sully smiled. "Well, then, I guess it served its purpose."

Contemplating, I looked out the window. I was sure that whoever put the statue on that ledge had done it with a different purpose in mind. Still, if they hadn't, I might have died. Of that I was certain. If only I could be certain of what else had happened yesterday. The conversation with Donovan seemed as real as the crash, so why couldn't I accept him as truth? Why couldn't I bring him back?

I tried to remember the details of our conversation. Donovan said he'd been with me since my baptism, since I was a child. I remembered knowing that he was with me. I could even conjure up scattered images and conversations. Why couldn't I remember him over the last decade or more? Why was it so hard to believe as whole-heartedly as I had when I was a kid?

It was like trying to remember how it felt to earnestly believe in Santa Claus or the tooth fairy. I had been so sure that all of those things existed too. As a child, it's easier to accept the impossible as reality. Donovan was different, though, because I knew that my faith determined whether or not he was possible, whether or not he was real. That made him all the harder to accept.

To accept him as reality was to accept that there was indeed a loving God in the heavens, and not only that, but a God who cared enough about me to send someone to protect me. That was the hard part to accept, especially when the last decade and a half seemed to prove the exact opposite.

Great train of thought to have at church, I thought as we pulled up the driveway. It was bustling with people, some of which I recognized. Sully parked the truck, and we walked the stone walkway. Gram and Nadine were seated on one of the marble benches beside the main entrance. Gram chatted away with Evelyn, who stood beside her decked out in a leopard print jacket and scarlet heels. They smiled and waved to us as we approached.

"Gram," I said, stooping to embrace the small woman.

She wrapped her feeble arms around me and patted my back. "It's so nice to see you again, Tina. You look lovely, my dear."

I stood and looked to Nadine and Evelyn and whispered, "She still thinks I'm Mom."

"But she's feeling quite well today," Evelyn smiled.

"I'm sorry, Kiddo," Sully mouthed and gently brushed the hair from my forehead.

Gram noticed the now purple knot on my head.

"My goodness, what have you done to yourself?" she said, studying the lump.

"Oh. Just a little accident, Gram, nothing to worry about," I assured her.

Sully motioned us inside. "Why don't we find a seat before it fills up?"

Gram and Evelyn followed Sully inside. Nadine turned to me with a grin and grabbed my hand. "It's so good to see you again, Alexandra."

"You too, Nadine," I said. "How is Gram doing?"

She gave my hand a pat as we followed Gram inside. "Well, she's been in and out for a couple of days now. Seems she's more gone than with us nowadays." She glanced at Sully and sighed. "It's to be expected."

I looked around at the inside of the church, admiring the arched ceiling and oval windows. The pews, the walls, and the altar were all crafted out of the same golden oak. Everything was as I remembered, down to the simple silver chandeliers that hung from the high ceiling. The church was small, but spectacular and filled with glowing warmth.

Sitting between Gram and Nadine, I mentally prepared myself to take on the role of my mother for the day. Sully said it was best to go with it, so I would. I longed for the old Gram, the one I could talk to about anything. I needed her right now. Glancing over, the small, frail woman looked expectantly around at the congregation as they filed into their seats. She looked like the old Gram, only weakened, as if her essence were being drained from her a little with each passing day. She looked lost, trapped inside herself.

"Oh, look, there's little Ricky," Gram suddenly declared with a smile. "My, he looks all grown up."

I followed her gaze. Rick Brightman walked the aisle of the church, looking for an empty seat. Confused, I turned to Gram. "You mean, Rick? The contractor? Do you know him, Gram?"

"Of course I do, and so do you, silly. The poor dear." She sighed. "It's a shame what happened to that family. Just a shame."

Sully bent forward from where he sat on the other side of Gram. He looked as confused as I was. "I think you're confusing him with someone else Mom. Mr. Brightman is from out of town."

Gram shook her head and scowled. "I most certainly am not. That is Ricky Brightman. Don't you remember, dear?" She turned to me. "You bought the house from his poor mother."

Clueless, I looked to Sully for help. I didn't know anything about who my mom bought the house from. Sully had been there to help with the purchase. He stared at Gram for a minute, searching his memory.

"You mean Mallory Blackwell's son? Wrong last name Mom, though I do think his name was Ricky."

Gram shook her head, frustrated. "Ricky was from her first marriage, remember? HIS name is Brightman. I never forget a name or a face," she chuckled.

Sully and I exchanged knowing glances. He thought for a minute and then nodded.

"You know what? You might be right, Mom. I don't know why I didn't put that together before." He scratched his head. "It's strange that he hasn't said anything."

I watched Rick find a seat across the aisle. When I recalled our conversation on the plane, I wondered the same thing.

"I bet he just didn't want to bring up those bad memories. It looks to have aged him quite a bit. He was just a teenager not too long ago," Gram said as the organ began to play the first hymn.

I stood when the congregation stood and sang when they sang, but I was just going through the motions. My mind kept wandering back to Rick. What happened to his family? Had Mom really bought the house from his mother? Why in the world didn't he mention any of this during our conversation? He'd made it seem as though he were just a visitor passing through.

During the sermon my mind shifted to thoughts of the previous night. I couldn't help but to think of Donovan. Why couldn't I see him this morning? He said he would be here. I still had so many questions. What if I had imagined him after all?

I must have been staring in a daze, lost in my thoughts for a while. A waving hand from across the pews brought me back. Rick smiled to me from the other side of the church and laughed silently when I finally blinked and responded with a nod. I directed my attention back to the front where Pastor James was passionately delivering his message.

"Sometimes God pushes us to the very edge of our faith, to the end of our limits, before he offers His deliverance," he was saying. "He wants more than anything for you to reach for Him in times of need."

What did it mean to be pushed to the edge of your faith, though? Did allowing my parents to be killed by a madman right in front of me qualify as pushing me to my limits? If that was the case, I wanted nothing to do with it. My mother had been a woman of tremendous faith. Where was her deliverance?

Anger began to well up to the surface. I shifted in my seat in a vain attempt to quell the urge to leave. I conjured Donovan's image in my mind. It was all I could think to do. *"You must believe,"* he'd said.

"If we cry out to God, he will hear our prayers. We are never truly alone. He never leaves our side no matter what circumstances you face. And sometimes, he answers our prayers in ways we may never have imagined," Pastor James continued from the pulpit, and when I looked up, it seemed as if he were looking directly at me.

Suddenly, I felt very uncomfortable. Grabbing a Bible from the pew in front of me, I opened it to a random page and pretended to read. My mind was whirling, thoughts hurling back and forth like a kite in a storm. I was agitated by Pastor James' words about faith and the things that Donovan had said to me last night. *"You must believe."*

Nadine smiled and leaned over to me. "Excellent sermon, isn't it?"

"Ah, yes. Pastor James is great," I said, trying to be polite.

Nadine looked down at the Bible opened haphazardly on my lap. She gave her finger a lick, then gave the pages a quick flip.

"I think that passage is more what you are looking for," she whispered and then turned her attention back to the sermon.

I looked down at my lap, to where her finger rested on the page. Curious, I began to read.

"For He will command his angels concerning you; to guard you in all your ways; they will lift you up in their hands, so that you will not strike your foot against a stone."

My heart quickened. I snapped my head up and looked at Nadine. A slow smile spread across her lips as she placed her hand back in her lap. She nodded, still looking forward.

"Yep, that's my favorite part too."

"But . . . how . . .?" I began to ask, but was interrupted when Pastor James called for the congregation to rise and sing the last hymn.

I stood, reluctantly singing the familiar hymn with the rest of the congregation, all the while sneaking looks at Nadine who sang loud and proud beside me. When the hymn was over, the congregation began to file out of the pews with waves of greeting and handshakes. I followed Evelyn, Sully, and Gram out the front doors where Gram stopped to chat with a neighbor. Nadine went with her and I tore my gaze away from her to look around for Rick. I was hoping to have a word with him before he left, but I couldn't find him in the crowd assembled in front of the church.

Scanning the parking lot, I spotted him climbing inside of a small, white pick-up truck. I'd seen that truck before. It was the same one that flew past me on the street when I went for my walk to the station. I was sure of it. Why would he not stop and say hi?

Before I could think about it for too long, Sully called me over to where he was talking to a group of smiling faces. I recognized some, but none by name. He introduced me, and we exchanged the usual pleasantries. When the conversation turned to my mother, I was again reminded of just how much I looked like her. The mention of her name made me ache to go visit her grave once again. When the opportunity presented itself, I excused myself and made my way to the back of the church.

I'd barely reached the grounds of the cemetery when I heard Nadine call my name. When I turned, she was walking up to meet me, arm in arm with Gram.

"I think it would be a great idea if you took Gram for a walk out there with you," Nadine suggested with an encouraging smile.

I shook my head and glared knowingly at Nadine. Gram couldn't see Mom and Gary's graves. Not while she still thought I *was* Mom. "I . . . I don't think that's such a good idea."

Gram brightened at the suggestion. "Oh, a walk would be wonderful, dear. The grounds are so lovely this time of year. You're not spooked by a little ole' cemetery, are you now?"

She grabbed my arm and started walking. I looked back to Nadine in a panic.

"No, I'm just worried that you might see . . . something, eh ... upsetting."

Nadine waved me on with a smile and took a seat on the cement bench beside the stone entryway. I trusted her. She was with Gram every day. She wouldn't let something bad happen to her, would she?

I grew more and more nervous as we entered the cemetery. How could I walk Gram to Mom's grave? She was sure to see Gary's resting place beside it. Would it not be cruel to let her see her son's grave when she was currently stuck in a past where he still lived? Gram commented on the fall colors and the well-kept lawn while I groped for the answer.

What do I do? What do I do? I cried out in my mind as we got closer and closer to the plots.

The answer came in a deep, melodious voice, beside me.

"Go," it said.

Stifling a gasp, I looked wide-eyed around me for Donovan, but there was no sign of him, only the scrutinizing eyes of Gram who eyed me suspiciously.

"What is it, girl? The spooks getting ya?" She chuckled and patted my arm to comfort. "There's nothing to be afraid of, Tina. It's just a place for those we've lost. Nothing to fear here."

I took a deep breath and feigned a smile. She hadn't heard his voice. Of course she hadn't.

"You're right. I guess I get a little jumpy," I said.

Donovan was here with me. That knowledge gave me comfort and the courage to do what he said I should do. Looking back, I saw that Sully was still engaged in conversation, his back to me. So I steered Gram towards Mom's and Gary's plots.

"There is something I would like to show you, Gram," I said, guiding her to the far corner of the grounds by the eastern fence.

We stopped in front of the white lilies still scattered atop Mom's grave. I motioned to it, my hand shaking.

"I know this is going to be hard for you to understand, but my name is not Tina. Tina was my mother . . . and you helped me bury her here," I said as tenderly as I could.

I watched Gram, my breath caught in my throat, waiting for her reaction.

"But that can't be . . . you just bought the house. And Sullivan . . ."

Gram paused and stared into space as if she were watching images play through her mind. I could tell that she was trying to make sense of them, and I waited, breathless, to see what I'd done. With a sudden gasp, she looked to the grave and then back up to me. A single tear ran down her cheek.

"Alexandra?" she whispered.

My breath rushed out in a sob, and my eyes welled with tears as Gram looked at me for the first time with admiring recognition. I nodded yes as she cupped my cheek in her hand. She took in every inch of my face.

"I've missed you so much, Gram," I cried, unable to hold back the tears.

Gram gasped with joy and grabbed me up into her arms and cradled me there as I sobbed against her shoulder. "Oh, my baby, Alexandra. I love you so much. I'm so sorry. I don't know what's happened to my mind. I . . . I just get so confused . . ."

I sniffed. "I know, Gram. It's not your fault."

Gram held me out at arm's length in order to look into my face again.

"I have missed you something awful! Good God in heaven, you're all grown up now, and so beautiful. You look just like . . ." Gram trailed off and then stiffened.

I looked into Gram's face, which was frozen in contemplation. I watched as her blank stare turned to a mask of fear and panic. She grabbed me by the shoulders and looked me square in the eyes.

"Listen to me now, Alexandra," she whispered urgently. "You can't trust him. It's all a lie! He was there that night, all those years ago. He'll kill you too. You have to leave this place and never look back."

I twisted in Gram's tight grip, her fingers digging into my arms.

"What are you talking about, Gram? Who was here?" My palms began to sweat as her words registered. "Do you know who killed Mom and Gary?"

Gram dropped her grip. The intensity of her face twisted into an expression of confusion and dismay. She looked around her as if she wasn't sure of where she was.

"Gary? Something's happened to Gary?" she cried, shoving me to the side. "What are you talking about, Tina?"

A cry rose up into my throat, and I forced it back down. She was gone. Lost again to an ocean of misplaced memories. I reached for her, but it was too late. Gram saw Gary's headstone.

"My boy? What happened to my boy?" she screamed, collapsing to the ground.

Not knowing what to say, I tried to calm her. I tried to coax her into leaving with me, but she sat staring at the gravestone in a state of shock and grief.

"What happened to my boy?" she shouted over and over.

I looked helplessly towards the church and was relieved to see Sully running towards us, Nadine close on his heels. When Sully reached us, he stooped down to his mother and wrapped his large arms around her shoulders. He whispered into her ear until she reluctantly stood and put her arms around him. He led her slowly away.

"Oh, Sullivan. What happened? Why?"

"Sssshhhh, it's okay, Mom. It's okay," he whispered.

When they passed me, he turned to look at me as Nadine reached me and put her arm around me.

"What the hell were you thinking?" he hissed.

"She . . . she remembered me. I'm so sorry. I'm sorry . . ." I stammered, bursting into fresh tears against Nadine's arms as he led Gram away.

Seven

"I just don't understand what you were thinking." Sully shook his head and paced the kitchen floor. "I told you it was best to just go with it, just let her think what she wants."

I sat at Sully's kitchen table, head hung, counting the number of times Sully stepped on the squeaky floorboard. I felt awful, despicable even. Upsetting Gram was the last thing I ever wanted to do, but I was also glad that it had happened. Did that make me a horrible person? I wasn't sure. I'd gotten my Gram back, if even for only a moment. For those few minutes, when I looked into that smile of recognition, the world felt right again. She told me that she loved me. I wouldn't take that back for all the world.

"She wanted to go. She was fine. Uncle Sully, she recognized me. She was fine," I protested, knowing it was no use but trying anyway.

"What did she say? Before she got upset?"

"She called me by my name. MY name. She told me that she loved me. Then she got all upset and started making no sense. That's when she saw Gary's grave."

Nadine entered with a sigh and sat across the table from me. "She is resting now. She should be just fine when she wakes up. There's no need to beat yourself up about it."

"I still can't believe this happened. I stopped to talk to someone for one second. . ." Sully continued.

"Now, don't you let him make you feel worse than you already do," Nadine said, patting my hand where it rested on the table. "It was my idea that Gram go with you in the first place. The blame is on me."

"You don't have to . . ." I started to say.

"Have to what?" Sully asked sharply, shutting me up.

"No, child, you listen here," Nadine said. "I thought it would do you and Gram a lot of good going out there, and I think it did."

"I think going out there did some good too," I agreed, and I held my chin high when Sully gaped at me in shock.

"How can you say that? You saw how upset it made her!"

I sighed, understanding exactly why Sully was so upset. I got it, I did. He was responsible for her, and he knew his days as caretaker of Gram were numbered. She was getting worse every day. How could he possibly understand how much that moment had meant to me while he had been losing her bit-by-bit in front of his very eyes for years?

"I saw how happy she was before she got confused," Nadine said, looking me in the eyes. "You can't know true happiness if you have never experienced despair, and as I am always with that woman, I can tell you that she has been through her share of despair and grief. I know it seems cruel to say, but Gram lost her son a long time ago. She already felt that pain and grief before. Somewhere in that beautiful mind, she remembers that sorrow. What she NEEDED was the joy of seeing her beautiful grandchild. Somewhere inside, she remembers that too."

Tears welled in my eyes as she spoke. I mouthed a thank you, and she smiled.

"And even if it was only for a moment, that one moment of pure joy broke through years of sadness and loss. She carries that bit of joy with her now. So, yes, I think it did you both a world of good."

I looked over at Sully who was examining his boot, frustration still evident on his face.

"Look, Uncle Sully, I know she got really upset and for that I am so very sorry, but she remembered me. Somewhere in her mind, she knows that I'm here for her. That can't be a bad thing, right?"

Sully leaned against the counter, defeated. He rubbed his eyes with a sigh. Nadine squeezed my hand. "Now you listen to me, Miss Alexandra. You take to heart every single thing your Gram said to you. Don't you feel bad for a minute, you hear?"

I nodded, knowing that I would never forget my moment with Gram. I would cherish all of it, even the ominous warning she'd given me before she was lost again to the past. *Don't trust him. He was there that night."* Was there anything to what she said? Or was she just ranting off some memory from her past? I wanted to ask Sully about it, but I didn't dare worry him further. I tucked the questions away when Sully sighed.

"Look, Kiddo, I really don't want to argue with you. What's done is done. We'll just have to see how she is when she wakes up in the morning."

Before he could say any more, his cell rang. He retrieved it from his pocket and, scowling at the number, put the phone to his ear.

"This is the chief," he answered, then shook his head. "You've got to be kidding me. Again? Okay, I'll hurry on up there now. Yeah . . . meet you there in ten."

"Is something wrong?" I asked.

Sully went to the door and grabbed his coat.

"Oh, just Old Man Pinket shooting at the Henley's hounds again. I swear that old man is going to accidently kill someone trying to protect those damned chickens of his," he said, then turned to me.

"You want me to drop you off really quick? May not be a good idea for you to be here in case Gram wakes up. You know, until we know where she's at."

"No, I agree," I said grabbing my coat, "but I think I want to walk. You need to hurry, and I could use the fresh air to clear my head."

Sully looked concerned as he contemplated.

"It's not that far," I reassured him.

"You sure you're feeling up to it?" he asked, motioning to the lump on my head.

I waved him off. "I'm fine. You go ahead."

"Okay, well, I'll be out for a while. Usually takes us a good hour to get that shotgun out of Mr. Pinket's hands and even longer to calm the neighbors. If I don't see you, I'll swing by in the morning."

"Sounds good. Hey, Uncle Sully?" I called to him as he left the house. He poked his head back in. "I really am sorry about Gram."

Sully smiled at me. "I know, Kiddo, me too. Everything is going to work out."

I watched Sully's truck pull out of the driveway and went back inside to grab my purse. Nadine was waiting at the door.

"Thank you, for everything," I said. "I really hope she's going to be okay."

"Don't you worry about your Gram. That's my job. You've got enough to worry about."

Before I left, I paused at the door and turned again to face Nadine. I had to ask.

"In church today . . . when you pointed out that passage. How did you know?" I asked.

Nadine patted my cheek and grinned at me, the wisdom of the universe in her eyes.

"Sometimes you just know," she said softly, motioning me out the door.

With a nod, I turned to go. It was hard to leave Gram, but Sully was right. It wouldn't be good for her to see me right away. Better to let her mind settle into wherever it was comfortable. That's what my sensible, sensitive side was saying. Selfishly, I wanted to make her remember me again. I wanted so much to be able to talk with her about the past and the things she'd said. What was she so afraid of?

I wanted to talk to her about the future and everything that was happening now. I wanted to talk with her about Donovan. She would understand it. She may even be able to help me understand it.

Donovan. My one good motivation for going home. I longed to see him again, even if for just a moment reflected in the antique mirror on the wall. I knew he was with me. I heard him so clearly in the cemetery. *Go*, he'd said, and Gram came back to me, even if for just a short while. I owed that moment to Donovan. I wanted to thank him.

As I made my way home, I wished that I could make my mind accept his presence. Why was it so hard to allow myself to just believe? I remembered the passage that Nadine showed me. *For He will command His angels concerning you; to guard you in all your ways.* I'd read it over and over. It was right there in black and white, and yet still so unbelievable.

I turned down the gravel road as the sun lay hidden behind the grey clouds rolling in. It was even darker than usual. Adding to the eerie effect was the fact that the road was narrow and surrounded by dense wood on either side, and it was unnervingly quiet. I considered jogging the road to get to the end all the faster, but I didn't want to risk the headache running was sure to cause. Deciding to walk it as quickly as I could, I chastised myself for how ridiculous I must look.

Lost in my thoughts, I was making fairly good time when I rounded the last curve. Soon I would be comfortably in my own neighborhood. As I maneuvered around some low-hanging foliage, I saw a vehicle parked in the middle of the road ahead of me, brake lights glowing. As I got closer, the small white truck and the rental plates gave me pause. It looked like Rick's truck. Waving my hands, I started towards it in the hopes that he would see me and I could finally get a word with him.

As I got closer though, the engine revved, the tires spun in the gravel, and the truck took off, sending up dust and debris to hover above the road in a gray cloud.

"Rick, wait! Rick!" I yelled after him, but the truck sped off noisily down the last quarter mile of dirt road and disappeared in the distance.

I stood staring, wondering if he'd heard me. *Maybe it wasn't Rick*, I considered. Maybe I'd stumbled upon a couple of teenagers in their favorite make-out spot or sneaking a smoke. Neither of those probabilities sat well with me though. I recognized those plates. It was beyond strange that Rick would speed off like that.

When I reached the end of the dirt road, I took a deep breath, relieved. I scanned my street, but there was no trace of the white truck. Shrugging it off, I climbed my driveway and fetched the key from my purse. I dropped my stuff in the entryway and went straight into the kitchen for something to eat. Grabbing a can of raviolis, I heated them up in a saucepan and then went to the fridge and pulled out the wine.

"A bit couldn't hurt," I sighed and poured myself a generous glass.

After dumping the dishes in the sink for later, I swigged the remainder of my wine. It was starting to numb the dull ache in my temples. I looked out the window above the sink and watched the sky grow steadily darker. Another storm was rolling in. I suddenly wished I would have considered storm season when deciding to make this trip.

It wouldn't have mattered though. My decision to get on the plane had been a hasty one at best. I'd willed myself to make this trip before I lost the nerve to.

This time I turned off the downstairs light before going upstairs. When I got to my room, I held my breath and looked straight to the mirror, expectant. Donovan was not there. With a heavy sigh, I collapsed on my bed, my head in my hands.

"I don't know how to see you. I don't know how to stop the doubts. I want more than anything to be able to hear your voice and thank you for today," I whispered.

I looked up again, hoping that Donovan would appear in the reflection, but only my own disappointed face stared back at me. Cursing my weak faith, I grabbed my pajamas and went into the bathroom for another soothing shower. When I emerged dressed for bed and followed by a new cloud of steam, I again checked the mirror. When the steam started to form a fog, I squinted and searched the hazy glass for his dark figure. I stepped closer to the mirror and tripped over the box from the attic, spilling its contents all over the floor.

"Son of a . . ." I squealed, landing on the bed and rubbing my shin before bending down to gather up my mess. Something caught my eye. I plucked the yellowing envelope from where it was wedged between the pages of my baby book. It had my name on it. For a minute I sat motionless, starring at my mother's handwriting.

When I finally opened it, I found a hand-written letter. I hesitated, feeling the tears draw into my eyes before I could stop them. I blinked them back and began to read.

> *My Dearest Alexandra,*
>
> *Your due date was today. I guess you're just too comfortable where you are to come out into the world just yet. I can't wait to see you, my sweet one, and hold you in my arms. There are so many things I want for you. I was hoping to bring you into a loving, complete family, but it seems the Lord had other plans for us.*
>
> *I am very sorry about your father. I don't think I'll ever understand why he left in order to someday explain it to you. I guess it's just one of those things you have to trust will work out for the best. As soon as we can, I promise, my angel, we are going to find a place to call our own, a safe place where we can start over and where we will be surrounded by wonderful people. You deserve that.*
>
> *I want so much for you, baby girl. I want you to be happy and to grow up to be a woman of tremendous faith. That is my biggest prayer: for you to always see the good in things and to have faith in yourself and in God no matter what. Just remember, as I am remembering right now, that you don't always have to understand the twists and turns in life. You just have to have faith that the journey will make you into who you were destined to become. You are meant for amazing things. I can feel it. I pray that the Lord always protect you and guide your steps in all that you do.*

I love you so, so much, my precious baby girl. I cannot wait to be able to tell you to your little face. This world will be so much more beautiful with you in it.

Love always,
Mom

Tears dropped onto the paper as I held it shakily in front of me, staring at the words but not seeing them anymore. I couldn't imagine the kind of pain my mom was in when she wrote them, yet she was able to look past all of it. She wanted to find a place where we could be happy, a place where we could start over, a place to call our own. Saluda had been that place. The house, I thought with a heavy heart, had been the culmination of that dream.

I thought about Gram, and Sully, and Gary, and all the loving people of this small town and realized that Mom had found all of the things she was looking for. For me, for us. Everything my mother had prayed about had come true, except for one thing. I wasn't the great woman of faith that she had hoped I would be. It was her greatest wish, and I'd let her down.

"I'm sorry I couldn't be what you wanted me to be," I sobbed, hugging the letter to my chest.

"Oh, but you are," I heard his velvet voice say against my ear.

My head snapped up, and I blinked the tears from my eyes. Donovan's image appeared in the mirror. He smiled at me encouragingly. Instinctively, I looked from the mirror to my side where he should be standing, but saw nothing there.

"No, I'm not," I said looking back into the mirror at Donovan. "I've been trying all day to have enough faith, to believe enough to be able to see you, but I couldn't."

I watched through the mirror as Donovan leaned over me. He placed his hand over where mine rested on the letter.

"You see me now. You heard me today in the cemetery. Why do you think that is?"

I could feel his warmth, warmth like I'd never felt before, tingling the skin on my hand. The gentle strumming vibrated against me, soothing me.

"I don't know," I whispered.

"It's because in that moment, just like now, you weren't *trying* to see. Faith isn't something you can will into being. It comes when you let go, when you stop trying to understand. You have great faith, Alexandra, when you stop telling yourself that you don't."

I shrugged, not entirely certain that what he said was true, but wanting it to be true more than anything.

"You cried out in faith in the cemetery that an answer would come, and it did. You are speaking with me now because your mother's letter shattered the doubts in your mind that I could exist. You are doing this, Alexandra, not me. You are exactly the woman your mother hoped you would be," Donovan continued.

A faint sob escaped my throat at his words, and I fought to keep the tears away. "Then why can't I see you here beside me? Why can't I open my mind enough to see?"

"That will come with time. Right now you just need to remember that I am here with you, even when you can't see me," Donovan answered, gently.

"Where do you go? When you're not with me? You can't be with me ALL the time . . ."

Donovan smiled. "I exist separately from you as I've said. Where I am, time does not exist. For you, things are linear. Life progresses on a forward line. It's not like that for me at all. For me, everything is a series of moments . . . thoughts, feelings, all separate from time. I am always with you in that way, and in that way . . . I always have been."

"Why me?" I asked.

"Why not you, Alexandra? He protects all of his children, just like you read in that psalm today. What's special about you, is you've been given a unique gift. The gift of sight. You can see me, feel me, and speak to me as you are right now. That is rare. It could be because of your mother's prayers that you were given this gift."

I contemplated what he said, not feeling like anything special. My mother had been the special one. So why then was I here while she was gone?

"Where was my mother's Guardian then? Or Gary's? Where were they that night? Why wasn't anyone protecting them? What about my childhood prayers for them?" I asked, trying to keep the anger that rose from my gut from spilling over.

Donovan bowed his head and sighed, pain showing on his face. "All I can offer you is assurance that it was their time to leave this world, and it wasn't yours. Your purpose is not finished."

"My purpose? So what was my mother's purpose? To die young? To be violently murdered?" I spat, my words sounding too harsh even for me.

"No, Alexandra," Donovan soothed. "You can't judge a life by how it ended. Just know that her beautiful existence had a purpose. We all have one, even me."

"And what is your purpose exactly?" I sighed, the fight going out of me.

"To protect you," he said looking into my eyes.

His words and the force of his stare made my heart quicken. "Protect me from what?"

"From an evil that would keep you from fulfilling your own purpose."

"I . . . I don't understand." I stood, pacing the floor in front of the mirror. "What evil are you talking about?"

Donovan watched me pace, keeping his eyes locked on mine. He spoke slowly. "From the same evil that took your parents away from you fifteen years ago."

I froze mid step. "The murderer . . . you know who he is?"

Donovan shook his head in the mirror. "No, I don't know anything that you don't. I just . . . sense things," he tried to explain.

"But . . . you were there that night! I remember you. You had to have seen him!"

He raised a hand to rest it on my shoulder. "I saw only you. That is all I was meant to see. This is your journey. I am not meant to interfere, only to ensure that you are able to see it through."

I sat back on the bed, throwing my hands up in frustration. "What does that even mean?"

Donovan motioned to the letter in my hand. "It's like what your mother wrote in that letter: '*You don't always have to understand the twists and turns in life; you just have to have faith that the journey will make you into who you were destined to become.*' Your mother understood that after your father left. She accepted that his leaving was part of her journey. Just like her death and what you must go through now will make you into who you are meant to become."

Sighing, I laid back on the bed. I didn't know what to think. So much was going through my head. I'd never thought about my mother's death that way. The anger and dejection was more comfortable to me. Donovan was forcing me to reevaluate the last decade and a half of my life.

"What if I don't want to become what . . . HE wants me to be?" I asked. "What if all I ever wanted was to be happy with my family? Why was that plan not good enough?"

Donovan sat beside me on the bed. I expected to feel the movement of his weight sinking into the mattress, but I didn't.

"Sometimes it's not about what we want. It's about having faith that His plans for us are better than our own, even if we don't understand them, or in your case, even if they seem cruel. There's a bigger picture, a puzzle that you can't always see, but you don't have to see it to believe in it."

My anger was beginning to deflate, the weight of so many years easing with every word from him. Even if I didn't understand everything he was saying, I could feel that he understood me. After being alone for so long, that was enough.

"So, it all comes down to faith again, huh?"

Donovan smiled. "Everything does."

"So, what exactly is the plan then? If there IS a murderer coming back here . . ."

Donovan's smile vanished. "He's already here."

"What?" I asked, jumping up. "What do we do?"

"I keep you safe," he said, standing beside me.

Again I felt the slightest tingling heat. I saw in the mirror where he held my hand, then looked down to where his hand should be and saw nothing. *Would I ever get used to this*?

A rumble from outside made me jump. "How can you be sure he's here, that he's after me? You don't know who it is. It's been fifteen years. What could he possibly want from me now? Hasn't he done enough?"

"It's like I said before. I can sense it. I felt it as soon as you arrived in Saluda. It grows stronger each day." The concern on his face made his words all the more frightening.

"I can't leave now though. I just got Gram back, and Sully. . ." I said. "This is where I feel closest to her . . . this is where she wanted us to be."

"I wasn't suggesting that you leave. In fact, I think you're meant to stay. You have to see this thing through, even if I don't like it."

"What do I do?"

"You trust me." Donovan held my gaze in the mirror, and looking into his earnest face, I knew that he would do anything to protect me. That he always had. "No matter what happens, you have faith. Have faith that you can overcome this evil. Have faith that there is a greater plan at work. Have faith in me. I won't let anything happen to you."

A crack of thunder erupted, and seconds later a flash of light illuminated the darkened sky. I jumped and shut my eyes tight.

"Can you make this storm go away? I hate storms."

"Sadly, no," he answered with a laugh. "But I can promise that it will not hurt you."

"Well, what kind of Guardian are you, then?" I teased, trying to mask my fear with humor. "I mean, you don't even have any wings or anything."

Donovan laughed again. I could listen to that warm laugh forever. It was the sound of comfort. "Would you feel better if I had wings?"

"Maybe."

"Then believe that I have wings," he said.

"Wait," I struggled to understand as rain began to pelt against the window. "You're saying that you don't have wings because I don't believe that you do?"

"I am saying that your mind accepts me this way, so here I am."

"You are great at giving confusing answers. Seriously, it's a talent. You should give up this whole Guardian thing and go into politics."

"And you are great at over-thinking questions and deflecting serious situations with humor. Perhaps you could be my campaign manager."

I chuckled, rubbing my temples where the steady ache persisted. I knew that soon it would be a painful throbbing, but I didn't care. "Great, I got the protector with a sense of humor."

Donovan got up from the bed. "You, me . . . we are all created alike. I laugh, I cry . . . I love."

Our eyes met again through the glass reflection. I watched emotion well up inside him though he fought to keep it from his face. I wished I knew what he was hiding behind those kind but sharp features. He walked to the head of the bed and motioned for me to follow.

"I can also tell when you've had enough for one day. You need to get some rest. I've kept you up too long. Please, come lie down."

"I'm not tired," I lied.

I didn't want the conversation to end, not when so many questions remained unanswered. With the storm raging outside like some kind of ominous warning of things to come, I doubted I could even sleep.

"You can't lie to me, Alexandra. Now please, I asked you to trust me. You're going to need your rest," he pleaded.

I was reluctant, but not wanting to let Donovan down, I climbed into bed and laid my head on the pillow. Immediately, the pain in my temples lessened, and I realized I was much more tired than I'd thought. Still, I couldn't let him out of my sight. I didn't trust myself enough to be able to see him in the morning.

When I looked back into the mirror, Donovan was sitting at the foot of my bed. He smiled at me, but I thought I saw concern in the depths of his eyes.

"You'll need to turn off the light if you expect to sleep," he said.

"But if I turn off the light, I won't be able to see you anymore."

"Doesn't mean I'm not here."

With a sigh, I reached up and switched off the light. I focused on the strumming sound that I knew was him. It filled the space between growls of thunder and kept me from panicking despite the storm and Donovan's warnings. My mother's murderer was close, and that thought made me tremble in the darkness. A loud clap, like the cracking of a whip, sent my pulse racing. I clutched at the corners of my pillow.

"Donovan?" I called out into the dark.

"Yes?"

"Do you ever get scared?"

"Yes," he answered. "Sometimes."

It made me feel better to know that he too had fears. "Of what?"

For a long breadth he didn't answer. When the answer came, it was a whisper.

"That I will fail."

Sighing, I closed my eyes again. The answer should have scared me and made me doubt him, but it didn't. I felt better knowing that I wouldn't be the only one forced to face their fears. Somehow, not being alone in that too steadied me. Not being alone was everything.

Donovan understood me and my fears and in that moment, as the sky exploded with fury, nothing else mattered. Soon my breathing fell into a steady rhythm with the gentle strumming beside me, and my mind drifted closer to sleep.

"Donovan," I whispered.

"Yes?"

"Stay with me. Please . . . all night."

I felt his touch, like warm static, on my hand, and my fingers eased around my pillow. The warmth stayed there as I followed the strumming into the peace of deep sleep. Before I was lost, I heard him whisper.

"I'm not going anywhere."

Eight

"Alexandra, wake up!"

I heard him call to me in the dreamless expanse where my mind drifted.

"Alexandra, I need you to get up now!" his voice called to me again, the urgency jarring me back to consciousness.

I opened my eyes to the dark, quiet room. The storm had passed, and Donovan was still there.

"Alexandra, you need to get up," he pleaded. "Someone is in the house."

My mind whirled. I noticed his warmth on my face as I considered his words. When the weight of them finally registered, I shot up in the bed, my heart pounding.

"What?" I gasped.

"Ssshhh," he whispered, "be very quiet, and listen carefully to what I say. You're the only one who can hear me. I'll guide you through this, okay? Stay quiet, and follow my voice. I need to get you out of the house. Can you do that for me?"

With a nod, I stood as quietly as I could and tried to control my breathing. *Was this really happening?*

"Good, now you need to open the door as silently as possible. Stay as close to my voice as you can." Donovan's tone was calm, steady.

I crept to the door. The only light for which to navigate came from the moonlight that seeped in between the slats of the closed blinds. Turning the knob as slowly as I could with shaking hands, I opened the door, praying it wouldn't squeak. When it didn't, I let out a jagged breath and waited for Donovan's instructions.

"Good, now wait right there until I tell you to come out into the hallway," his voice sounded from the hall in front of me.

I stood frozen in the doorway. The darkness beyond was thick and oppressive. My hearing was heightened by the lack of sight, and I searched the darkened house for sounds of movement. That's when I heard it. A slight shuffling came from down the hall. It was hard to tell exactly where it came from. Stifling a scream, I willed my heart to stop pounding. The sound of it was sure to give me away.

Slow, heavy footsteps came into the hallway from one of the rooms and just as quickly disappeared into another. The intruder was either in the hallway bathroom or in my old room. I couldn't tell which. *Were they looking for me?* The thought made my legs tremble. I couldn't breathe.

"Now!" Donovan called from just outside the room. "Get down the hallway as fast as you can without making a sound. Stay to the right, and don't stop. Follow my voice."

I hesitated, unable to make my legs move.

"Now, Alexandra. You have to trust me. You'll be fine if you go now!"

I bolted noiselessly into the hallway and found the far wall. Making my way shakily towards the stairs, I kept my footsteps careful but fast. I followed Donovan's voice.

"That's good. Just keep moving. Quickly. You're almost there," he called from just ahead of me.

As I passed in front of the two rooms, I heard shuffling within one of them. I stopped, fear nailing me to the floor where I stood. A dark figure moved in the bathroom, catching my eye. I held my breath. Rendered immobile by panic, I knew I had to keep moving, but I couldn't find the courage to do anything but stand there.

"Keep going, Alexandra!" Donovan cried out. "No, don't stop!"

His words jarred me to attention, and I broke out into a silent run towards the stairs, but it was too late. The figure turned in the doorway and lunged for me. I screamed, dodging the hands that clutched at me.

"Run, Alexandra! This way!" Donovan yelled, leading me to the staircase.

When I got to the bottom of the stairs, I heard the intruder dive for me. Strong hands clutched my ankle and flung me face-down into the floor. The pain was acute. I screamed and kicked against the hand that squeezed my ankle like a vice, but I had no impact. My attacker began to drag me back up the stairs. I clawed at the carpet, frantically trying to get away.

"Donovan!" I cried out, trying desperately to grab onto something, anything.

"Kick him, Alexandra!" I heard him yell, so I kicked my right leg as hard as I could.

The figure reeled back, and I yanked my ankle free. I turned to run, but he lunged at me again, this time grabbing onto my calf. Again, he began to drag me back up the stairs towards him. As he reached for my thigh, though, he was yanked backward by a violent, unseen force. I kicked him away.

When he reached again, he caught me by the same ankle. I cried out in pain, flipping onto my back to kick as hard as I could with my free leg. In the darkness I saw a head, cloaked in black, writhing as he tried to lunge for me. Something was holding him back.

He reached for me with his free hand over and over, gaining a little space with each angered thrust forward. I sat up and pried at the fingers that gripped me. The hand was covered with a leather glove.

Terror consumed me anew as I remembered the gloved hands that had reached for me from the front seat of our mangled car all those years ago. *The same evil . . .*

"Use your nails!" Donovan's labored voice yelled.

I clawed at the arm above the gloved hand, which held steadfast to my ankle like a bear trap. When I felt moisture beneath my fingernails, the hand released its grip with a squeal. I kicked free.

"Run, Alexandra! Find help." Donovan strained to shout. "I can't hold him much longer!"

Stumbling to my feet, I raced to the front door. My breath was knocked from my lungs when I slammed into something solid. I swung my arms out, ready to defend myself. My hands gripped the piano and with relief, I struggled to straighten up and get a breath. The reflection cast into its surface by a single ray of moonlight from the window made me pause. Donovan was at the top of the stairs. He was bent over, gripping the intruder's leg with both hands. He held him back with all his might, the veins in his muscular arms popping. The black figure struggled and writhed beneath him.

"Go! I can't hold him!" Donovan screamed, and I turned and ran for the front door.

When I tried the knob, it turned, but the door did not budge. I struggled to release the deadbolt, the panic making my movements clumsy. Finally throwing the door open, I ran as fast as my legs would allow down the driveway and into the street. I looked both ways, searching for someone, anyone who could call the police. It was so late. Not one porch light remained lit. There were no signs of life anywhere.

Running in the direction of town, I spotted a squad car parked under the street light. My bare feet scraped against the cold pavement as I ran towards it, not daring to look back. *Please let someone be in the car*, I prayed.

As I got closer to the cruiser, I heard footsteps running behind me. They were running towards me. Crying out on terror, I sped up, frantic to get to the cruiser. When I reached it, there was no one inside.

"No!" I screamed, running around to the back of the car, hoping against all hope that one of the doors was unlocked. None of them were.

The footsteps grew louder as they approached. Frantic, I looked up the street for somewhere to hide and saw a porch light come on a few houses back up the way I'd come. Knowing I would never make it to the station, I took off from the car towards the lighted porch.

I only made it a few steps when I ran head-on into someone. With a scream, I flailed my arms, trying to break free as they grabbed at my arms. They were too strong.

"Alex, it's me! It's okay!" Will said, trying to hold me close. "It's okay. I've got you."

I took in the crisp Saluda Police uniform, then looked into Will's concerned face and stopped struggling. Peering around him, I searched the street but didn't see anyone coming after me. Looking back up at Will, I collapsed, a sobbing mess, into his arms.

"He's in the house . . . He came after me."

"Ssshhh, it's okay now," Will said. "Who was in the house? Who attacked you?"

"I . . . I don't know. He had on a mask."

Will held me out at arm's length and looked me over. "Are you hurt?"

I shook my head. "No, I don't think so."

"Good," he said, looking me in the eyes. "Is he still in the house?"

"I don't know. It was so dark. He was . . . stuck when I got away. By the stairs . . . he could still be in there."

I finally caught my breath, but couldn't keep my eyes off of the house. Where was Donovan? Was he still holding off my attacker? Will unlocked the patrol car and reached in for the radio.

"Galia to station," he said, holding down the button.

"Go ahead," a male voice answered back from the console.

"I'm going to need some backup at 127 Baker Street for a B&E and assault. Ring the chief. He's going to want to come right away. Over." Will dropped the radio and turned back to me.

"Okay, get in the car. I'm going to go have a look. You'll be safe in here. I'll leave the keys. If you see anyone come out of the house other than me, lean on the horn. Understand?" he said, taking his gun from the holster on his belt.

"What?" I shrieked. "You can't go in there by yourself! Just wait for Uncle Sully . . . or one of the others."

Will gave my shoulder a reassuring squeeze and then motioned me into the car. "If I wait, we may never know who did this," he explained. "Do not move from this car."

"Will . . ." I tried to argue, but he shut the door and motioned for me to lock it. Then he jogged towards the house, shouting to the concerned neighbor to go back inside.

I watched as he disappeared around the bushes in front of the driveway.

"Please let him be okay. Please let him be okay," I whispered, my eyes glued to the house.

"He'll be fine, Alexandra," Donovan panted from the back seat.

With a squeal, I jumped and whirled around but saw no one. When I heard the slow strumming, I knew that it was Donovan. Breathing in the relief, I looked into the rear view mirror. He smiled weakly.

"Are you sure he'll be okay?"

"Whoever it was," he breathed, "ran out the back door. I couldn't . . . hold him any longer. I sensed you were out of danger . . . as soon as he ran."

"Thank you," I cried, relieved. "Thank you for getting me out of there before . . ."

"You don't have to thank me . . . This is why I'm here," he said, looking me in the eyes so I could see he was serious. He took a shallow, labored breath. "But, Alexandra, you must trust me. You hesitated . . . That's why he saw you. I can only interfere so much. You have to listen to me. Trust what I say if I'm to protect you."

I nodded, frustrated with myself. "I know. I panicked. I froze. Wait . . . are you okay?"

In the mirror I watched Donovan struggle to sit up. Sweat beaded at his brow.

"When I interact with the physical realm . . . it takes more strength. It drains my energy quickly. I'm not meant to be a part of your world . . . only to guide you through it. Next time, you have to do exactly as I say," he warned.

"Next time?" I croaked, my heart back in my throat. "There's going to be a next time?"

"I'm afraid this was only the beginning," he whispered.

Donovan laid his hand on my shoulder, and I felt the warmth of his touch. His touch was unlike the familiar touch of another person, flesh on flesh, which is felt on the surface. When he touched me, I felt the warmth permeate my skin, my muscles. I felt his warmth from the inside.

He took a deep breath. "Do you trust me?"

"I trust you."

"I told you, I'm not going to let anything happen to you, Alexandra."

Looking deep into his eyes, I could see emotion flowing in them on an ocean of topaz. I could see his concern, his care for me, and I knew that he spoke the truth. He would protect me at all costs.

"I believe you," I said, reassured.

Up the road, the glare of headlights flashed as they turned into my driveway. The rumble of a large engine let me know that it was Sully. I looked into the mirror at Donovan.

"Go, the danger has passed. Listen for me," he said. "I'll be right there with you."

I got out of the car and for the first time noticed the stinging cold of the night air on my bear arms. My ankle was sore and stiff, but the pain wasn't enough of a concern to stop me. When I made it up the driveway, I saw Sully, fully dressed in jeans and a heavy flannel, on the porch questioning Will. He looked tired.

"She's safe. She's in my squad car up the street. I told her to honk if she saw anyone at all," Will was saying. "The house is clear, but Chief, you have to come see this."

"See what?" I asked, running up the porch steps.

Sully searched me with his eyes, surveying me from head to toe. Then he hugged me to him tightly. I met Will's scowling eyes.

"I told you to stay in the car."

"It's okay," Sully said, letting me go. "Did they hurt you?"

"My ankle is a little sore from where he grabbed me, but other than that I think I'm good thanks to . . ." I stopped myself short. There was no way I could tell them about Donovan. They would think I was crazy for sure. Hell, a part of me might still agree with them.

"Your survival instinct?" Sully looked impressed, but then turned serious as he looked me in the eyes. "Do you have any idea who did this?"

"I wish I did," I sighed.

"Chief, I really think you should come upstairs and have a look. It might give you some idea of who we're dealing with here," Will said, motioning him inside.

Sully turned and followed Will into the house, and I followed after them. All of the lights were on, making the events of the last hour seem like nothing more than a bad dream. When we reached the foot of the stairs, I stared at the spot where my attacker got hold of me and shuddered.

"I don't think she should see this," Will said, turning to Sully.

"No, I want to see," I protested, meeting Will's concerned glare. "This is my house. I have the right to know what he did to it."

"Suit yourself," he said, leading us through the upstairs hall.

Even with the lights on, I could see nothing out of place. Will passed the first bedroom and motioned us toward the bathroom. Sully went inside. I hung back in order to gauge his reaction.

"What in the hell?" he said.

My curiosity got the better of me, and I stepped into the room with them. At first I didn't see anything out of the ordinary. The towels hadn't been touched, and the shower curtain was drawn back, exposing nothing strange in the shower. I looked at both Sully and Will confused, then followed their gazes to the bathroom mirror. There, written in black marker was a message:

You're a whore just like she was. Leave, or you will die like she did!

Gasping, I covered my mouth with my hands, trying to force the bile that rose in my throat back.

"Why would someone write something like this? Much less break in here to do it?" Sully asked.

I could only stare at the mirror in horror. Through it, I saw Donovan step into the room. He held my eyes with his.

"I was just wondering the same thing." Will shook his head.

There was a commotion on the stairs as two officers emerged and joined us in the small room.

"Jones, I'll need you to get a picture of this for a handwriting analysis. Dust it for prints. Conley, check all the doors and windows for signs of forced entry," Sully ordered.

"Yes, Chief," they nodded and got to work.

"You won't find any prints," I said, still in shock. "He was wearing gloves. Leather gloves, just like that night . . ."

Sully looked at Will. "I'm getting her out of here. Come on outside."

Breaking my gaze from the mirror, I ran into my room to grab my robe before following Sully and Will out to the porch. I sat on the swing while Sully questioned me. Will leaned on the banister to the side, deep in contemplation.

"Were both doors locked?" Sully asked.

I sighed. "I don't know for sure. When I ran out of the house, I had to undo the deadbolt on the front door, so I know that one was locked. I don't know for sure about the back door. I've never checked it. It could have been unlocked this whole time."

"Did you see anything else as you were running from the house? An unusual car, or someone hanging around?"

"No, there was nothing. That why when I saw Will's squad car, I ran for that. That's when I bumped into Will."

Sully turned to Will, his eyebrow raised.

"What exactly were you doing out here at this hour anyway?" Sully asked.

Will repositioned himself against the banister. "I was just running a patrol of the area. When I heard screaming coming from the house, I went to check it out. The front door was locked, so I was making my way around back when I heard another scream and saw her bolting towards the street. I ran after her to see what the hell was going on."

"You were patrolling at one a.m.?"

Will stood tall and looked Sully in the eye. "Hell, you know I don't sleep. I was just making the rounds."

"The rounds?" Sully scoffed.

"I was taking a drive, clearing my head. It's not like there are a ton of neighborhoods to choose from, Chief," Will retaliated.

"Well, I for one am glad you were here when you were," I offered.

Sully sighed and rubbed his temple before turning his attention back to me. "Is there anything else you can remember about this perp? Height? Weight? Hair color?"

I shook my head. "I told you, it was dark and, he had on a mask." Hugging my robe to my body, I looked into Sully's worried face. "It's the same man, isn't it? The one who killed Mom and Gary. He's back, isn't he? Only this time he wants to finish the job."

Sully sat next to me on the swing. He put his arm around me and hugged me to him. Will watched intently from where he leaned.

"Let's not jump to conclusions just yet. We don't know who did this. It could be anyone," Sully assured me.

"But that message . . . Whoever wrote that on the mirror had it out for Mom. I don't get it. Why would anyone want to hurt her? It doesn't make any sense."

With a sigh, Will shook his head and looked off into the distance. "If this is the same person, it would mean that their murder was not just some robbery attempt or random act of violence. It would mean it was planned, premeditated."

"It would also mean that they've been here this whole time, all these years later," I mumbled.

"Or they came back," Will agreed.

"But why? Who would have been angry at Mom? She never did anything to hurt anyone. And why would they call her . . . a whore? That doesn't make any sense. None of this makes any sense."

I searched my memory, but I couldn't remember there ever being a time when my mother had done anything but make people smile.

"We can't be certain that this is the same person. It could just be someone trying to scare you away," Sully said.

"Away from what?" Will asked.

"Could it have something to do with the house? Do you remember what Gram said about Rick?" I asked, recalling her strange reaction to him at the church.

"Ricky Brightman?" Sully asked confused. "Why would he have anything to do with this?"

I stood and faced them both. "The first day I was here a white truck sped past the driveway while I was walking to the station. It was the same truck that I saw Rick drive away in after church. It's the same truck that took off down the dirt road when I came up on it walking home from your house this afternoon. At the time, I thought it was strange that he would be parked up that street, but he had a clear view of the house from there. Maybe he was watching me."

"Why didn't you say anything about this before?" Sully asked, astonished at my revelation.

"I only just thought of it," I confessed. "Gram said something today about Mom buying the house from his mother. Could that have something to do with this?"

Sully was lost for a moment in thought. He paced the porch a ways before finally stopping in front of me again.

"I suppose it could, actually. Your mother was only able to afford this house because they were forced to foreclose on it. The bank auctioned it off. She was the only buyer. I co-signed on the loan."

"Maybe they didn't want to sell the house, and Mom was in their way. Maybe he wants it back," I said. "Could he be scaring me into selling it?"

Sully nodded, his face tensing. "Rick's working up at the elementary school. I just signed off on all the permits. I think I'll ride up there tomorrow and have a little chat with him."

"I'm going with you," I declared.

"The hell you are," Sully argued. "I'm not sure I shouldn't put you on the next plane out of here at this point. This makes two incidents now that have been too close for comfort."

I took a deep breath, surprised by the rage that welled up from my gut. A sudden urgency replaced all fear. Taking a step towards Sully, I squared my shoulders. "I ran from this bastard fifteen years ago when he took my parents from me. I won't run from him this time."

Sully sighed and looked down at his feet. "You didn't run. You were ten years old. I knew it was best that you leave here. We all did. You needed to move on with your life. I was protecting you then, just like I am now."

I stood firm. "I'm not leaving. Mom wanted this to be my home, and I am not leaving it. Not this time. Take me with you to see Brightman. Either I go with you, or I'll find some way to see him myself."

"Alexandra, no . . ." I heard Donovan whisper against my ear. I took a step back.

"I'll take her," Will spoke up from where he leaned against the railing.

Sully spun on him. "You stay out of this."

"She's our only witness to any of this," he reasoned. "I think she should go."

Sully shook his head, letting out a loud breath as he contemplated. The two officers from inside stepped out onto the porch. Sully looked up, obviously thankful for the distraction.

"There are no signs of forced entry, Chief, and no prints. All the windows are locked up, but the back door was cracked. The perp probably left it open when he ran. Either that door was unlocked when he came in, or he had a key," Conley reported.

Sully looked at me. "I can't remember if it was locked up before you got here. Haven't had a need to lock anything around here before. This could all be my fault."

"No," I argued. "I never checked it. It's my fault. Although . . . would Rick still have a key? I mean, have the locks been changed since he and his family lived here?"

"No, they've never been changed," Sully said, his jaw tightening. "Like I said, never had a reason to worry about that kind of thing before."

"Well, you have a reason now." Will sighed.

"Either way, you're coming home with me tonight until I can get these locks changed in the morning. It's not safe for you here," Sully said.

I shook my head. "No, I want to stay. I'll put something in front of the doors or something. There are only a few hours till morning anyway. You have Gram to think about. You said it yourself. It's best I wasn't there, remember?"

"A lot has changed since I said that. You were attacked, Alex. We're just going to have to take our chances that Gram will be fine."

"No, Uncle Sully. I'll be fine. I can't upset Gram again," I protested. Sully stepped toward me ready to insist, but Will stepped between us.

"I'll stay," he said.

"I don't think so," Sully growled. "Why in the hell are you so eager to help all of the sudden?"

"Because you're being too protective to use your head!" Will shouted. "If the perp comes back, I can be here to intercept him. We can catch the guy!"

"Don't think I don't know what you're really up to," Sully said, getting into Will's face.

I stepped between them, arms raised. "Fighting isn't going to solve anything right now. I am staying here, in my house, and that is final. I won't upset Gram again."

Exhaling, Will took a step back. "Look, I just want to catch this guy. Alex is right. There are only a few more hours till daylight. I doubt the guy will try anything again tonight anyway. If he does, I'll be right here waiting for him."

Sully looked at me, and I shrugged. I wasn't thrilled with the idea of being assigned a babysitter, but if it meant I could stay home, then so be it. He let out a deep breath and stared me in the eyes as he considered, the frustration evident on his face. He finally dropped his shoulders in defeat and turned to Will.

"Okay, Mr. Helpful. You stay," he said and then turned to the other officers. "Jones, I want you to keep watch from your cruiser. I want you patrolling the street. Call me if you see anyone, and I mean ANYONE suspicious. Conley, you get back to the station and log those pictures. I want to run that hand writing analysis first thing in the morning."

"Yes, Chief," they both answered, hurrying to their vehicles.

"Will doesn't have to stay. I don't need a babysitter," I said, knowing my argument was futile but trying.

"He stays, and that's final," Sully said, patting me on the shoulder.

"And if I don't want him to?"

"Now THAT would be a moot point," he winked, then stalked down the porch stairs.

I rolled my eyes as Sully opened the door of his truck and turned to Will and me.

"I'll be back in the morning to pick you up, Kiddo. You and I will go see Brightman together," he said, earning a smile from me. Then he pointed to Will. "You hear anything unusual, you call me immediately."

"You got it." Will waved as Sully pulled out of the driveway. Then he turned to me with a smile. "Looks like we get to have a sleepover. Let's make popcorn and take turns painting one another's toenails."

Glaring at him as I passed, I went into the house, letting the screen door slam in his face when he turned to follow me.

"What? I'm lightening the mood," he said and followed me inside. He locked both the knob and the deadbolt behind him, then walked to the back door and did the same.

I went into the kitchen and got down a glass. I poured myself a small amount of wine and slung it back just as Will walked in.

"Do you want a glass?" I offered.

Will stared at the bottle in my hand for a second. He swallowed hard, shrugging his shoulders. "I'm on duty remember?"

"Right," I said, pouring more into my glass. "More for me."

"Go easy on that," he said. "I need you to stay coherent."

I took another sip. "I'm calming my nerves. This seems to be the only thing that helps lately. Plus, I have one hell of a headache. I'm just going to finish this glass, and that's it. Promise."

He seemed satisfied with my answer and rubbed his hands together. "Right, so first thing's first. Do you have any nail polish remover?"

I raised an eyebrow over my glass. "I'm not painting your toenails."

"That's a shame," he scoffed. "I was going to get that marker off the mirror upstairs. You shouldn't have to look at that."

"Isn't it evidence?" I asked.

"We have pictures of it, and no prints were found. Unless you like it there . . . I mean, it's not to my taste, but it does rather match the black hardware in there. Up to you."

"All joking aside, just why ARE you being so helpful?" I asked. "No offense or anything, but you've always sort of struck me as kind of a jerk. Or at least that's how you seem to want to come off. Why the Nice Guy act?"

When Will shrugged and looked away, I knew I'd struck a nerve. "Because you never asked for any of this. You've already been through enough for one lifetime, and believe it or not, I have a heart." He clenched his fists. "And because your mom was always patient and nice to me, even when I gave her hell. I owe her this much."

His eyes were a dark well of emotion, and I believed he was sincere. There was a lot more to Will Galia than I'd ever thought. I caught myself wondering just how deep the well went.

"Okay then," I said, breaking away from his glare. "I have some polish remover in my bag upstairs."

I kept my eyes averted when we passed the upstairs bathroom, never wanting to see those horrific words again. Will turned to go in, and I continued into my room. My feelings bounced between fear and dread to overwhelming anger and rage. The wine helped to calm me, but my head was spinning in a thousand directions. Had my mother's murderer been here in Saluda all along? Had I seen him? Passed him on the street? Spoken with him?

I reached into my bag, and when I emerged with the polish remover, I caught Donovan's image in the mirror. He looked down on me, a worried expression on his salient face.

"Be careful," he warned.

I glanced behind me to make sure I was alone. "Why, do you sense something? Is the man who attacked me coming back?"

"What did you say?" Will called from the bathroom.

"Nothing!" I shouted toward the hallway, then looked back to Donovan.

"No, I don't think you are in any immediate danger. There's . . . just something about him." Donovan nodded toward the hall. "You shouldn't get too close."

"What . . . Will?" I began to ask, then stopped short when Will's image appeared in the mirror as he came to stand in the bedroom doorway. I looked from Donovan's image to Will's, waiting for a reaction from Will. My words caught in my throat.

"Did you find any?" Will asked, oblivious.

I took a breath, relieved. Of course Will couldn't see Donovan. I should have known I was the only one who could.

"Here," I said, tossing him the polish remover.

"Can I use one of the towels in there?"

"Sure, whatever you need. I don't use that bathroom. Just get it off however you can."

Will turned and went back down the hall. I looked back to the mirror at Donovan who stood with his arms crossed against the wall by the door. Shrugging at him, I grabbed a pillow and blanket from the bed, then reached for one of my books and went into the hall. I paused by the bathroom, but didn't look in.

"Is it working?"

"Yeah, I think. It's definitely permanent marker, but it's coming off with some elbow grease."

"That's good," I said, relieved. "I've got a pillow and blanket for you. I'm going to put them on the couch."

Downstairs, I set the pillow on one side of the couch and the blanket on the other, then tossed the book in the center. Going back into the kitchen, I finished off my glass of wine. I was exhausted, mentally and physically. Too much happened in too little time, and my brain was scrambling to keep up.

Will came into the kitchen as I was resting my aching body against the counter, waiting for the wine to numb away what it could.

"You don't look so good," he said, coming to lean on the counter beside me.

"Again with the flattery." I smiled.

"No, I mean it. How are you holding up?"

"I'm just tired," I sighed. "I think I'm going to try to get some sleep. I don't know how possible that's going to be though."

"Yeah, you should get some rest," he said. "Don't worry about anything. I'm right by the doors. I'll hear if anyone tries to get back in. Jones is right outside too. You don't have anything to worry about."

"Thank you," I said. I wanted to correct him, to tell him that I had everything to worry about. My mother's murderer was out there somewhere, nearby, and that thought alone threatened my very sanity.

"Help yourself to anything in here if you're hungry," I said. "Sorry I don't have a television or anything to help you pass the time. I put one of my books on the couch for you. Best I could do, sorry. I never planned on staying here very long."

"Thanks. Those look like Gram's cookies over there. You may be missing a few in the morning," he smirked. "And don't worry about me. I can occupy myself."

"Help yourself," I said, leaving him in the kitchen. "See you in a few."

"So how about now?" Will asked before I made it out of the room. I turned and met his waiting gaze.

"What do you mean?"

"How long do you plan on staying now?" he asked.

"Now? I can't imagine leaving." I walked away, but out of the corner of my eye, I thought I saw Will smile.

Upstairs, I went to my room and shut the door. I looked into the mirror, but there was no sign of Donovan, which was fine. It gave me some time alone to think. I sat on the bed and let the events of the night hit me.

Sully thought that the attacker from tonight might be a different person from that night fifteen years ago, but I knew better. Even if Donovan hadn't warned me of this "same evil", I would have known. Those gloved hands that came after me were the same. Their furious determination to hurt me was the same. No one could convince me otherwise.

Rolling up my pajama leg, I exposed my tender ankle. Fingerprints, red and swollen, throbbed from where the intruder had gripped me. The skin there was turning a sickly shade of yellow and purple. I found the small scar just below my hairline and rubbed it. This was twice now that I'd escaped those hands.

A tear fell from my eyes, and I wiped it with the back of my hand. I didn't know if I was more afraid or enraged. I thought about what Donovan said earlier that night, about having to see this thing through, and wondered what he meant by it. My thoughts were broken when I felt his warmth on my ankle. The pain soothed and relaxed. I closed my eyes and heard the gentle strumming and let the ache melt away.

"You knew something was going to happen, didn't you?" I asked into the empty room. "I saw it on your face tonight."

"I sensed it. I couldn't know for sure," Donovan answered into to my ear.

"Why didn't you tell me?" I asked, opening my eyes to look into the mirror. He was sitting on the bed beside me, his hand on my ankle.

"I'm not meant to interfere, only to guide."

"And protect, right?"

"That's right." Donovan looked pained. "Sometimes that means NOT telling you something."

"You want me to trust you. How can I do that if you don't tell me everything?" I asked confused.

"You have to." He sighed, lifting his eyes to mine in the mirror. "You have to trust that if I'm not telling you something, it's for a reason."

I looked away. "Am I ever going to find out who killed my parents?"

"I hope so."

"Do you think it's Brightman?"

"It's a possibility. That's why I'm not sure you should go out there to speak with him tomorrow."

I looked back into the mirror and met his concerned expression. "I have to go. If it's him, maybe I'll know. Maybe this whole nightmare could finally be over. Uncle Sully will be with me, and you. I'm not afraid."

Donovan shook his head. "That's what worries me the most."

There was nothing to say. I knew that I should be afraid, and a part of me was. Someone out there wanted to hurt me or worse. It was the same person who brutally murdered my parents. A new fear was rising inside of me, though, one that overshadowed all of that. I was terrified that this man would never be found, that he would never pay for what he'd done to my family. I feared that I would never know who he was.

For the past fifteen years, I'd lived with the knowledge that this monster roamed free while I was left bound by the scars he left.

Now he'd resurfaced, and my desperate need for justice outweighed all other fear.

"You need to get some rest," Donovan said.

"That's what you said this evening, and I was attacked a few hours later."

Donovan nodded his head, sorrow showing on his face.

"I'm sorry," I whispered, immediately regretted the remark. Donovan saved my life again tonight, and for that I was grateful to him. The words to express how glad I was that he was here evaded me. I hoped he knew, even though the anger boiling inside me kept me from being able to say them.

"No, I'm sorry, Alexandra," he whispered. "I can't keep evil from coming for you, only protect you when it does. But I can promise that no harm will come to you again tonight. You should sleep."

Sighing, I switched off the light and laid my head down on the pillow. I wrapped my robe more tightly around my body, not relaxed enough to get into the covers. There was no denying how exhausted I was. If I could only quiet my mind enough to sleep.

"Donovan?" I whispered.

"Yes."

"Tell me about where you . . . live. Where you are when you're not with me here."

"You want me to describe where I was sent from? Where I exist in the spiritual realm as well as here with you?"

"Yes."

"It's hard to explain to someone who has never seen," he said.

"Try, please."

Donovan took a deep breath as he searched for the words. "It is filled with light, a brightness unlike anything in this world."

"Are there more there? Like you?"

"There is no one else with me here, though I can feel the presence of many. I can feel love."

"So you're all alone up there?"

"No, never alone. It's so hard to explain," he struggled to continue. "For me, every moment is with you. Seeing you, being here with you, it's all that matters. Not what's come before, not what will come after. It's as if I've only ever been here with you."

My blood warmed at his words, and my mind wandered through my life's memories. I remembered feeling him with me. He was always a part of my life. Up until the day my mother was taken from me.

"Why did you leave me when she died?" I asked, tears forming anew in my weary eyes.

The strumming grew louder against my ear. I felt his warmth on my arm.

"I never left you," he whispered. "I've been with you this whole time, always. You just needed to come back here, to your home, to remember. You needed to remember who you are, to see that the accident doesn't have to define you and your faith. I've always been right here at your side."

Wiping my eyes with the corner of my pillow, I thought back. All this time I believed that I was alone, that I was wandering through this life on my own. How wrong I had been. If only I'd seen it before, maybe I would have had the courage to come back home sooner.

All the years I missed with Gram came to mind. I should have been here to help take care of her. How many more moments could I have had where she recognized me? And Donovan. Now that I'd found him again, I couldn't imagine how I ever forgot him, especially when he had never forgotten me.

My mind swam in the space between memories, fading more with each one. In every memory I visited, I heard his soft, gentle strumming, playing like the score in the background of my life.

"Sleep now, Alexandra," Donovan whispered against my ear.

Nine

I could hear my mother's screams above the crunching of metal as the car came to a smashing halt against the great oak. The panic that rose in my throat as Gary's was sliced open raced through my veins and threatened to consume me. Then the serpentine knife came for me.

Donovan was there. He was with me, telling me to sink into my seat, but this time I didn't listen. I wanted to see. I needed to know who the man with the knife was. Nothing else muttered.

Struggling against my confines, I strained to get an arm free. I inched forward, staring through the dark into the front seat. When lightning flashed, I could see that the man was wearing a mask. I reached out. I could almost grab it.

"Who are you?" I screamed as the blade came at me over and over again.

I didn't feel the pain, only noticed the fresh wounds sliced into my arms. I didn't care. Continuing to reach forward, I used all my strength to force myself free from my seat even as the gloved hands grabbed at me and hurled the knife into me over and over. I could feel the metal gouge my throat.

With the next lightening flash, I watched my bloodied arm reach for him. I forced out one last bone-chilling scream and lurched forward to claw at his face. As the blade came down on my throat for the last time, I ripped off the mask.

I shot up in the bed, my face soaked in sweat, and gasped for air.

"It's okay, Alexandra. It was just a dream. Sshhh, it's okay. You're okay," Donovan whispered.

I felt his warmth on my face. Taking a deep breath, I looked around. It was still dark. I glanced at the clock. It was just past 4 am. It had been less than two hours since I laid my head down.

"The dream," I panted. "I could almost see who he was."

"It was just a dream."

"I know, it was just . . ." I stopped short when I heard the music. "What is that?"

"Your friend seems to have taken to the keys," Donovan said. "He's been playing for a while."

"Will?" I said, rubbing my eyes. "I forgot he was even here."

I got up from the bed and straightened my robe, then turned on the light and ran a hand through my hair before going to the door.

"What are you doing?" Donovan asked.

"I'm going to see what he's up to," I answered, opening the door.

The music became more distinct as it traveled up the stairs. Though he played lightly on the keys, I recognized *Fur Elise*.

"Please, you need to keep your distance from him," Donovan pleaded.

I looked back in the mirror, into Donovan's worried eyes. I knew that there was something he wasn't telling me. "What is it that you sense about him exactly?"

He shook his head, frustration evident on his face.

"I can't . . . explain it to you," he said. "You shouldn't trust him, Alexandra. Right now, you shouldn't trust anyone."

"I'll keep my distance." I left the room, not looking back into the mirror. I heard Donovan's sigh of disapproval behind me.

Downstairs, a single lamp on the piano shone like a spotlight on Will while he focused on his hands at the keys. I stopped at the bottom of the steps and watched as he slid his fingers over them with tremendous focus, missing the occasional note as he played.

I watched the intensity on his face, his mind was somewhere else entirely. His eyes carried so much pain and anguish that it made me want to reach out to him. I was eager to know more about him. Donovan was right, I didn't know him at all. I waited until he finished the song before I spoke up.

"I didn't realize you still played," I said.

Will whirled around, his sullen expression turning to a grin. "Your mother was a great teacher. I bet you play beautifully."

"I was okay at one point, I guess."

"I hope I didn't wake you."

"Not at all." I shrugged. "Bad dream. Happens sometimes."

Will sighed. "I know the feeling."

He straightened and scooted to one side of the bench. "I know what will cheer you up, though. There's only one other song that I remember how to play."

He started to play the melody to *Chopsticks* and patted the empty side of the bench with his free hand,

I shook my head. "No, I can't."

"Oh, come on," he said. "It would cheer ME up."

Hesitating a moment, I decided it was the least I could do. Not only had I wrecked the man's car, but now he was forced to babysit me all night. It was a wonder he was nice to me at all. I took in a deep breath and sat next to him on the bench, waiting for my entrance. When the opening came, I played the rhythm. Will smiled, bobbing his head up and down to the music.

"See? We're pretty good," he said, then hit a wrong note.

I laughed and Will concentrated, getting himself back on track. Mischievously, I sped up the rhythm, forcing him to go faster. Will's fingers raced to keep up. I sped up again and tried not to lose focus when Will's tongue poked out of his mouth as he bore down on the keys in utter determination.

"I got this!" he said, his fingers flying across the keys.

He hit more and more wrong notes, and when I sped up again, he lost his fingering and finally threw his hands up in surrender.

"Okay, you got me. I give. You are the *Chopsticks* master," he said, laughing.

I stopped playing, the laughter coming uncontrollably. It felt good to laugh. "My mom and I used to play that song all the time. Now SHE was the *Chopsticks* master."

Will nodded in agreement. "She was amazing on the piano, that's for sure. I think you may have inherited her musical genius."

"Yeah, well," I said, bowing my head, "I haven't really played much. Not at all actually, before I came back here."

"Well, then, I'll consider that butt whooping you just gave me a privilege. Thank you for humoring me."

I laughed in spite of myself. "You're welcome. I figured I owe you for crashing your car into the side of a mountain and all. Think we're even now?"

Will's smile vanished. His mood shifted from laughter to concern. Maybe he was finally upset about the loss of his prized car. I regretted the joke and felt terrible all over again.

"Will, I'm sorry. I didn't mean . . ."

Will shook his head. "No, it's alright. There's just something I have to tell you."

I stared at him, confused. He shifted in his seat and continued.

"It's why I really came over here tonight," he confessed. "I wasn't just taking a drive like I told your uncle. I was here to keep an eye on things, on you."

"What do you mean you were keeping an eye on things? How could you have known . . ." I started to ask, confused.

"I think someone wanted you to crash my car," he interrupted, looking me in the eyes.

"What? What are you talking about?"

"I went to the shop today to see what the hold-up was on the brake report. It turns out that Hank, the mechanic, had a family emergency and left in a hurry for Charlotte. So I took a look at the brakes myself," he explained.

I stared at him, waiting for him to go on. The urgency in his voice made my heart begin to race.

"Alex, it looks like someone cut the brake lines, but not all the way. It was a clean cut most of the way through. The rest must have snapped after you hit the brakes a few of times. Whoever did it wanted the car to be driven a little while before the brakes went out."

I shook my head in disbelief. It took me a minute to process what he just said. None of it made any sense. "But, no one knew I was going to borrow your car."

"Do you remember seeing anyone at the cemetery that afternoon?"

"No, no one was there except for Pastor James," I said, "but I was in the cemetery for a while. You can't see the parking lot from there. Someone could have gotten to the car then, I guess."

Will shook his head. "I don't think so though."

"Why not?"

"Because I know my keys were in that drawer. They are always in the front of the drawer. When I went to hand them to you, they were gone. There were not in that drawer. I think someone took them and then put them back later. They wanted the car to stay in the lot so they could cut the lines and be sure that you'd be the one driving it when they snapped."

"But why? Who?" I asked, trying to remain calm.

Will shrugged. "It could have been anyone. All they would have had to do that day was wait until I was in the back office to snatch them."

"How would they have known where to look?" I asked.

Will shrugged. "I mean, they weren't exactly hidden."

"But still, no one knew about me borrowing your car."

"I thought about that too." Will scooted closer. "We were talking right beside the door, and those doors are like a hundred years old. You can hear right through them. Anyone could have heard us from out there."

"I didn't see anyone."

"Doesn't mean they weren't there," Will said.

I glared at him. That's exactly what Donovan would say, and they were both right. I thought back to a couple of days ago.

Then it came back to me. I covered my mouth with my hands, my eyes widening.

"What is it?" Will asked.

"Rick! Rick was there!" I cried. "I bumped into him when I left the station. Right after I talked to you, I opened the door, and he was right there. I almost knocked him over."

"That makes sense," Will agreed. "What's his motive though? Why would he want you dead? Or your parents? Over a house?"

"I don't know," I growled, "but I am sure as hell going to find out."

Will furrowed his brow. "Maybe you should let me go up there with Sully tomorrow. If it is him, he'll be extremely dangerous."

"Oh, don't you start now," I snapped at him. "I am going up there. I'm the only one who's seen this bastard. I'll know if it's him."

Will raised his hands with a smirk. "Okay, okay. At ease soldier. I doubt he'll try anything with Chief there, anyway."

I took a deep breath. Anger broke way to fear as I thought about this new information. If all of it were true, I was in more danger than I thought. Donovan was right.

"You really think someone cut the brake lines?" I asked again, hoping he would show some sign of doubt. I wanted him to be wrong.

"I know so," he answered.

"I could have gone off the mountain. I almost died the same way . . ." I collected myself. "Just like the message said on the mirror."

Will bowed his head. "I know."

"Does Sully know about this? Did you tell him?"

"No. I want to wait for the actual report from Hank. The chief likes hard proof," Will said. "Plus, he would freak out. You'd be quarantined at the station or sent back to Chicago on the next flight."

"You're right. He would totally freak out." I raised an eyebrow at Will. "So what, you just decided to keep an eye on me yourself then?"

"Something like that," Will said, looking away.

"But why? Why do you even care?"

"It's my job to care, and like I said, I owe it to your mom."

I studied him closely. The muscles in his sharp jaw were clenched. He was hiding something. "There's more to it though, isn't there? Not about me at all, but about you."

Will took a minute and then looked back at me. His eyes, brimming with red, were haunted.

"I couldn't let it happen again," he whispered.

I moved my hand to cover his on the bench, but my fingers bumped something hard that clanged to the floor with a metallic thud. Will rushed to pick it up, but I reached the object first. I held the cool metal flask in my hand and stared with shock into Will's horrified face.

"What is this?" I asked and then sniffed the lid. "Whiskey? What happened to being on duty?"

"You're not the only one who likes to calm their nerves," he spat, grabbing the flask.

I got up from the bench, disgusted. "Some protector you are. What were you going to do if the guy came back to attack me again? Breathe on him?"

Will grabbed my arm and forced me to face him. I tried to yank my arm free, but his grip was too strong.

"I only had a few sips. Sometimes, my head gets away from me," he pleaded. The desperation on his face made me stop struggling. "Can you understand that? Can you understand having thoughts . . . memories that constantly haunt you? That threaten to drive you crazy? Sometimes I don't know who I am anymore . . ."

The pain in his eyes tore at my heart, and although their intensity made me uneasy, I felt compelled to listen. I did know what it felt like. I knew exactly what it felt like to lose yourself in the pain of the past. I lowered myself back onto the bench, keeping my eyes glued to his. He removed his grip on my arm as I sat.

"You said you couldn't let it happen again. Let what happen? What happened to you, Will?"

He looked away, contemplating. Taking a deep breath to collect himself, he turned back to me. "It was an accident, about five years ago. My wife and I were living up in New York at the time. We had a nice little place right outside the city."

"Your wife?" I whispered.

Will only nodded. "Our son, Tristan, was only four years old. We had just thrown him his first real birthday party. We'd just gotten him his first big-boy bed, one of those car beds. My wife made him this cute little football cake. He loved watching football with his old man."

Will smiled joylessly at the memory. I placed my hand on his shoulder and braced myself.

"It was my fault," he continued, his face glazing over into a mask of sorrow. "I got home late that night. My partner and I spent all night staking out a suspected drug shipment. I wasn't thinking straight. I put my holster on the kitchen table to grab something to eat."

I closed my eyes, afraid of where the story was heading, not wanting to hear more but listening anyway.

"I didn't even remember I'd left it there until we heard the shot go off in the morning," Will's voice broke.

I looked into his face as tears streamed down my own. Will stared into the room with a blank expression, lost in that moment five years ago.

"I killed my baby boy. It was my fault," he said between clenched teeth.

He looked into my eyes, searching for some kind of empathy in them. I knew his pain. I knew the guilt, the loss, the anger. How much more must he be feeling though, to have lost a child to his own mistake?

There was so much I wanted to say, but I couldn't find the words. I wanted to tell him that he shouldn't blame himself, that accidents happen, but I knew all too well how little comfort those words would be.

I thought about all of the things that Donovan said to me about purpose and plans, but for the life of me, I could not see the purpose in the loss of a child. I prayed silently for the right words. What I heard in return was gentle strumming.

I looked into the glossy finish of the piano and saw that Donovan was there. He sat on the base of the stairs, facing away from us, his hands folded across his knees.

"Right now, he just needs you to listen," he said to me. "He needs you."

I reached for Will's hand. Will looked down at our joined hands and then up into my face.

"Melissa left me shortly after. I couldn't blame her. Every time she looked at me, she saw the man that killed our son. So I came back here to Saluda, to the only other place I ever called home."

Will sat up, trying to shake the demons from his head. "Sully was looking for someone with some experience and was kind enough to give me a chance."

He laughed suddenly, releasing my hand.

"I don't even know why I am telling you all of this."

I wiped a tear from my cheek and squeezed his hand. "Because I'm listening, and because you know that I've lived in that same dark place. The place where you wish it were you that died instead."

Will's face brightened with recognition. "That's it exactly. There are so many evil people in this world who deserve to have their life taken from them, me included. Tristan died because I was careless. He was an innocent child. I'm the one who deserved to die. I've done so many horrible things in my lifetime. He was the one thing I did right. He made me feel like I could start over, as a father. I can't tell you how many times I've wished I would have been killed in that stakeout. If I had never come home, my son would still be alive."

"I get that. I do," I said, with a nod. "I often wish that I would have died in the crash instead of Mom and Gary, or that I could at least have died with them. I saw the car coming, the one that ran us off the road. I could have warned them. If I hadn't been so afraid, I might have saved their lives."

I realized in that moment that I had never admitted that to anyone. It was a release in a way, having the words free from my mind's prison.

"What I've come to realize since coming back here though," I continued, "is that there's a bigger picture than what I can see. I'm still here for a reason, and so are you. You're not an evil person, Will."

Will's head dropped. "You don't know me, Alex. You don't know what I'm capable of."

"I know enough. Your life still has purpose," was all I could think to say.

I was at a loss, wanting so badly to say something that would give him hope, the way Donovan had done for me.

"You have to tell him that his son forgives him," Donovan said from where he still sat on the stairs, head downcast. "He needs to forgive himself."

I cleared my throat and shook my head, looking at him through the piano. I couldn't say that to Will. Who was I to tell him that his dead son forgave him? Why would he even believe me?

"You need to tell him, Alexandra, because it's the truth, and he needs to hear it. You know it because I know it. This is your gift. If he cannot forgive himself, he will always be lost."

I looked back at Will and took a deep breath, forcing back my tears.

"I know that it's not my place to say, but you need to know that your son forgives you," I said. "He would want you to forgive yourself."

Will looked at me and stared blankly into my eyes, tears forming in his own. He grinned and blinked them away, then cleared his throat. "I don't think I can. That's why I came over here tonight. I almost did it again. I let you borrow that damned car, and it almost got you killed."

"There was no way you could have known a crazed lunatic was trying to kill . . ." I stopped short, unable to say the words. I looked to Donovan's reflection for comfort. "It wasn't your fault."

Will gently took hold of my chin and forced my eyes back up to his. "Still, it was my car, and nothing like that is going to happen on my watch. Never again, I promise you that."

I felt my face flush, the intensity of his eyes burned into mine. "You don't have to take responsibility for me. None of this has anything to do with you, Will."

Will kept a firm hold on my chin and drew my face close to his. My heart sputtered and raced inside my chest at his proximity. I breathed him in. The pungent scent of whiskey mingled with a hint of leather and fresh rain.

"I'm making you my responsibility," he said softly.

"Why?" I whispered, lost in the darkness of his eyes.

He gently swept the hair from my cheek with his free hand.

"Because you make me feel something that I haven't felt in a long, long time," he whispered and then closed the space between us.

I closed my eyes as he brushed his lips against mine. My breath caught in my chest and I parted my lips, aching for more of him. He found my lips again and let his hand fall from my chin as he took my mouth with his. I felt the heat between us boil in my blood, threatening to carry me away, if only for a little while. Away from the fear and pain, away from the loss and darkness. I wanted to lose myself in him completely, but I could hear the strumming behind me, and Donovan's solemn, pleading voice.

"Alexandra, please. You can't," he whispered, his voice full of angst and desperation.

I jolted back from Will, taking a breath to clear my head. "We can't do this."

"You're right. I'm sorry . . . That's not why I'm here." Will looked at me, worried. "I'm sorry. I shouldn't have . . ."

"WE shouldn't have," I corrected. "It's not that I don't want . . . I guess I just need this whole thing to be over before I can think about . . . this."

"No, I totally get it. I completely agree," he said, giving me a reassuring smile. "It will all be over soon."

I smiled back, wanting to believe that he was right, that this whole nightmare would end soon. Then I remembered what Donovan said in the car. Tonight was only the beginning.

"I hope you're right, but I'm not so sure," I said.

"Trust me." He stretched his long arms. "In the meantime though, I feel like crap all over again. Your fault, by the way. So, I demand a rematch."

Will poised his fingers above the piano keys and smirked at me with a twisted grin.

"Oh no, you couldn't possibly be suggesting that you can keep up with me," I laughed, grateful for this change of mood.

Will started to play the *Chopsticks* melody again, focusing on his fingers on the keys. "I've seriously got this now."

"You think so?" I smiled and began the rhythm, matching his tempo. "You know, you really should feel like crap."

I sped up the rhythm, and Will's tongue poked back out of his mouth as he concentrated.

"Why is that?"

I sped up the rhythm even more. "You're a terrible kisser."

Will lost his focus, hitting a throng of wrong keys and the music fell apart. He turned to me horrified, mouth agape.

"I am not, you cheater! And you know it!" He placed his fingers back on the keys and smiled. "I declare a rematch. No distracting me with your obvious and outrageous lies this time."

Laughing, he began the rhythm again. We played over and over, letting the piano distract us from the rest of the world while the sun began to peek above the horizon. As dim light seeped into the room, I looked into the piano for Donovan. He never budged from where he sat at the base of the stairs, facing away from us, his gaze lost in thought. Waiting.

Ten

I emerged from the shower refreshed despite the lack of sleep, eager to see what the day would bring. I hoped it would bring Brightman to justice. Though I tried not to jump to conclusions, I couldn't help it. Everything added up.

Wiping the fog from the bathroom mirror, I studied the lump on my forehead. It was healing at least, the shades of black and blue were fading into a greenish yellow. Noticing the dark circles under my eyes, I dabbed on some concealer. Then I put on a pair of jeans, a tank top, and my favorite red sweater.

I made a point to not look into the bedroom mirror as I laced up my sneakers. I knew Donovan was there, I could hear him, but I wasn't ready to talk about the last few hours. Not before I could figure them out for myself.

"You have feelings for him," he said softly.

I continued to tie my laces. "I don't know what I feel, if you want to know the truth."

"You probably feel less alone," he said, and I finally met his eyes in the mirror.

"I already felt less alone, as soon as I found you again," I said.

Donovan sat at the edge of the bed. He was leaning over, his forearms resting on his thighs, fingers laced. He looked worried.

"You feel understood, because you see the same pain and emptiness in him that you've lived with for so long."

I couldn't deny any of what he said. I didn't have the words to even try.

"Bonding over tragedy is natural. The closeness you feel for him is normal." Donovan sighed, looking away from me. "But Alexandra, you mustn't get that close to him. You have to trust me with this. Keep your distance."

"But why?" I asked. "You can't just say something like that and not explain yourself."

Donovan shook his head. I thought he wanted to tell me something, but couldn't. Or wouldn't. "Besides what I'm sensing, I already told you. You shouldn't trust him. I think he's hiding something from you."

"Like what?" I asked.

"I'm not sure," was all Donovan said before the sound of Sully's heavy truck interrupted us.

"Chief is here!" Will yelled from downstairs.

"It's go time," I whispered, suddenly anxious.

"Listen for me." In the mirror I watched as Donovan took hold of my hand reassuringly. "I'll be with you the whole time."

Focusing on his warmth, I took a deep breath. I was about to come face to face with the man that could be my mother's murderer. As much as that thought nauseated me, I willed myself to stand up and walk to the door. I turned to look once more at Donovan and saw him standing beside me. Reassured, I left the room.

When I walked into the kitchen, Sully was leaning back on the counter with a cup of coffee in hand. He offered it to me, and I took it gratefully. Will was at the stove scrambling eggs. He nodded at me and went back to stirring.

"Long night?" Sully asked, an eyebrow raised.

"We got by," I said, taking my first scalding sip.

Sully inspected my face, obviously trying to decipher what he'd missed. "Right. Well, I've got a locksmith coming by to change all the locks. Should be here any minute. We'll head on out to the school and have a word with your friend Rick once they're done."

I flinched. "Ugh, don't call him that. Makes me sick to my stomach."

"I told you. We can't go jumping to conclusions about the man," Sully said. "We're going to need some hard evidence that links him to last night's break-in, or to your mother's accident. We can't work on only assumptions here."

I stole a glance at Will who gave me a told-you-so shrug. If Sully wanted hard evidence, I was determined to find him some. If Brightman was the killer, he was not going to go free again.

Suddenly I was even more anxious to get to the school. I needed to see Brightman. I needed to gauge his reaction to our questions. I needed to know.

"Can we just go now? The locksmith could take a while and I don't think I can sit here that long," I pleaded. "We can have him come back."

"Why don't you have something to eat?" Will suggested. "I mean, I know I'm not the greatest cook, but you should eat something."

"He's right. Maybe by the time you're done, the guy will be here," Sully said.

I shook my head. "No, I can't. My stomach's a mess. I just want to get up there. I have to know. I can't rest until I see his face."

Will sighed and dished eggs onto a plate. "More for me, I guess. You guys go on. I'll stay here and wait on the locksmith."

"Really?" I asked. "You wouldn't mind?"

Sully held up a hand. "I don't know that I like this idea. I wanted to see to it personally that Alex and I were the only ones who touched those keys. No offense, Deputy."

Will took a sip from his coffee cup and met my pleading eyes.

"Look," he said, "as SOON as the guy is gone, I will lock up and take the keys straight to the station and lock them both in the safe. You'll probably be back by the time I get there anyway, in which case I'll hand them right to you."

"That's a great plan, Sully," I pleaded. "We're just going up there to ask Brightman some questions, right? We won't be gone long."

Sully tugged from his coffee cup and looked from me to Will. "Fine, but only because I have somewhere to be later." He jabbed a finger at Will. "I want those keys in that safe or in my hand. No one else so much as looks at them."

Will nodded and shoved a forkful of eggs into his mouth. "You got it. No one else sees them."

I gulped down my coffee and gestured for Sully to do the same. HE took a long drag, then grabbed a fork from the counter and scooped some eggs from Will's plate into his mouth as Will gawked at him.

"You're right. You're not the greatest cook," Sully said, then taking one last sip of coffee turned to me. "Okay, Kiddo, let's go."

Will took another bite of his eggs and shrugged as Sully walked out of the kitchen.

"Thank you," I said to Will.

"Just don't let me regret it," Will said. "Be careful. Feel the guy out, but don't push him. Let Sully handle it. If he's the one, we'll find a way to prove it."

"Got it," I said. "I'll see you later then."

Jogging out the door, I hopped into Sully's truck as he started the massive engine.

"Now we are just going to ask Brightman some very basic questions about the house and what he may know about the break-in last night. Let me do all the talking," he instructed.

I nodded, turning my attention to the window while Sully navigated us to the road that would lead us to the school. The morning was overcast with a crisp, bone-chilling breeze that announced the approaching winter. The darkened sky muted the fall colors, adding a grayish tinge to the atmosphere.

I stared, mesmerized, out the window. I hadn't ridden this road since that night when we were coming back from my recital. How fitting it was, I thought, that we were driving up to confront the man who murdered my parents off this very road. Why? That would be my first question to him. Why?

As the truck hugged the curves of the road, I held my breath, and I looked at the steep drop on the left side. We were getting close to the accident site. I turned to Sully who was focused on the road. He turned to me and smiled, oblivious. I'd almost forgotten that Sully was still in Iraq when the accident happened. He didn't know the exact spot. When we turned the next curve, I remembered vividly.

Turning back to my window, I saw the small side street coming up on my side of the road, the side street the killer had sprung up from before hitting our car. Jutting up from below the tree line, the road was covered in overhanging brush. I stared at the spot as we passed and tried to remember that split second before our car was struck. I remembered the headlights speeding up from below.

Closing my eyes, I fought to bring the image from the past into my current reality. When I did, I recalled that the headlights were higher up, above my eye level. They weren't like the headlights of a sedan or a smaller car. No, the vehicle had been taller, wider than a car. I concentrated, pulling the image closer in my mind.

Red.

There'd been a glint of red from between the headlights. Gasping, I opened my eyes. Sully looked at me, concerned.

"What is it?"

"That was the road . . . the one the vehicle that hit us came from."

Sully's eyes widened, and he nodded with sudden understanding. He grabbed my hand and gave it a squeeze. "God, I'm so sorry. I don't know why I didn't think of it. This was the road . . ." he sighed. "I shouldn't have let you come up here. I wasn't thinking."

"No," I interrupted, "it's fine. I needed to come."

Squeezing his hand back, I smiled. I didn't want to tell him what I remembered just yet. I didn't want anything to distract him from the task at hand. Talking to Rick was all that mattered.

"We're almost there," Sully said, letting my hand go.

I looked out the window, at the incline in the road. The school was at the top. My heart began to race with fear and anticipation. How long had I dreamt of this moment? How often had I prayed for a chance to see justice served? I closed my eyes and focused on the strumming coming from the back seat.

When the truck reached the top of the incline, I stared at the red brick building trimmed in navy blue, which sat among the tall oaks and pines. The school was smaller than I remembered, but had the same quaint charm. Scanning the parking lot for the white pickup truck, I spotted it by the main office where it was parked next to a work van and larger pickups filled with lumber and metal extension ladders.

"There's his truck," I said, pointing it out to Sully. "That's the one I keep seeing."

Sully parked beside it, and turning off the growling engine, he turned to face me. "Now remember, we don't know anything for sure yet. We can't just go accusing people of murder or break-ins on a hunch. I'll do the talking. You just hang back and see if you can pick up on anything, okay?"

"Got it." I nodded, telling myself he was right.

We got out of the truck and walked to the main entrance. I wrung my hands as Sully tried the door. It was locked. Then we heard the humming of a table saw coming from the side of the building.

"This way," Sully said, motioning me to follow.

When we turned the corner, we found Rick with a half dozen other men in the courtyard between the main office building and the rest of the school. They'd set up shop in the center with heavy equipment and lumber. A tent of plastic film covered the opened wall of the auditorium. Rick was bent over a long folding table in the center of the courtyard looking over plans while men sawed and carried plywood and insulation from the side door. I stopped short when he spotted us and flashed us his signature smile.

"Chief, Miss Nolan, to what do I owe this pleasure?" he asked. "I hope nothing is wrong with the permits."

Sully shook his head, taking the hand that Rick offered him. I stayed back, suddenly without words.

"No, sir, nothing like that," Sully said. "I was wondering if you wouldn't mind taking the time to answer a few questions. Do you have a minute?"

Rick looked from Sully to me, the smile disintegrating from his face.

"Certainly. I hope everything is alright. Shall we?" Rick gestured to the parking lot and walked passed me.

I could only stare, taking in his heavy work boots and long sleeved flannel shirt. He looked different out of his business attire, but that smile was just as off-putting in jeans and a baseball cap. I could imagine his hands covered with leather gloves.

We walked back to our vehicles where the sounds of hammering and sawing were muffled. Rick stopped in front of his truck and turned to Sully.

"So, what can I do for you, Chief? The look on your face tells me this has nothing to do with our job here."

Sully sighed and rubbed his chin before starting. "There was a break-in at the house last night. Someone attacked Alex."

Rick's eyes widened with shock, and he looked at me. "My God, are you all right?"

I took a step back, not liking his eyes on me. I didn't dare speak for fear of saying something Sully would regret later. Glaring back at him, I gauged his response instead. Sully stepped between us.

"Well, here's the thing, Mr. Brightman," Sully began casually, focused. "Alex remembers seeing your truck on two separate occasions near the house prior to last night's incident. I know your family owned the home before Tina . . . before Alex's mother purchased it from the bank. I was wondering if you might have an idea as to who might want to scare Alex out of the house. Have you seen anything unusual?"

Rick looked from Sully back at me, taking in Sully's words. He nodded and turned to look Sully directly in the eyes.

"Oh, I get it. You think I had something to do with it," he said. "What, because I drove by the place a couple of times?"

"Now, no one's accusing you of anything," Sully said, clearing his throat. "Do you mind telling me, though, just why you were up that way?"

Rick took a labored breath, obviously upset by the direction of the questioning. He stared at me, his grey eyes piercing into me, pinning me to the pavement where I stood.

"I haven't been in Saluda for years. I wanted to see the old house. I have a lot of memories tied to that place. Some good, some bad. I was just trying to get a feel for the old neighborhood, you know?" he said, staring Sully down. "Last I checked, Chief, that wasn't a crime. I'm sorry if you thought I had anything to do with that break-in. I hope you find your man. I really do."

Rick began to stalk back towards the school. Desperate, I looked at Sully to see if he was going to stop him. Sully only shook his head at me and sighed. This couldn't be it. No, this wasn't over yet. In a fury, I stepped forward.

"Why didn't you mention that you were from Saluda on the plane?" I called after Rick who stopped and turned to me.

"Alex, no . . ." Sully grabbed my arm, but I shrugged him off.

"What do you mean?" Rick asked.

I took another step towards him. "On the plane, when you asked me about my roots in Saluda, why didn't you mention that you were from here? You made it seem like you had only ever been here on business."

Rick contemplated and then, growing impatient, walked up to me.

"Careful, Alexandra," Donovan whispered beside me. I stood firm knowing he was with me.

"What do you think I should have said?" Brightman spat. "'Hi, my name is Rick, and your mother took away the one thing that mattered most to my dying mom.' Would that have been better for you?"

Sully scoffed and motioned for me to get into the truck. "Let's go, Kiddo. This is doing no good."

Rick snickered, taking another step towards me. "Oh, he never told you? Why does that not surprise me?"

"What is he talking about?" I turned to Sully.

"Get in the truck, Alex," he answered.

I turned back to Rick, rage mingling with fear in my throat. "My mother bought the house at auction. Your family had already lost it."

A vile sneer twisted on Rick's lips. "You're right. We did lose it to the bank. When Mom came down with cancer, she couldn't work anymore. My dad had to take on three jobs just to keep food on the table and the power on. When the medical bills got out of hand, they put a lien on the house."

Rick stepped even closer. I could smell the sawdust on his clothes.

"We had to sell everything we owned, called every family member we had," he continued. "We could have bought the house back."

"There was no way you were going to get the house back," Sully argued, coming to us. "It belonged to the bank straight out."

Rick kept his eyes on me, unblinking, his voice rising with every word. "We could have bought the house back at auction if there hadn't been any other bids on the table. Your mom bought the house right out from under us. That house was everything to my mom. Her heart and soul went into that house. Her children were all born under that roof. She loved that house more than anything. She was devastated when we lost it. She died less than a month later."

Looking into Rick's eyes, I could see unadulterated pain and blazing hatred staring back at me in cold slate. I leaned into his face, my own anguish and anger screaming in protest within my soul.

"Alexandra, please . . ." Donovan pleaded, but I was too far gone.

"My mother loved that house more than anything too. She just wanted a place to raise me, a house where we could grow together as a family. She also loved her life. We were just starting over. I lost everything when she died. She was MY life, and she didn't deserve to die."

Rick took one final step towards me, his face contorting into a humorless, grotesque smile inches from mine. I could feel his hot breath on my cheek as he bent down close. Sweat beaded my brow, but I set my chin and met his glare. He chuckled and squinted his eyes.

"Well, then," he growled, "I guess we're even."

"Alexandra! Get out of the way!" Donovan screamed, and I stepped back just as Sully lunged for Rick.

"You son of a . . ." Sully screamed, taking a swing at Rick and connecting with his jaw.

The two men grappled on the ground exchanging blows until workers from the site came running towards the commotion from around the corner. They dragged the two apart as I watched in frozen astonishment. When they were on their feet, Sully yanked himself free from the men that held him at distance from Rick. Rick struggled against the two men that restrained him, his chin bloodied, and his flannel shirt ripped at the sleeve.

"I'll have you for assault!" Rick screamed as the men started to drag him away.

Sully wiped at his scraped lip and walked to the driver side door of the truck motioning for me to get in.

"Come by the station. I'll have my secretary draw up the papers for you!" he yelled back, then turned to me. "Let's get the hell out of here."

"Wait," I shouted, spotting something on Rick's exposed arm. "What is that?"

Rick wrenched free of the men and glared at me.

"On your arm?" I asked pointing. "Did you hurt your arm?"

Rick rubbed the large bandage covering the lower part of his forearm. "Not that it's any of your damned business, I got snagged by a 2x4 unloading the truck."

I stepped towards him, adrenaline propelling me forward. "Let me see it!"

"Alex, get in the truck," Sully instructed, but I kept my eyes on Rick.

"I don't have a damned thing to prove to you or your boyfriend there. I can see he's just as caught up in you as he was in your mom. Well, you win again, Chief. You've got the house and another Ms. Nolan. You win. I don't have to prove a damned thing to either of you." Rick snarled, turning his back and huffing away towards the site with the rest of the workers.

I stared after him, the pit of my stomach lurching. Looking at him made me want to vomit.

"Alexandra, it's time to go. It's alright," Donovan said. I felt his touch on my shoulder. "There's nothing more you can do. Let's go."

Taking a shaky breath, I willed myself to back away. I climbed into the truck but kept my eyes on Rick until he disappeared around the corner of the building. Sully started the engine and hurled us back onto the road before looking at me.

"You're trembling," he said, patting my knee.

"It's him. You heard that. It has to be him. Did you hear what he said to me?"

"Oh, I heard it, the bastard. He's got one hell of a nerve."

"He had a bandage on his forearm."

"Yeah? So what? The guy's in construction. I'm sure it happens all the time," Sully said, watching the road as he maneuvered the truck onto the descent back.

"Last night when the intruder grabbed me, I scratched him. It must have been pretty bad too because I heard him scream when he let go of me. It would have been in the same place on his arm."

Sully looked at me considering, then turned his attention back to the road. "I don't know, Kiddo. As much as I dislike the guy, there's still no proof that it was him last night OR fifteen years ago. He would have been just a kid, barely out of high school at the time."

I thought about that for a minute. "Mom bought the house when I was seven, and Rick said his mom died shortly after that. He had a few years to brood it over. If he really blamed Mom for taking the house . . ."

"Even so, we don't have anything else but a hunch and some harsh words to go on," Sully said, sighing.

"Aaaahh!" I yelled, bringing my fists down onto my lap. "If I could only remember something that would. . . Wait a minute."

"What is it?" Sully looked alarmed.

"On the way up, when we passed that side road, I think I remembered something. I'm not sure if it will help."

"What exactly did you remember?" Sully asked, looking back to the road as he took a tight turn. I braced myself against my arm rest.

"I only remember the headlights really. I remembered that they were up higher than where I sat in our car. It couldn't have been as small of a car. More like an SUV or a truck."

"Were they as high as in this truck?"

"No," I contemplated. "Not as high as this, but higher than a car. Maybe a smaller SUV or a Jeep even. Something like that. I also remember seeing a flash of red between the lights. I think the vehicle was red. Does any of this help at all?" I asked, looking Sully in the face.

He thought about the new information, nodding as chewed on it.

"It might. I mean, it's something," he said. "I can cross reference some things when I get back to the station and see what turns up."

I sighed, sitting back in my seat. It was a start. I thought about the encounter with Rick and all of the things he had said. "Was what Rick said true? Did Mom buy the house out from under them? Did she know?"

For a minute there was silence. I glanced at Sully, who looked to be deep in thought, and waited.

"Your mother knew that they had lost the house and that it had gone to auction. That was all she needed to know," he finally answered.

"So you knew?" I asked. "You knew they were trying to get the house back?"

"I knew they were trying. The bank didn't think they had much of a chance." Sully looked at me. "Your mother deserved that house every bit as much as they did. I wanted her to be happy, and she was. You both were. Sometimes one person's loss is another person's gain. That's life, Kiddo."

"What about the other thing he said?"

"What other thing?"

"What he said about you and Mom. He thought you two were involved. He called you my boyfriend," I said.

"He doesn't know anything about anything. He was a kid back then. He was just trying to get a rise out of us," Sully huffed. "I want you to stay far away from him. Even if he's not our man, I don't want you near him, okay?"

Conceding to nothing, I turned to the window and noticed where we were. We turned the next corner and the crash site came into view. I'd never forgotten the way the tops of those trees looked, just peeking over the slope on that side. As we got closer I noticed something white lying on the side of the road at the spot where our car went over.

"Stop! Stop right here," I shouted. Startled, Sully hit the brakes.

"What's the matter?" he asked, pulling over to the side of the road. I jumped out.

"Maybe I can remember something else. This is where it happened," I yelled back as Sully got out of the car to stand with me.

I walked to the spot where I remembered our car had left the road. Lying on the ground was a bouquet of fresh white lilies. Bending down to pick them up, I inspected them for a card. They were the same kind of flowers that were left on my mother's grave.

"I wonder who left these here," I said as Sully came up beside me. I looked at him while he gazed into the deep expanse over the side.

"This is where the car went off," I explained while he stared blankly ahead. "The vehicle came up from the other side of the road and rammed us straight-on. We flew right over the side."

I walked to the edge of the embankment and braced myself before looking over the edge. The brush was overgrown, but I could make out the base of the huge pine tree that had broken our fall. It was so far down. Much farther than in my dreams. I blinked back the tears that threatened to escape my eyes.

"Do you remember anything about that night?" Sully asked. "Anything else at all?"

I took in a shaky breath. "Besides the gloves, brown leather . . . and the knife? I can still see the snake handle when I close my eyes, how it coiled around his hand. I will never forget that," I shuddered. "But that's all I remember."

"I think about that night all the time," Sully said, still looking out into the expanse. "I wonder what I was doing. What was I thinking at that moment? If I hadn't have left for Iraq, things would have been so different. They might still be alive."

"No, Uncle Sully. You can't think like that," I said. "You were protecting our country. You were already our hero. There's nothing you could have done. It was just their time. I'm starting to accept that, I think."

"If only I had stayed. How different things might have been," he whispered.

"Everything happens for a purpose. I think it's our purpose now to bring whoever did this to justice. He can't get away with it. He can't," I said.

"It's been so long," Sully said, lowering his head.

"I know what I have to do," I said as an idea hit me. "I've got to get down there, see if I can remember something else. Maybe if I get to the actual spot where it happened, I can remember something else about him. It's not that bad of a climb down. . ."

"No. That's not a good idea," Sully interrupted. "We're not prepared for that sort of climb."

"Oh, come on. It will only take thirty or so minutes. I think I can remember . . ." I gauged the first step down, contemplating how I could maneuver the steep decline when I heard the strumming right beside me.

"You have to leave now, Alexandra," Donovan ordered in my ear. "We can't stay here any longer. You're in danger here. We have to leave. Right now."

"I told you. It isn't a good idea. Get back from there and get into the truck," Sully insisted, and I could see the urgency in his eyes.

My heart sped in my chest. I looked around at the dense woods that surrounded us and the fall below. I could feel it. The air had grown thick, and tension seeping up from the drop below hovered around us like a fog.

"We have to go now," Donovan repeated. I could hear the desperation in his voice despite his trying to retain a calm tone.

Setting the flowers back down on the side of the road, I took one final glance over the edge before jogging back to the truck and jumping in. Sully's face was hard to read, a mixture of sorrow and fear. He pulled the truck back onto the road and made a swift three-point turn to get us going back towards town. I scanned the wilderness outside my window for signs of danger. No one was out there, no other cars on the road. Perhaps Rick had followed us . . .

"It's okay now. I don't feel it anymore," Donovan whispered from behind me. "You're safe."

I tried to steady my shaking hands. I had to know what was going on.

"So, what was that all about?" I asked out loud, directing my question towards the back seat.

"It just wasn't a good idea. I'm not fond of heights either." Sully shrugged. "Plus, if anything happened, no one would even know we were down there."

I looked behind me to where I knew Donovan sat, pleading for him to answer. I wished more than anything that I could see him.

"I'm not sure," he said. "It came out of nowhere. A strong sense that you were in grave danger, but from what or whom, I don't know. It was everywhere all at once and then just as quickly vanished into nothing. I'm sorry. It makes no sense. You're safe now, but I'm not sure what that was."

Reclining in my seat, I took a steadying breath and looked back to Sully. "If I'm going to remember anything, I have to get down there."

"I just don't think it's a good idea. It's too dangerous down there. We'll find another way to tie Brightman to the scene. We have an idea of the size and color of the vehicle that hit you. That could give us a lead."

"You think you can place him in the vehicle that night?" I asked, hopeful.

"It's a long shot, but maybe. I'll run some searches when I get back to the station this afternoon."

"Where is it you're in such a hurry to get off to anyway?" I asked, changing the topic.

I was going to make my way to the crash site with or without Sully's help. That much I was certain of. I just needed to know how much time I had in which to do it without his knowledge.

"Well, Kiddo," he sighed. "I'm taking Gram to a home in Hendersonville today. It's time. I just can't give her the care she needs anymore. She needs to be in a constant care facility."

It was as if he had slapped me in the face. I wasn't expecting the blow.

"What? But I thought she was okay at home with . . ." I stopped short. "Is it because of what happened yesterday? This is my fault, isn't it?"

"No, no, this isn't your fault. It's just time. I've avoided it for long enough," Sully tried to comfort. "We have to think about what's best for Gram."

I blinked back my tears. "Do you want me to go with you?"

"I think it would be best to take her alone. She won't react well to sad faces." He squeezed my hand. "She'll be confused enough as it is."

I feigned a smile for Sully's benefit, knowing this was hardest on him. He'd taken care of Gram ever since she had first been diagnosed with Huntington's disease. He had barely graduated from high school. He'd been with her ever since, save for the year he was deployed to Iraq when Gary came to live in the cabin in his stead. That's when Mom met Gary, while he was taking care of Gram. I felt guilty all over again for having made Gram upset, for not being here for her for so long. Now it was too late.

"I'm so sorry, Uncle Sully. Is there any way I can help?"

Sully smiled at me and pulled the truck onto the main street. "This was NOT your fault. I don't want you blaming yourself. I've known this day was coming for a long time. It's better this way."

I looked away, not wanting him to see the tears that fell onto my face. I wiped them with the back of my sleeve. Sully was trying to make me feel better, but I still felt responsible. Would Gram have been better off if I hadn't come back? Would everyone have been better off?

"Can I visit her soon? I won't upset her. I promise. I'll go along with whatever she says."

Sully pulled up behind Will's squad car in front of the station and cut the engine. He turned in his seat to face me and gave my hand a final squeeze.

"She would like that a lot. As soon as she gets settled in, okay?" Sully said with a sad smile. "Now, you let me worry about Gram for the time being. You need to focus on you right now. We're going to get to the bottom of this."

I followed him into the station and immediately searched for Will. The station appeared empty. The only indication of Will's being there was a small stack of folders lying upside down on his desk.

"Will must be in the back. Listen," Sully said as he poured himself a cup of thick, black coffee from the readied pot. "As unhappy as I know this will make you, I want you to stay here at the station till I get back. I mean it, don't go anywhere with anyone. Can you do that for me?"

I crossed my arms. "It's the middle of the day. I really don't need to be in quarantine. I'm not a kid anymore, Uncle Sully."

He took a long sip of strong brew and winced. "I know. I know you're not a kid anymore. So do this for me as the police chief asking his witness, okay?"

I looked into his big, puppy-like eyes and nodded, not promising anything. "Just take care of my Gram, okay? Don't even worry about me. I'll be right here when you get back."

Sully patted my cheek and took another sip of his coffee. "Just let me grab those keys from Will. Make yourself at home. Evelyn's probably out to lunch. She should be here within the hour. She'll keep you plenty of company, I'm sure."

I waited for Sully to disappear into his office and then quickly made my way to Will's desk. If he was really interested in helping me find my mom's murderer, then the files on his desk might be about the case. Keeping an eye on the office door, I examined the stack of small folders. Flipping them over in my hands, I read the tab on the top one. It was labeled with the date of the accident. *Jackpot.* I flipped through the contents, noting reports from various officers who described the scene from that night, taking care not to read the details. Being there had been enough.

The back of the folder held pictures. My breath caught in my throat when I came face to face with a picture of the accident scene, captured in fading color. I dropped the rest of the folders with a gasp, but my eyes remained locked on the photo.

The car lay upside down against the great pine, broken chunks of metal and debris scattered among the brush. The photo was taken after I was rescued from the car, after the left rear door had been removed. I brought the photograph closer, squinting, and could make out a hand dangling from the driver's seat.

Clasping my hand to my mouth, I choked on the bile and sobs that rose up from my gut. Then I looked with curious dread to the right side of the vehicle, to where my mother would be lying. The photograph was blurry there. Squinting did nothing to help bring the image into focus this time.

Wiping at the moisture standing in my eyes, I looked again. That part of the picture was smudged. I ran my finger across the glossy surface of the photograph and felt where that edge of the picture had been rubbed raw, maybe with an eraser. Someone had wiped out my mother's image.

Commotion from the office sent me scrambling to put the picture back in the folder and reaching down to gather the rest. Flipping them over, I set them back on the desk and began to walk away when I noticed a paper I missed lying on the floor. Snatching it up, I glanced at the fine black print. It was another statement, made by someone who had been at the accident site.

When the office door opened and I heard Sully's deep voice as he paused to finish his sentence, I opened the top folder in order to cram the paper back in. The name on the statement made me pause. William Galia's name was there in black and white. Will had been there that night.

Shutting the folder, I walked away from the desk just as Will followed Sully out of the office.

"The handwriting analysis should be here by the end of the day," Will said as they walked into the room. "Jones sent in the photos of the mirror as well as a snapshot of Brightman's signature from one of the permits. It's not much, but maybe we can get a match."

Will nodded to me. I grinned back and had a seat at the table near the coffee pot. My mind was reeling. Will had been at the accident scene. He'd made an official statement about what he saw. Why would he not have told me?

"Good." Sully walked to the coffee pot and refilled his cup. "Call them back and tell them to call me directly on my cell. I don't want to miss them if I'm not back in time. If the analysis points to Brightman, I'm hauling that bastard in tonight."

"Will do," Will said, going to his desk.

I watched from the corner of my eye as he swept the stack of folders into his top drawer, keeping an eye on Sully's back as he did. Sully handed me a key, and I focused back on him.

"Here you go. Make sure you hang onto this at all times. Put it in your pocket, and don't let anyone else touch it. I've got the only other one for emergencies, so we don't have to worry about someone letting themselves in," he said, taking a swig from his cup before setting it down.

Stuffing the key into the front pocket of my jeans, I wished I'd brought my purse with my key ring or even my jacket, which had much deeper pockets. I was in such a rush I'd forgotten both.

"Okay, I have to get going. I should be gone for a few hours," Sully said to me. "Just stay here, okay? If you get hungry, have Evelyn call down to the diner to send something over. Tell them to put it on my tab."

"I said not to worry about me," I said. "Just take care of Gram, please."

"That's the plan," he said with a sigh and then turned to Will. "Remember, pull up anything you can on Brightman. I want to know everything there is to know about that man. We'll go over what we've got when I get back."

"I'm on it. Don't worry about a thing," Will assured.

Sully gave one final glance from me to Will, contemplating, before he finally turned and left the station.

Once he was gone, Will came had a seat on top of his desk and folded his hands.

"How are you holding up?" he asked. "Chief told me what happened with Brightman. What are you thinking?"

"It's him. It has to be," I said, looking Will in the eyes. "You should have seen his face when he talked about my mom. Nothing but sheer hatred."

"Sounds like he has some serious issues over how your mom got the house. I guess it would make sense that he would want to try and scare you out of it."

I rubbed my face and leaned back in my chair. "I don't know. It just seems so . . . so crazy. To kill someone over a house? It just doesn't make sense to me. How could someone DO that?"

Will nodded in agreement, coming to the coffee pot for a clean cup. "It sounds like his beef had more to do with the loss of his mother, not so much the house," he said, pouring himself a cup of coffee. He sniffed it and winced, but took a sip anyway. "Do you think he still wants the house back?"

I took the pot from him and sniffed its contents. Disgusted, I put the pot back and watched in shock as Will took another sip and winked at me.

"Well," I continued, shaking my head, "it makes sense with what was written in the mirror, I guess. Maybe he found out I was coming to take possession of the house. I just wish I could remember something else."

"Something else?" Will asked, his eyebrow raised.

"Didn't Sully tell you? I remembered a little about the vehicle that hit us that night. I remembered that it was taller than a car, like a jeep or small SUV. And I remembered that it was red."

"No, he didn't say anything."

"Yeah, well, that's probably because it does no good whatsoever," I pouted.

"I don't know. It could be useful. It would be pretty easy to see what kind of car was under Brightman's name at the time. Cross reference his vehicle's description with accident reports or mechanic shop submissions on or around that day. Hitting you guys with that kind of force must have done some pretty significant damage to the perp's car as well, right?"

I found new hope in his words. "You think it's possible to track down the vehicle then? Is there anything helpful in those files you have?"

Will looked up, mid sip, from his cup. "What files?"

I pointed to his desk. "The ones you hid in your top drawer as soon as Sully had his back turned. What are you doing with those anyway? And when were you going to tell me that you were there that night? That you gave a statement?"

Will let out a long breath and set his cup on the table. "I've been looking over the files from the accident, trying to find something that can tie Brightman to the scene. I haven't found anything."

"You were there, Will," I said. "Why didn't you tell me?"

He walked to his desk and retrieved the files from the drawer. "I was there that night, yes. I was walking home from a friend's house and saw your car crashed over the side of the road just as the paramedics and police were pulling up. They took me in for questioning, but I didn't see anything. There was nothing to tell. See for yourself."

He tossed me the statements folder. I caught it and pulled his statement from the pile, reading it over as he watched.

"Why didn't you tell me? It says here you helped get me out of the car. I don't remember any of that."

"Well, you wouldn't. You were pretty banged up and unconscious at the time."

"Answer my question, Will!" I demanded.

"I didn't say anything because I can hardly remember a thing myself. I was walking home from my friend's house because I was wasted. He took my keys so I got pissed and started walking, okay? Not one of my prouder moments."

"Did you see a SUV? A red one? Did you see anything?"

Will sighed and shook his head. "By the time I got close enough to realize what was going on, the paramedics and police were already swarming the place. The guy was long gone by then. It's all a blur anyhow."

"Did you see her?" I whispered.

Will shuffled his feet.

"Did you see her?" I repeated.

Will shook his head. "No. She was covered with a sheet when I got down there. All I saw was . . ."

"Was what?"

"I saw you. I saw what that monster did to you." Will walked closer, bending down to look me in the eye. "And for the first time I stopped thinking about only myself. I wanted to help you. I wanted to DO something, but there was nothing else I could do but help them get you out of that car. It's why I decided to be a cop, Alex. I wanted to keep things like that night from happening to anyone else."

"Why were you hiding the files from Sully?" I asked. "Does he know you were there?"

"I don't think he knows. I doubt he ever cared to read the accounts of that night. It's a tough read. I don't blame him," Will explained. "I was hiding them from him because I know he wouldn't like me meddling. He doesn't want to admit that the person who broke into your house the other night could be the same person who murdered your mom and his brother."

"It is," I insisted.

"I agree with you. That's why I looked up the files. Sometimes a fresh pair of eyes can catch things that may have been overlooked. I found your account really interesting." Will turned, having a seat behind his desk and grabbing another folder. "I didn't realize you got a good look at the murder weapon."

I closed my eyes and shuddered. "The snake handle . . . sort of hard to forget. I just wish I could remember more. If I could just get down there, to the place where it all happened, maybe I can remember something else."

Will held up his hands. "That's a great idea. Why don't we?"

"I wanted to earlier with Sully, but he didn't like the idea. Said it was too dangerous. He's probably right. It's pretty steep and a lot further down than I remembered," I said, then considered my next words before I spoke them. "And something felt . . . off about the place."

Will stood again. "It can't be easy to go back to that place. Feeling uneasy is natural, but I think you need to get down there. It's the only way you're going to remember anything that can help us find the killer, especially if you remembered something already today."

I became aware of the strumming that surrounded me, a warmth on my shoulder.

"I don't like it, Alexandra. It's too dangerous." Donovan said against my ear. "There has to be another way. I don't trust him, I knew he was hiding something."

"I know a guy in my neighborhood," Will continued. "He's leant me some rappelling equipment in the past. I can go get it, and then we can get down there and see."

I shook my head. "Sully will blow a gasket if I do. He doesn't want me to leave here at all. He's got enough to deal with today without me worrying him more."

Will glanced at the clock. "He said he was going into Hendersonville. That's a good twenty or thirty minutes away. It will take me about that long to grab the gear and get back here. We could be there and back before he even leaves Hendersonville."

"I don't know . . ." I said.

Desperate to get back to the site to see if I could remember anything else, I considered my options. I was afraid that the danger Donovan had felt, that I'd felt, would still be out there. I'd promised to trust Donovan, and to do what he said. But this killer could not go free, and I was the only one who could stop him.

"What about Evelyn? She'll tell him we left."

Will chuckled, and taking the files with him, grabbed his coat from the rack at the front door. He turned back to me with a smile.

"Let me take care of Evelyn. You just be ready to go as soon as I get back."

"I don't know about this," I said. Before he left, Will looked me right in the eye and winked.

"Trust me," he said, and then left the station.

Eleven

Five minutes later, Evelyn breezed into the station in a blaze of neon pink polyester and heavy perfume. She smiled when she spotted me attempting to brew a fresh pot of coffee.

"Well, hey there, darling. I wasn't expecting to see your beautiful face this afternoon," she said and hung her shiny coat on a hook.

Her hot pink sweater dress matched her six-inch heels. Trying not to stare, I wondered how she could be comfortable wearing Stilettos all day. I'd never attempted to wear shoes of that height myself, but I was certain that if I ever tried, I would last about a minute before nosediving into the pavement.

"I've been quarantined here until Uncle Sully gets back from Hendersonville. It was an exciting night."

"Quarantined, my goodness. Is everything alright?" she asked, positioning herself behind her desk.

"Someone broke into the house last night and attacked me," I explained, "so now I'm on station arrest."

"My word!" Evelyn gasped, putting a manicured hand to her chest. "Are you alright, hun? That is just awful. Who would do such a thing? In Saluda?"

I shrugged. "That's what we're trying to figure out."

"Well, the chief will get to the bottom of it. If anyone can figure it out, it's Sullivan. Once that man has it in his mind to do something, he'll see it through. Don't you worry your pretty little head about it."

I remembered the way Sully laid out Rick an hour earlier.

"He's on it, alright," I said, then poured out a cup of coffee. "Would you care for a cup?"

"Oh, no, thank you. I don't trust a thing that comes out of that pot." She giggled.

I sniffed my cup. It smelled more like coffee and less like burnt rubber this time, so I decided to chance it and took a tentative sip. The hot liquid scorched my tongue, and the bitterness made me gag, so I set the cup down.

"I can see why," I coughed. Evelyn laughed as the phone on her desk rang.

"Saluda Police Department," she answered in a cheerful voice. "Oh, hey, Gertie! How are you this afternoon, sugar?"

I marveled at the perfect Hollywood Southern belle that was Evelyn and wondered if I would have picked up that overly-charming accent if I'd gotten a chance to grow up here. Would I have picked up a liking for sweater dresses and big hair too?

"You're kidding. Really? My birthday isn't until next week. They didn't say who it was from? Well, butter my butt and call me a biscuit. Isn't that the sweetest thing," Evelyn said, then covered the receiver with her hand in order to whisper to me. "Someone booked me a hair appointment for today. Isn't that just darling?"

I nodded in simulated enthusiasm. Then I remembered what Will had said and chuckled to myself. *Let me take care of Evelyn.* Brilliant.

"You should totally go now. I'm stuck here anyways. I can answer the phones," I offered. "Will should be back any minute anyway. Go enjoy yourself. You deserve it."

"Well aren't you the sweetest," she said, and then took her hand away from the receiver. "Well, Getrie, I haven't had my roots touched up in a coon's age. I guess I'll be right over."

Evelyn hung up the phone and turned back to me. "Are you sure you don't mind? I really shouldn't . . ."

Smiling, I waved her off. "Of course not. Get on out of here."

Evelyn stood and bounced happily in her heels. "Why, this is so unexpected. You know, I bet Jack Lovell up at the tavern is responsible for this."

She giggled as I helped her into her jacket. I held back my laughter. "He's had his eye on me ever since the divorce, bless his heart."

"I'd say he's probably in good company."

"Thanks hun, but if it weren't for miracle workers like Gertie, I could scare dogs off a meat wagon," she said, grabbing her purse from her desk. "I'll only be a couple of hours. If anyone calls with an emergency, just forward the number on to the chief."

"Will do," I said, as she grabbed her coat and tinkered out of the station.

Relieved at the ease at which Evelyn was disposed of, I wandered back over to the coffee pot and picked up my cup, desperate for caffeine. I regretted skipping breakfast too. My stomach was starting to growl. Taking another sip, I grimaced. The brew tasted very little like coffee and more of what I thought an old gym sock might taste like.

Grabbing three dusty sugar packets from a little basket on the table, I dumped them in and stirred the white crystals around with a tiny straw. Holding my nose, I tasted it again. The sweetness overpowered the dank bitterness and made it a little easier to tolerate.

The phone on Evelyn's desk rang and made me jump, spilling a small amount of coffee on the floor. I stared at the spill, half expecting it to dissolve the tile in a wisp of chemical smoke. When the phone rang again, I went to the desk and considered a moment before picking it up. What if it was Sully?

"Saluda Police Department," I answered in my best Southern drawl, trying to mimic Evelyn as best I could.

The voice on the line laughed. "You've been watching too much Andy Griffith."

I recognized Will's voice and sighed with relief. "It was my first attempt at Southern charm. Give me a break."

"I'm guessing by your performance that Evelyn fell for it?" he asked.

"Faster than a hot knife through butter," I tried again.

"That was better," he said. "I'll be there in five minutes."

"I'm still not sure about this . . ." I started to argue.

Will cut me off. "Be ready to jump in the car, Aunt Bee."

When the line went dead, I retrieved my coffee. Sitting back down, I heard the strumming behind me.

"This isn't a game Alexandra," Donovan said.

I spotted movement from the top of the desk and noticed a small vanity mirror sitting to the side of a stack of papers. Through it I could see Donovan leaning against the door, his face stern.

"Do you really think you have to tell me that this isn't a game? I know it's not a game. In fact, I am scared out of my mind to go back there," I confessed. "I have to do this, Donovan. I'm the only one who can stop this guy."

Donovan sighed. "I don't like it."

"What did you sense back there? Was it him?" I asked.

"Yes, I believe so. Only it was different. I couldn't tell where he was coming from. The danger was everywhere all at once. It came out of nowhere," he said. "There was something else too. A . . . sadness I haven't felt before."

"Sadness? I don't understand," I said, looking in his eyes through the mirror.

"As much hatred and anger that was closing in, I felt an overwhelming anguish and desperation. I don't like the idea of you going back there. It isn't safe, Alexandra."

"Nowhere is safe. You said so yourself," I argued. "You can't stop evil from coming for me."

"That doesn't mean you should go looking for it."

I thought for a moment, terrified by Donovan's description of what might be waiting for me at the bottom of that ledge. Nothing however, could squelch the desperation for justice that swelled up from my soul. The need for it consumed me. The cost of putting this monster away didn't matter anymore.

"I have to go down there. It's the only way I'll ever remember more about that night. I could remember something that will put my mother's murderer away for after all these years. I have to try," I pleaded.

In the reflection I could see Donovan shake his head. His jaw twitched as he glared at me with those sapphire eyes. "You know I can only do so much to protect you. I'm here to keep you away from danger, not march you right into the face of it."

"Is this about me going down to the site, or the fact that I'm going down there with Will?"

I studied his reaction in the tiny mirror. He looked away for a minute, his eyes fierce. When he looked back at me, I saw the sorrow he tried to hide.

"You can't trust him, Alexandra," he whispered. "I fear that you're not safe around him. You need to keep your distance. Please, Alexandra."

"What do you know that you're not telling me?" I demanded.

When Donovan looked away again, I knew I was right. There was something about Will he wasn't telling me. But why?

"There is no way to know anything for sure," he said. "Can't you just trust me on this?"

"What about me? Can't you trust me? Why can't you tell me what you think you know? Is it so important that you'd stop me from trying to remember more? We could end this today! Fifteen years of my life I've waited, and it could all end right now. Can't you see how important this is to me? I can do this." I wiped a tear from my eye before it could escape, but I knew he saw.

Donovan's voice lowered, and he looked back up to me, compassion replacing his stern tone. "Alexandra . . . he's dangerous."

From the window I saw the squad car pull up in front of the building and heard a single honk. I turned from the mirror to where I knew Donovan stood. I focused on the spot where he should be and willed my mind to conjure up his image, but it was no use. I saw nothing but the peeling green paint of the door frame. I angled my chin to where I guessed his face would be.

"Look, I know that you have a job to do, and I know that I'm making it difficult. If you can't help me, I understand. But I have a job to do too. I have to stop this bastard. I'm the only one who can. I have to do it for them, and I have to do it for me." I was surprised by how shaky my voice sounded. "I'm sorry."

Stifling a sob, I locked the door from the inside before going out. I almost turned back when I heard Donovan's hushed voice behind me.

"You've never been a job," he whispered, but I was too upset to let his words phase me.

I tried to look normal as I hopped into the squad car beside Will. Giving him my best smile, I fought to not let my nerves show.

"Are you ready for some repelling?" Will grinned next to me.

I rolled my eyes at him. "You are enjoying this entirely too much."

"Beats sitting in the office all day," he teased, handing me a white paper bag. He motioned to a large coffee cup in the cup holder. "I grabbed you a muffin and a coffee. It's not as good as the amazing breakfast you passed on this morning, but I figured you could use it."

Taking the bag gratefully, I pulled out the huge blueberry muffin and took an excited bite.

"Thank you. I was dying," I admitted, wiping my mouth with the back of my hand. "And sorry for bailing on breakfast, but I had to get out there and see that bastard face to face."

Will nodded and pulled the cruiser onto the road. "How do you feel about him now that you've had a chance to think about this morning? Since you've seen his face, gauged him a bit? Still feel like he's the one?"

I swallowed a sip of coffee. "It has to be him. He's the only one with any kind of reason for wanting to hurt us . . . for wanting me out of the house."

Will gripped the steering wheel tighter. "You're not entirely convinced, are you?"

I sighed and shook my head. He was right. There was something off about it all. "It's like I said before. Why would anyone kill people over a house? I know it meant a lot to his Mom, and he blames the loss of the house for his mother's death, but it's still just a damned house. Then again, looking into his eyes when he talked about my mom, seeing the disgust and hatred there . . . it scared me."

"I don't know," Will said, taking the curves of the road faster than Sully had, forcing me to grip the side of my seat to remain steady. "Some people are just messed up in the head, and there isn't a rhyme or reason for it. It doesn't have to make sense to you, just to them. People who do this kind of thing aren't rational. Remember that."

Contemplating his words, I turned to my window. A grey pall still hung over the trees, and the threat of rain darkened the skies. The sound of Will's cell phone turned me back to him. He fetched it from his pocket.

"Galia," he answered. "Mmhmm, yes, that is very interesting. That could be our vehicle. Stay with it, and call me if you get anything. Thanks, man, I owe you one."

I stared at Will as he hung up the phone and put it back into his pocket with his free hand.

"Was that about the information I gave you earlier? About the red SUV?" I asked excited.

"It was."

I set down the muffin and glared at him. Waiting for him to go on.

"I called an old friend who's still on the force up in New York. He has a talent for tracking down information. He says a red Bronco was surrendered to a scrap yard in Waynesville the morning after the accident. The shop records indicate there was major damage to the driver's side of the car . . . the exact kind of damage that, based on what you've said, the vehicle from that night would have sustained. It's a long shot, but it could be something," Will explained, keeping his eyes on the road.

"How can we know if it's the same vehicle that hit us?"

Will braked as we came up to the last curve before the crash site. "There's not much to go on. No record of who surrendered the vehicle. My buddy is doing some digging on the Bronco's VIN number. If we're lucky, it will tie to Brightman."

"Pray we luck out then," I said, turning again to the window just as we passed by the small side street.

Will slowed the cruiser and, taking a look in his mirrors, made a three-point turn in the middle of the road and parked beside the lilies which still adorned the embankment. He got out, and I followed as he retrieved a long rope, a harness and some metal carabineers from the trunk. Then he leaned into the back and brought out the gun holster, which he flung over his shoulders.

"Why are you bringing that?" I asked, startled by the sight of the gun perched in its holster at Will's side. "Are we going into battle?"

Will gathered up the rope and harness into a small pile and motioned for me to grab the rest.

"I figure it can't hurt," he said, then took in my worried face. "Look, someone is after you. I hate this thing more than anyone. You know that. But I would rather have it and not need it than need it and not have it."

I considered the possibilities and shuddered, remembering the danger that had been so thick in the air just an hour ago. As much as I hated the thought of Will having to use his gun, I hated the thought of being caught helpless without it even more.

"I guess you're right. Just . . . be careful with that thing," I said, grabbing the rest of the gear and shutting the trunk.

I followed Will to the base of a large tree where he handed me the end of the rope.

"Here, hang onto this," he said, taking the rest of the rope and carefully wrapping it around the tree trunk. He slipped here and there on the moist leaves and pine needles that blanketed the forest ground. When he came back with the other end of the rope, the knees of his uniform were speckled with damp soil and moss.

Will devised a complex knot so quickly that I couldn't keep up with each end of the rope as it entwined through his fingers. He pulled the now free end tight, and the slack hugged the base of the tree. Will picked up the harness and motioned for me to put it on.

"Ladies first," he grinned.

"Oh, no," I protested. "You're going down there first. I'll follow."

Will sighed and wiped his brow with the back of his hand. "I would rather be the one to go first, believe me, but I'm afraid it's not an option unless you know how to put this harness on and attach it to the main line."

I thought for a moment, fighting to find a way around the fact that I had never rappelled before and therefore had no clue how to strap that dog leash looking thing onto my rear end. Grunting, I surrendered with a shrug. Will smirked as he strapped the harness around my right thigh.

"I'll be right behind you, okay?" he reassured.

I contained the urge to argue and raised my arms so he could adjust the straps at my waist. Once he had me strapped into the harness, he led me to the edge and steadied me with his hand while he secured me to the rope using carabiners. I chanced a look behind me at the drop and suppressed the urge to vomit.

"I suddenly remembered that I'm deathly afraid of heights. Of the height from here in particular," I panted.

Will finished strapping me in and placing both hands on my shoulders, looked me in the eyes. "That's completely understandable, considering . . . You're going to be fine. You can do this."

"Just tell me what to do," I said, taking a shaky breath.

Will handed me the line and showed me how to hold it and let out slack. "Just keep two hands on the line and squeeze. I'll be right here to pull you up if anything goes wrong."

Suppressing the growing panic, I nodded. "Okay."

Will helped me over the edge. I told myself not to look down, but just as quickly as I thought it, I forgot, and peeked behind me. My heart jumped into my throat at the sight of the expanse below and the base of the great pine that had broken our fall fifteen years ago. It looked to be miles down.

"Good, now just ease up on the rope and start walking down with your legs," Will instructed.

I took two steps and eased my grip on the rope. When the line jolted me backwards, I squeezed as hard as I could and hugged the line to me. Gasping, I shut my eyes and waited for the world to stop spinning. Panic consumed me.

"Alex, you've got to get a better grip on the line. Ease off slowly, and then walk it down," Will yelled. "I know you're scared, but we don't have a lot of time."

Fear filled my ears with the sound of my own heartbeat, and I lost Will's words to the thundering in my chest. I willed myself to move. I just had to get to the bottom.

When the strumming surrounded me, I gasped. Tears of relief came to my eyes. Donovan was there.

"You were right. I shouldn't have come," I whispered. "I don't have the strength."

"Yes, you do," Donovan said against my ear. "We'll do this together. I won't let you fall."

I felt his warmth on my hands, which were clenching the rope so tightly that the grooves were beginning to burn into my flesh.

"It's okay," Donovan whispered. "I've got you."

Easing my fingers, I let the rope slide through my palm ever so gently. Slowly, we lowered into the brush. I used my legs to maneuver around shrubbery and bushes, all the while concentrating on the warmth on my hands, knowing that Donovan was in control of the rope. I knew he wouldn't let me fall.

A few feet farther, the brush began to thin. The base of the great pine was just below. I took slow, steady steps towards the tree, getting snagged here and there on a prickly branch or protruding twig, but continuing on. I couldn't help but to notice the strange quiet that pervaded the woods around us as we descended. It was as if even the birds and crickets avoided this place. The thought sent a cold shiver down my back.

"Do you feel that?" I asked Donovan, wondering if he was picking up on the same foreboding energy.

"I do, and I don't like it."

"I should have never come," I said. "You were right. I'm sorry."

"No, you were right about coming down here. You need to do this," Donovan said. "What you were wrong about is thinking that I would not be with you."

"I don't deserve you," I whispered. "I'm making your job so hard. I know that."

Taking one final glance behind me, relief washed over me at the sight of the ground. The embankment flattened out, and I was able to stand, once again, on level ground.

"I could leave you if I wanted to," Donovan said, his warmth leaving my hands as I stood. "We've all been given free will to choose. You have never been a job to me, Alexandra. You've always been my choice. You're all that matters. Now, let's do what we came here to do. I'm right here with you."

Overwhelmed with gratitude that Donovan was with me, I wiped my tears and used his strength to continue my mission. Wiggling out of the harness, I yelled up to Will to pull the harness back in.

Walking over to the base of the pine, I placed my hand on its trunk, remembering. Everything else around me vanished except for the tree and the strumming keeping watch over me. I closed my eyes, trying to make sense of the storm of emotions welling within me at the sight of the tree that had saved my life, but in the same instant had claimed my mother's.

Taking a deep breath, I opened my eyes and looked out over the sloped landscape. If the tree had not stopped our fall that night, our car would have rolled and fallen hundreds of feet farther.

"This tree stopped our fall," I began, my voice coming out as a hoarse whisper.

"Yes," Donovan said.

"It also killed my mom. When we crashed into it, it killed her." I forced out the words through clenched teeth.

I felt Donovan's hand on my shoulder and I closed my eyes again, seeing the twisted metal and bloodied hair. "No, Alexandra. Evil killed your mother. It's that evil that I have to keep you from now."

Crashing in the bushes beside us jarred me from my memories. Will emerged from the brush and unclipped himself from the main line.

"That wasn't as steep as I thought it would be. We could have gone it on foot after all, I think. It gets steeper farther down though," he said, taking in my solemn expression. "Did you remember something already?"

"No," I said. "Not yet."

Will studied me a second more and then took a look around. "Be careful where you step. There's a good drop on the left here. It looks fairly flat along this ridge though."

I stepped away from the tree to where I guessed the car had come to a rest all those years ago. Will followed me with his eyes.

"What is it?"

"I remember his footsteps," I said, focusing.

"Footsteps?"

"When the killer finally gave up trying to get to me, when the police were coming, he ran that way." I pointed back the way we had come down, but did not look. I kept the image in my head. "I could hear him running away."

"That makes sense," Will agreed. "He would have left his vehicle up the road where it's not as steep, where he could hide it in the trees. Do you remember anything else?"

Will's eyes burned into me, but I was too lost in memory to look at him. I concentrated instead on every image and every sound that I could conjure from that night. I closed my eyes, but all I could see were flashes of light and a gloved hand wielding a serpentine knife.

"No," I said, opening my eyes to Will's intense stare. "Nothing."

"Are you sure? Try as hard as you can. I have to know . . . We have to know," Will persisted, coming closer. "Maybe if you put yourself in the exact same spot . . ."

Taking a step back, I focused on the tree. I strained to remember, through the flashes of light and memory, where I'd been pinned in relation to the tree. I took another step back, my eyes transfixed to the tree before me, but seeing into the past.

In my mind, the brisk fall air and autumn colors melted into a torrent of rain and smoke and shadow. I looked out through the shattered glass between bursts of light and plunging darkness. When the angle was right, I sat down and closed my eyes, immersing myself entirely in that moment fifteen years ago. I narrated what I saw for Will.

"The windows were smashed on this side," I said gesturing, but not looking. "There was a lot of smoke and the rain. It made it hard to see. The car was upside down. I was pinned underneath the back seat. I could see . . ." I took a shallow breath. "Gary, hanging from the front seat. And Mom . . ."

My voice broke.

"You don't have to do this, Alexandra," Donovan whispered beside me, his voice filled with concern.

"Go on, Alex," Will urged. "What else did you see?"

"There was blood where her seat used to be. So much blood . . . and her hair . . . her hand . . . She was thrown from the car," I continued, tears falling unnoticed down my cheeks. "I tried to yell for Gary. Then footsteps."

"What did you see, Alex?" Will's voice was tense.

"All I could see was a shadow. A tall figure . . . heavy steps. He crossed to Mom's side of the car first and just stood there . . . looking. I called to him, but he didn't respond. He just stood there! I screamed for him to help her. The gloved hand . . . it stroked her hair."

I heard Will sigh and let out a troubled breath. It was drowned out by the thunder in my reverie.

"Then he left her. . . . He walked to the other side of the car. Gary started to wake up. I screamed for him to wake up!" I cried out, lost in the memory. "Wake up!"

"Alexandra, you have to stop," Donovan called to me from some distant shore in my mind.

"I heard Gary scream! And then it was quiet. All I could hear was the rain. I didn't understand what was happening. And then I saw him . . ."

"What did you see? Did you see his face?" Will was shouting, the urgency in his voice permeating the darkness.

"A knife!" I squealed. "He had a knife. He tried to get to me . . . again and again. I couldn't move. All I could do was scream. He wouldn't stop . . . He wouldn't stop!"

"His face! Concentrate on his face!" Will yelled. "Who was it, Alex? Who was it?"

"No, Alexandra," Donovan called.

"Did you see who it was? Did you see?" Will yelled again. "Focus, Alex!"

"Damn it. Why are you pushing her so hard?" Donovan screamed at Will, but it fell on deaf ears.

"Alexandra, you need to get up now. We have to go!" I heard Donovan plead to me in the distance.

In my mind, I could see him in the back seat with me, instructing me, saving me. *I am with you*, I heard him say, the strumming soothing me in my greatest time of need. I concentrated on his face. For the first time, I remembered the tears that glistened on his cheeks.

"You're in danger, Alexandra!" He screamed to me now. "We have to go!"

His velvet voice, thick with apprehension, jarred me from my memories. I opened my eyes to see Will standing over me, his face tense and reddened.

"You saw something, didn't you?" he demanded. "What did you remember?"

"I couldn't see his face. I was bleeding . . . and the rain," I managed.

"You saw him, didn't you?" he yelled.

"No, damn it . . . his face, it was covered . . ."

"Alexandra!" Donovan yelled.

"Ssshhh!" Will shot up abruptly, holding a hand up to silence me.

I stood and wiped my eyes, following Will's gaze behind me, but saw nothing.

"What is . . .?"

"Someone's coming," Will whispered, not taking his eyes off of the direction we came. "On my say, run that way along the ridge as fast as you can. I'll hold him off."

"He's here, Alexandra." Donovan warned. "You have to run. Follow my voice."

Will drew his gun from its holster.

"What? No . . ." I stammered, panic tightening around my throat.

"Alexandra!" Donovan pleaded. "Run! This way!"

"Go now!" Will yelled.

I hesitated only a second longer before turning to run as fast as I could along the ridge.

"This way!" Donovan yelled in front of me, and I followed his voice into the woods.

Risking a look behind me, I saw Will raise his gun. I turned as a shot ripped through the unnatural silence around us and echoed like the hideous crack of a death drum. Screaming, I fell over my feet, landing noisily onto the damp, leaf covered earth. Donovan's voice was immediately in my ear.

"Get up, Alexandra. You have to run. Get up!"

I stumbled to my feet, finally getting my trembling limbs beneath me. I looked back for Will, but saw no one.

"Run!" Donovan yelled again, and I took off in the direction of his voice.

"What about Will?" I screamed.

"You can't worry about him right now. Just stay with me. You have to keep running!"

Before I could protest, another shot erupted from behind. Splinters of bark stung my flesh as the bullet punched a hole in the tree beside me. I covered my head with my arms and kept running.

"This way! Get lower to the ground," Donovan yelled just in front of me.

I could feel the warmth of his hand on my wrist, leading me through the trees and brush. Crouching down, I kept as low as possible. Heavy footsteps sounded on the ground behind me. I fought the urge to turn, if just for a second, to see who was after me, to see his face once and for all. The need to know outweighed all logic.

"Alexandra, keep running!" Donovan shouted, anticipating my hesitation. "Stay with me."

I forced myself forward. Another shot erupted and hit a tree just in front of me, sending more shards of tree bark into my face and arms. Ducking instinctively, I lost my footing and Donovan's grasp on my wrist. With a scream, I slipped over the edge of the ridge.

Sliding down the steep embankment, I smashed into bushes and shrubs, which snagged my legs and back. I clawed at the earth, trying to grab hold of a branch or a root, but I couldn't. I was moving too fast and with too much momentum. When I came to the bottom of the embankment, my body rolled uncontrollably until I finally came to a rest beneath a damp thicket of dead brush and fallen limbs.

For several seconds I was afraid to move, or even to breathe. With my eyes closed, I searched the silence surrounding me for the strumming. When I heard it, I felt Donovan's warm touch on my forehead, but it was different somehow. The strumming slowed. It was fainter than ever before.

"Alexandra, are you alright? Open your eyes for me," Donovan whispered into my ear.

I wanted to get lost in his velvety voice and could almost feel him beside me in the muck, solid and strong and in the flesh. When I opened my eyes, my breath caught in my throat. I saw him kneeling there, looking down on me. In that instant, I could see every feature of his magnificent face. His raven black hair . . . those magnificent eyes. I could see into their haunted blue depths as they looked over me with warmth and worry.

Startled at the revelation, I shot up and winced at a new, sharp pain in my right thigh. I looked down to discover a red gash through a fresh tear in my jeans. Straightening out my leg, I moved it around. Once I determined that it wasn't broken, I turned back to Donovan. His figure was gone. All that remained of his presence was the strumming, slow and fading.

I choked back a sob and started to get to my feet.

"No, wait!" Donovan warned.

Freezing, I listened. I could hear shuffling of feet as someone traversed the embankment above. My heart dropped and I looked around, frantic for an escape route. I knew I wouldn't be very quick on my feet if I tried to run, and the ground was littered with fallen debris, dead leaves, and shrubbery. Any kind of movement would be easy to hear and to track. As the shuffling grew louder my chance to escape diminished. Out of options, I decided to make a run for it and began to rise.

"No, Alexandra! Lay back down," Donovan instructed, his voice confident and firm. "You need to sink into these dead branches and leaves! Hide yourself in them."

Without hesitation, I laid back down and scooted into the pile of fallen brush where it was damp and muddy. Frantic, I covered myself with branches and debris, digging into the moist earth with my legs and arms.

"That's it, good. Cover your face. Hurry!"

I pushed a branch in front of my face. It was covered in dead, soggy leaves and smelled of mold and wet earth. The world around me grew dark as I covered my head as best I could. Bitter panic rose in my throat as I remembered the last time I'd wedged myself out of reach in the damp darkness.

I clung to Donovan's strumming, but didn't dare let my sight wander from the fissures of daylight seeping in through the cracks between the branches and leaves.

"Good, now stay very still. I need you to remain absolutely silent. Do not move!" Donovan whispered urgently beside me.

He was with me inside this murky, dank sarcophagus. I could feel the warmth of his arms around me, steadying me as the shuffling turned to heavy footsteps that jogged the remainder of the embankment and then began to stalk towards us.

I didn't dare move, didn't dare blink. I could only lie there motionless, listening to the heavy footfalls as they approached and grew louder with every crunch of dead foliage. I strained my eyes to see something, anything through the minuscule cracks around my face.

The footsteps came to a stop a foot from my head. I thought I might throw up, the fear manifesting as a whirlwind churning inside of my abdomen. Instead I focused on the strumming, on the gentle "ssshhh" against my ear and the feel of Donovan's warm arms around me. Then I was distracted by a flickering of light that danced in the shadows of my organic tomb.

Following the flicker with my eyes to a crack just above my face, a twinkling caught my eye. I stared at the play of light until my eyes focused. When they did, my heart stopped and my body stiffened uncontrollably. There shimmering in the daylight, inches from my face, was a knife. Its serpentine handle twisted around a gloved hand.

Twelve

"Ssshhh, it's okay, Alexandra. You've got to stay completely still." Donovan whispered, "It's almost over. I've got you."

Focusing on Donovan's voice, I realized with shock that I wasn't breathing. Worse still, I was shaking. In my panicked state I didn't dare take a breath for fear that the use of even that much muscle would make the shaking worse. *Maybe it would be better if I just passed out,* I thought as the light from the cracks ebbed and rippled in my vision. *Yes, just slip into a deep sleep and escape the terror around me. Escape it all . . .*

"Stay with me, Alexandra. Stay with me!" Donovan's words came out rushed and tortured.

Just then, all of the light from the crevices vanished as my pursuer took a step forward and blocked what little daylight shone on us through the blanket of trees above. I forced my eyes upward, intent on seeing, on knowing who was out there before I lost consciousness. All there was, was blackness. I closed my eyes and let it consume me. I longed to slip into it, to rest at last. The end.

"He's leaving. You did it, Alexandra. Hang in there just a few seconds longer." Donovan's voice pulled me back.

I forced my eyes open, and when I saw that daylight again permeated the darkness around me, I fought to keep them open. Donovan's smooth voice spoke calming words to me as I thought about that night, all those years ago, when his voice had been the only light in an impossible darkness. It had sustained me then, just like it did now.

A heaving cry of frustration erupted from the stillness around us, and then the heavy steps jogged off through the brush, crunching and snapping violently away. I took a deep, ragged breath but remained still, all my senses alert and vibrating. The footsteps disappeared into the distance and I waited, rigid, until several minutes had passed and I heard nothing. Only then did I allow my muscles to ease as I panted for breath until it seemed my lungs would explode from the amount of air I sucked in.

"He's gone. You did it," Donovan said, and the warmth around my arms lightened and faded. "We need to get you to safer ground,"

I was too afraid to uncover myself, my body remaining one with the muck and moist earth. My mind refused to process relief.

"It's okay. He's gone," Donovan whispered. "Trust me, Alexandra."

Donovan's voice pulled me from my shocked state. I brushed the branches and mangled leaves from my face and limbs. My muscles ached, and I noticed for the first time that I was cold. My jeans, now wet and clinging to my skin, held the frigid dampness against me, chilling me with each new gust of autumn wind. I stood on shaky legs and took stock of my injuries. Aside from the gash on my thigh, I was relieved that I'd suffered only a few scratches and scrapes during my fall.

"You're hurt."

The worry in Donovan's voice made me take a closer look at the gash in my leg. It was deep, but had stopped bleeding.

"It's just a scrape. I'll be fine," I answered, my voice wavering.

"We have to keep moving. He might decide to double back. Can you walk?"

"Yes." I nodded, following Donovan's voice. "Let's get out of here."

Donovan led me in the opposite direction from the footsteps. I took wide steps, which stung, in order to avoid the cluttering of downed branches and thorny bushes.

"Wait," Donovan said, and I halted mid-step.

"What is it? Is he coming back?"

"No. Take off your sweater," he urged.

"What? Why?" It was freezing.

"It's bright red," he explained. "You're easy to spot out here. You have to get rid of it. Bury it under some of this debris."

I pulled the muddied sweater over my head. The cool air nipped at my bear arms, but I was grateful that the tank top I wore beneath it was dry. I jammed the sweater beneath a pile of dead branches and covered it with leaves until the red was no longer distinguishable from the shades of brown covering it.

"Good, now let's go," Donovan urged, and I plunged ahead.

We traveled for a while wordlessly, me tripping over shrubbery and branches, eager to get somewhere where I could rest. The forest went on forever in a million different directions, and the sunlight was dipping farther and farther beneath the tree line.

"Shouldn't we go back up towards the road?" I paused to catch my breath.

"No, he would have thought of that. That's the first place he'll look," Donovan answered a few feet ahead of me.

"But it's also the first place anyone will look, right? The police . . . Will?" I urged.

"We don't know that anyone beside this man is out looking for you yet."

"But Will's car is up there. Will could be up there waiting for me to come back. He could be hurt," I pleaded to the trees before me, wishing I could see Donovan's face. "What about Will?"

"We can't worry about him right now, Alexandra. He doesn't matter right now."

I recoiled. "How can you say that? Because you don't like him?"

Donovan sighed, and his voice got closer. He spoke from right beside me now, his tone urgent and all business.

"I never said I didn't like him. What I said was that I don't trust him, and neither should you. Did you hear how hard he was pushing you back there?" Donovan paused, taking a loud breath before going on. "It doesn't matter if I like him or not. None of that matters right now. Do you understand? All that matters right now is you, YOUR safety. Nothing else matters."

I imagined him there, looking into my eyes, making sure I understood what he said. Glaring ahead in defiance, I shook my head. Donovan sighed again and his voice softened.

"Look, we have to think strategically about this, okay?" he said. "Whoever is after you will be expecting you to go back up to the road, back to the car. He will be expecting you to go back and look for Will or flag down some help. HE will be waiting, and it's not worth the risk of going up there in the hopes that he is not the only one."

Huffing, I lowered my eyes. He was right. I didn't want him to be, but he was. He always was. I wanted more than anything to go back and find Will and, and to make our way back to the station, but we couldn't. Whoever was out there would be waiting for me there.

I threw my hands up in frustration, knowing I had only myself to be angry with. It was my idea to come out here. I hadn't listened to Donovan or to Sully, and now my life was on the line. Will could be out there injured or worse. It was all my fault.

"Damn it. So, what do we do?" I asked. "Where are we going? It's going to be dark soon."

Donovan's voice came as calm as a whisper. "We keep moving, until we find a safe place to wait."

"Wait for what?" I shrugged, defeated and exhausted.

"For the Calvary," Donovan said.

My shoulders dropped. The thought of being stuck in these woods in the dark with a madman after me made my stomach twist around itself.

"Come on, let's keep moving," Donovan said, his voice moving in front of me.

I sighed, hurling myself forward. Every step made my legs ache and tremble. My arm muscles seized with the dropping temperature.

"You're doing great," Donovan encouraged as I brooded. "Just keep moving forward."

"Easy for you to say," I grumbled, but continued on. "You're celestial."

We journeyed through the thick, damp brush for what seemed like hours. My arms and fingers went numb as the sun dipped below the tree line, turning the evening sky an iridescent swirl of coral and blush. Shadows crept up from the ground, their black fingers extinguishing the remaining sunlight seeping in through the trees. Soon the sun would vanish entirely, and the forest around us would be lost to the oppressive dark.

I continued to follow Donovan's voice as he encouraged me to keep walking, pausing only for a minute when my legs throbbed. Then his warmth was on my hand, guiding me forward. I tried not to think of Will or how hysterical Sully must be by now. The guilt was unbearable. I prayed that Will was okay.

When it seemed my legs could move no further and exhaustion began to overpower me, a bed of moist leaves and soft earth called to me. I considered dropping where I stood and closing my eyes until the sun came up, but I heard Donovan call out suddenly.

"There!"

I looked ahead through squinted eyelids in order to see in the waning daylight. There was a clearing ahead. The trees thinned, and the foliage dispersed to either side of a browning meadow. Weaving through the middle was a thin trail leading off into more densely wooded terrain.

"A trail?" I asked, knowing I didn't have the strength left to hike even a marked path.

"It's a game trail. That means . . ." Donovan's voice trailed off ahead.

"That means what?" I asked, not understanding the excitement in his voice.

The black of night was closing in. There was no chance of me following the small trail into another stretch of wooded hell.

"Up there!" Donovan called ahead. "Come on."

When I looked up into the trees, I saw nothing. It wasn't until I followed Donovan's excited calls that a structure took form among the blackened leaves. Hobbling into the clearing, I looked up at the hunting platform. It poked out from among the branches of a large pine tree just off the game trail. One would have a clear vantage point of the trail and the woods below from that platform. Donovan's excitement made sense, but I was apprehensive.

"We're going to spend the night way up there, aren't we?" I shuddered.

Donovan was beside me again. "Only as long as we have to. Come on. It's almost dark."

When we arrived at the base of the pine, I found planks nailed along the side of the tree to use as a make-shift ladder up to the space. From this perspective, even in the dark, the platform seemed a mile high.

"Must I keep reminding people that I have an issue with heights?" I pouted.

"I know you do, but this height may just save your life," Donovan sympathized. "Take it one wrung at a time."

I looked once more at the height and then to the surrounding forest, now almost completely immersed in black. Then I began to climb. My legs wobbled and the gash in my thigh stung each time I lifted my leg to the next wrung. I had to rely on my arms to pull myself up each one. This time I didn't look down as I ascended bit by bit from the shadows below into the last fading shards of evening light.

Near the top, my knee buckled from under me, and my feet slipped free. I clung to the top wrung with all the strength left in me. Feet flailing and kicking, I groped for a foothold. Panic took hold of me when my arms lost strength, and I started to slip. I reached for Donovan and started to scream his name. Before I could, I felt his grip on my arms.

"I've got you," he grunted, and I felt his strength pull me. "I told you I wasn't going to let you fall."

Glancing up in the feeble, dying twilight, I could see his muscled silhouette stooped down to help me. Gasping, I realized I could feel his grip on me, warm and solid. At last my foot found its foothold on the wrung. I strained to keep my eyes on him as I pushed myself to the top of the platform. He pulled me as I flung my legs safely over.

I struggled to sit up, desperate to hold the image of him in my eyes. He sat beside me on the platform, his form no more distinguishable than a shadow. I reached out my hand to touch him.

"You can see me," he whispered.

"Yes," I answered, my eyes welling with tears.

Through moist eyelids, I watched Donovan reach for me as the last of the sun's light faded into black. I blinked back my tears and let them roll onto my cheeks. In the split second that my eyes were closed, his silhouette vanished and was lost to the darkness that consumed the forest around us.

Heartbroken, I cried out and bowed my head. I let disappointment and exhaustion seize me. "I can't . . ." I wept.

"It's alright," Donovan whispered. "I told you, when your heart is ready, you will see me."

I lifted my head and looked at the spot where I knew he looked back at me. "Right now, my heart has never wanted anything more in my whole life."

I felt Donovan's hand on my cheek. I closed my eyes and imagined him there in front of me.

"I thought I could do this," I whispered. "I thought I could bring my mom's murderer to justice, but I'm tired, Donovan. I'm tired of running from shadows. I'm tired of the sadness. I'm tired of being afraid."

I heard Donovan sigh into the darkness.

"I wish that I could tell you that it will all be over soon, but that's something I just don't know," he said, and I could feel the strumming, slow and gentle against me. "I do know that you will make it through this, that you are strong enough. You are going to persevere."

I let out a ragged breath. "How do you know that?"

His hand brushed the side of my face again. "Because you have to, and because I won't let there be any other option."

"You said before that you don't have to be here, that you want to be," I said, wiping my eyes on my shoulder. "Why?"

I heard him take a deep breath. I felt him pull away. "You are why I exist . . . why I even want to. You are everything to me."

I could hear the anguish in his voice, but didn't know what to say. How could I even begin to explain to him what he meant to me? He'd saved my life more than once, twice, a dozen times. I wanted to tell him that wherever I was, as long as he was with me, I was home. He reminded me that I was never alone, and I couldn't imagine my life without him. Before I could form the words, I heard him clear his throat.

"You need some rest," he said. "You'll be safe up here tonight. You should try and get some sleep."

When I wiped my face with my hands, I was startled by how cold they were. In fact, now that I'd stopped moving, the chill was becoming overwhelming. I longed for my jacket or even the muddied sweater I left behind.

Shivering and exhausted, I laid down as close to the base of the tree as I could in order to escape the razor-like night wind. Curling myself into a ball, I tucked my bare arms into my legs to harvest as much body heat as I could from my core. While the dense plywood beneath me was hard and unforgiving, I was thankful that my body could rest at last. I searched the darkness for the sound of Donovan and heard the strumming beside me. The fact that the strumming was growing faint and slow was worrisome, but my mind was too weary to question it. I was satisfied that he was there.

A hefty breeze stung my cheeks and arms and chilled my legs through my damp jeans. I waited for it to pass and then curled in tighter and braced myself for the next cruel gust. What came instead was soothing warmth. It wrapped around my chilled arms and held onto me, shielding me from the wind. The warmth covered the back of my damp, weary legs, and pressed against my head. My body eased and the shivering stopped. I knew that Donovan was lying beside me, holding me close to him.

"You'll make yourself weak, touching me like this. Your energy, what if you need it?"

"Right now you need it more."

I closed my eyes and let his warmth surround me. The strumming calmed me. I knew it would drain him, interacting with me this physically, but I was too thankful, too wrapped up in the safety of him to care. I rested against the strength of his arms and let the black, dreary night melt away.

"Talk to me," I whispered.

"What do you want me to talk about?"

"Anything. I just need to hear your voice," I answered. "Talk about those years in Chicago . . . those years I can't remember you. After the accident."

The night was silent for a moment, and then Donovan's voice, like smooth satin, filled my ears. "Do you remember that night you snuck out of your Aunt and Uncle's house? You were barely fifteen, and you took your uncle's Camaro out for a joy ride. You drove around town for an hour and then just parked on the side of the road in the middle of nowhere. Do you remember that?"

I snickered. "You saw that?"

"You climbed onto the hood and lay there for hours staring up at the sky until the sun started to rise."

"I remember," I said, my mind growing heavy with sleep. "That was so long ago."

"For me it was as close as yesterday. Your whole life, to me, has been a handful of days and at the same time forever," he whispered. "You talked while you lay there. It was as if you were talking right to me. Do you remember?"

"What was I talking about?"

Letting Donovan's familiar voice ease me into forgetting where we were and what we were hiding from, I journeyed with him into the past and closer to welcomed slumber.

"You talked about your parents, about missing this place," Donovan said. "You talked about school, about how different you felt from everyone else. You were angry."

"Teenage ranting," I shrugged. "Sorry you had to hear it."

"I'm not," he assured me. "I think you knew I was listening. I think you needed me to listen. Just like I needed you to tell me what you were feeling. You never spoke about what was going on inside until that night atop the car. Somewhere inside you, you knew I was there."

I could barely hear him speaking, my mind teetered on the brink of consciousness. The warmth of his body surrounding me filled me from the inside out. I tried to stay with him, tried to focus.

"I think I've always known . . ." I answered, more asleep than awake.

For a minute the only sound that filled the space around us was his gentle strumming. I drifted further away into the welcomed numbness of sleep, taking Donovan's comforting voice with me.

"You asked me a question that night. I'm not even sure you knew what you were asking," he continued, a whisper against my ear. "You said that if God never gave anyone more than they could handle, why did he have to make you so strong to begin with? 'Why me?' you asked. What made you so special?"

I sighed, barely aware that I was still speaking. "You . . . never answered me . . ."

I felt Donovan's warmth on my check and my breathing slowed and my mind was carried away with the sound of the muted, tender strumming. I heard his voice as it flowed with me, but the words lost their meaning as I was finally lost to blissful sleep.

"I did answer you," he'd whispered. "I said . . . everything."

Thirteen

Though I struggled and shoved against the seat that pinned me, I couldn't make it budge. The footsteps approached, crunching and snapping the dead leaves with merciless persistence. I tried to scream, but the weight on my chest crushed my lungs. Squeezing my eyes shut, I fought against the pain. I attempted to sink into my seat in order to hide, but I couldn't move. Then I heard a voice, smooth and deep, and a gentle strumming beside me.

"Alexandra, come with me."

Opening my eyes, I watched the dark figure reach for me through the open door. The seat that pinned me was gone, and my lungs gasped, unobstructed, the wet night air. Leaping up, I grasped the hand he held out to me, and he helped me to my feet. We ran though the darkened woods, my legs snagging on dead branches and prickly shrubs. I could barely see, but followed his dark frame as we delved deeper and deeper into the darkness.

Tripping on a fallen tree branch, I screamed out and lost my grip on his hand. When I looked up, I could not distinguish his figure from the surrounding shadows. The strumming was too faint. I couldn't tell which direction it was coming from. Searching the woods frantically with my eyes, my ears heard the strumming slowly fade into nothingness. Before I could cry out for him, I caught a glimpse of his figure standing in a clearing ahead.

Relieved, I ran to him, my arms outstretched. When I reached him, though, his image evaporated, and my arms embraced nothing but rain and smoke. As the haze dissipated, I stared in horror at the huge white fangs in front of me, glistening in the dim *moonlight. The massive red eyes of the great beast glowed and burned into my flesh. It snarled and barked at me, sending shrieking echoes throughout the sinister night. The last thing I saw before it charged was the glint from the amulet which adorned its neck. The twisted metallic serpent dripped with blood.*

I woke to total darkness, stifling a cry. My breath came in shallow pants as I struggled to remember where I was.

"It's okay," Donovan whispered beside me.

His warmth remained around me as I remembered with trepidation that we still rested in the hunting platform fifty feet in the air. The night still ruled the sky. I scolded myself for waking before the relief of dawn, but then I heard what woke me.

In the distance, interrupting the constant sway of the breeze through the trees, came the low, guttural barks of several large hounds. I shot up, the frigid night air assaulting my bare skin. The dizziness that followed had me reeling.

"Dogs," I whispered, holding onto the base of the tree. "Is it a search party?"

"I think . . . it may be," Donovan answered weakly.

"Why didn't you wake me up? We have to call to them!"

When he didn't answer, I searched the platform for his figure. Still unable to see him, I listened for the strumming. It was still there, faint and slow.

". . . Was waiting for them . . . to get closer," he half whispered, half groaned.

"You made yourself weak keeping me warm," I gasped. "You used too much energy."

I hesitated, concerned, and then strained to see out into the wilderness. The barking dogs were getting close. The leaves crunched beneath their prancing paws. I cupped my hands around my mouth to call out.

"Wait!" Donovan strained to yell.

I dropped my hands.

"Let's just wait . . . see who it is. To be sure."

Heeding Donovan's caution, I crouched down and waited, all my senses searching the night for movement. The dogs whined as they charged forward with precision upon the debris covered earth. Footsteps stomped and plodded behind them, hurrying to keep up. My heart rose into my throat, and my eyes fixed in the direction of the barking. When they got closer still, I could see a single stream of light darting and bobbing as it approached.

"Alex!" A familiar voice called into the darkness. "Where are you, Kiddo?"

"It's Sully," I sighed with relief, starting for the edge of the platform. Before I reached the edge to climb down, I felt Donovan's hand on my shoulder.

"Let's see . . . if anyone is with him," he panted, "before we give away your position."

Before I could argue, a second beam of light trailed behind Sully. It moved slower, the lighter footsteps straining to keep up.

"That could be Will!" I said, relief urging me forward. Climbing down on shaky limbs, I used all my strength to steady myself.

"Alexandra, please . . . be careful. I haven't got my strength. If he's still out there . . ." Donovan cautioned from the platform.

"It's okay now. I'm safe." When I got to the bottom of the tree, I paused to look up to where I'd heard his voice. "Thank you, Donovan . . . for my life."

"Don't thank me yet," I heard him breathe before I ran in the direction of the nearing flashlights.

"Alex!" Sully shouted into the woods again and again, desperation thick in his voice.

"Uncle Sully!" I cried back, my throat hoarse. "Over here!"

Sully's voice turned frantic as he yelled over the barking dogs. "Over here! I found her! Get on the radio, now!"

Fighting past the downed limbs and brush, my legs sore and unsteady, I rounded a final tree towards the lights. I came to a sudden stop at the sight of three frenzied Bloodhounds, which snarled and lunged at me, their teeth glistening in the moonlight.

"Down boys! Down!" Sully yelled, and the dogs sat obediently, their tails wagging.

I squinted as the beam of Sully's flashlight washed over my face.

"Alex!" he shouted in relief, and with a few tremendous crunching steps, I was in his arms. He hugged me tightly to him and petted my head. "Thank God. I've been looking for you all night. I found your sweater and thought . . . My God, you're freezing."

Sully removed his jacket and draped it around my shoulders. I sunk into its warmth, its enormity engulfing me like a blanket. My mind fractured, breaking into a million shards, each rambling thought trying to escape at once.

"I'm so sorry," I said. "It's all my fault . . . I'm so sorry . . ."

"Sshh." Sully kept an arm around me as we turned back towards the other flashlight.

I was lit with hope as the footsteps approached. When Officer Jones caught up with us, he panted, trying to catch his breath. My heart sank as he tucked his radio back into his belt.

"The others are heading back up to the road to flag down the ambulance," he said.

I turned to Sully, panicked. "Wait . . . ambulance? Where is Will? Is he hurt?"

Sully hugged me close. "The ambulance is for you, so we can get you checked out. We found Will's cruiser beside the road, but we haven't located him yet. When was the last time you saw him?"

My legs lost all their strength. I found myself leaning into Sully for support. "It was hours ago. We were just going to take a look around the site, see if I could remember anything new. Then he shouted that someone was coming. He told me to run. There were gunshots. He was here, Uncle Sully! It was the same man, the man with the knife."

My legs finally buckled from under me, and I sank to the ground. Sully bent down and lifted me into his arms, handing the dogs' leashes to Jones.

"What if he hurt Will? What if Will's out there somewhere . . . What if he's dead?"

"Don't you worry about any of that right now. We found you. We'll find him too," Sully assured me. "Let's just get you out of here."

"The dogs," I breathed, my head fuzzy as my body bobbed with every heavy step that Sully took, "can use them to find Will."

"Between me and Mr. Henley, we must have swept a five mile radius. I was just about to call it in for the night when I found you. It's black as pitch out here. He couldn't have gone far. We'll find him."

"It's Brightman . . . has to be."

"If it is, it's the last mistake he's ever going to make," Sully said behind gritted teeth.

I closed my eyes, the swaying movement of Sully's arms as he carried me proved too much for my weary head. Searching the darkness or the strumming, I found it faint and slow among the panting of the dogs and the loud footfalls over a multitude of branches and dead leaves. Assured, I slipped away.

When I opened my eyes again, I was in the back of the ambulance on the side of the mountain road. Clusters of light and movement surrounded me. It took a minute to process it all. A paramedic hovered over me, dabbing at my thigh with a wet cotton ball. It stung, but I was too disoriented to complain. Beyond the opening of the ambulance, I watched Sully talk to Jones and another man who leaned against a pickup full of wriggling Bloodhounds.

Sully nodded in agreement with whatever was being said. When I sat up, we locked eyes. The paramedic bade me to lay back down. I refused and was about to stand up when Sully appeared in the ambulance doorway.

"Please tell this gentleman that I'm fine. I can walk. I don't need to be lying in the back of an ambulance while Will is still out there!"

Sully gave the paramedic a dismissive nod. The paramedic threw his hands up in defeat before walking away to give us a minute.

"You've been through a lot tonight. You need to do what the doctors say."

"I'm just a little woozy," I argued. "All I need is some water, and I'll be fine."

Sully shook his head. "You need to go to the hospital and let them check you out."

Defiant, I rolled to my feet and wrapped Sully's jacket around me. I stood firm even though a strong gust of wind threatened to knock me off balance. We were parked further up the road from the crash site. From the headlights of the nearest squad car, I saw that the drop to the ridge was only a slight slope here. The crash site would be only a small hike from here.

"I'm not going to the hospital. There's nothing wrong with me other than a few cuts and scrapes." The paramedic handed me a bottle of water, and I thanked him. Then I turned my attention back to Sully. "We have to go back out there and look for Will."

"You'll be safer at the hospital for the rest of the night. Whoever is after you could still be out there too." He looked into my eyes. "Did you see anything, Alex? Can you give me a description? Anything at all?"

I took a swig from the bottle and then bowed my head. "I ran before I saw anything. Will screamed for me to run. I tried to look back, but I didn't see anyone. There were gunshots. Then I fell down the embankment and hid under some brush. I couldn't see his face, just the knife."

"Knife?"

I looked him dead in the face. "It was the same knife, Uncle Sully. It was the same man. I know it."

"Did you see anything that could help us identify this guy?" Sully prodded. "Any scars or distinguishing marks? What was he wearing?"

"I was covered in debris. All I could see were his hands. He had on gloves," I grimaced, furious with myself. "He was right there,

Uncle Sully . . . but I couldn't see him without giving myself away. He was right there!"

Sully put his arm around me and hugged me to him. "You did what you had to do in order to stay safe. I'm glad you did. Now you need to let us take care of this guy. This is why I told you not to come out here. Damn it, Alex, why didn't you just listen to me? I'm trying to protect you."

I hung my head. "I just wanted to remember something . . . anything that could pin the accident to Brightman. Will was just trying to help me remember. Have you tracked down Brightman? Has anyone questioned him?"

Sully sighed and let me go. "I sent Conley to track down Brightman. He'll call me if he finds anything. We'll find Will. In the meantime, you need to let these paramedics take you to get checked out."

"I told you. I'm not going," I insisted.

Sully glared at me. When I didn't back down, he sighed and shook his head.

"Fine, no hospital," he agreed. "But you are coming home with me so I can keep an eye on you myself."

"No," I cried. "We have to get back out there and find Will. He could be hurt. We can't give up yet."

"I told you. We made a wide sweep of the area. There's not much else we can do until morning. It's too dark. We'll send the dogs back out at first light if we haven't heard from him," Sully argued. "There's no way you are going back out there, Alex. You look like you could fall right over. When was the last time you ate something?"

I thought for a minute. The last thing I'd eaten was when I took a bite of the muffin Will gave me that morning. Though I was famished and unsteady, none of that mattered as much as finding Will safe and alive.

"I can't leave him out here, Uncle Sully." I looked into Sully's eyes, urging him to understand.

Sully sighed, looking from me to the pickup full of eager, whining hounds. He patted me on the shoulder and nodded.

"Okay, Kiddo. Henley and I will take another pass across the ridge with the dogs. Jones!" he yelled and the officer jogged up to us, his breath trailing in white wisps behind him. "I want you to take Alex home to get her stuff. Then bring her straight to my place. I want you by her side every minute, do you understand? Do not leave her until I get there."

Jones nodded, but I started to protest. Sully cut me off.

"You're not doing Will or myself any good by being out here. If you want me to find him, then I need you safely out of the way. Henley!" he called behind us.

"Yes, sir?" Henley yelled back from his pickup.

"Your dogs fit for another pass?"

I watched Mr. Henley remove his cap and wipe his forehead with the back of his hand.

"I'd give 'em another hour before they need to get inside and fed. Storm's on the way too. Best get moving if we're goin'," he said, gathering the leashes.

Sully turned to me and placed both hands on my shoulders. "One hour, that's all you get. If we haven't found him by then, we'll have to call it until morning. I'll meet you at my place exactly an hour from now. Jones doesn't leave your side."

I thought about arguing, but I knew it would do no good. Sully was being gracious by giving me this much.

"Okay," I conceded.

With one final pat, Sully walked to the pickup. I followed Jones to his squad car and climbed in the passenger side as the first smattering of rain began to fall.

"Wait," I called when we rolled up to Sully and Mr. Henley as they started down to the ridge.

Sully turned, and I shrugged out of his jacket, tossing it to him through my window. Sully grabbed it and flung it over his shoulder.

"You need this more than I do," I said. "Find him, Uncle Sully."

"One hour." He hollered back before he disappeared down the slope, and Jones pulled the cruiser onto the road.

When we pulled up to the house, I hopped out of the cruiser and ran through the stinging drizzle to the door. Lightning flashed in the distance, and the wind was picking up. Patting my pockets, I was relieved to find the new key still inside. Shivering, I turned the knob.

"Stop," Jones called from behind me. "Let me go in first!"

Sighing, I stepped aside so that the officer could get by. I followed him into the house and waited just inside the door as he flipped on the lights and meticulously checked every room and window. When he cleared the kitchen, I made a dash for the bag of Gram's cookies. I devoured three in the time it took Jones to come back into the kitchen.

"The bottom floor is clear," he announced. "I'm going to check upstairs. You stay right here."

"No worries. I lack the willpower to move from this spot and these cookies at the moment," I mumbled, my mouth full of oatmeal goodness.

By the time Jones came back into the kitchen I'd downed the entire bag. Though I felt better with a full stomach, I still shivered in my damp clothes. My body ached all over. I tossed the empty bag on the counter and headed out of the kitchen.

"I'm going to take a shower and grab my things," I said. "Please yell if Sully radios in about Will."

"I'm not supposed to let you out of my sight, remember?" Jones was all business.

I raised my eyebrow at him. "I just spent twelve hours buried in grimy underbrush or trudging through knee-high wilderness. I'm wet, muddy, scratched all to hell, and freezing. I am taking a hot shower, and I don't care if that means you are standing right there to hand me the soap."

When Jones didn't waver, I added, "Look, you already checked upstairs. No one's getting past you down here. I think you can relax a bit."

Jones eyed me, but backed down. "I'll give you twenty minutes. If you're not down here by then, I'm coming up. And it won't be to hand you the soap."

"Fair enough," I agreed, making my way painfully up the stairs as I gripped the railing for support.

Shutting the door of my room behind me, I looked into the mirror. My own reflection startled me. I was more of a mess than I thought. My once white tank top and blue jeans were now a sick shade of dirt brown. Small cuts and scrapes littered my filthy arms. My hair was matted with small bits of leaves and mud.

"Do you feel as bad as you look?"

Donovan's image appeared in the mirror beside me. He braced himself against the door. My heart warmed at the sight of him.

"I'll feel a lot better after a shower."

"Hurry, Alexandra," he whispered, still weak. "You shouldn't be here. It's too obvious. We need to leave as soon as possible."

Startled, I gathered clothes from my bag as quickly as I could. "Do you think he'll come here?"

Donovan hesitated. "I don't know, but . . . something . . ."

I caught the confused look on his face as he concentrated on something I could not see.

"Something what?"

"Something is off . . . I can't pinpoint what it is, but I don't like it," he said. I could see the concern in his eyes. "Hurry."

There was something he wasn't telling me, but I knew that there was no point trying to get it out of him. There was no need. I trusted him with my life.

Rushing into the bathroom, I started the shower. Within seconds, the room was filled with steam. I emerged minutes later warm, clean, and dressed in my most comfortable sweat pants and a long-sleeved shirt. I bandaged my thigh, and my muscles felt much less tense. A quick glance in the mirror assured me that I was looking much better as well. Then I caught Donovan's reflection.

He was leaning against the wall, ear to the door, the palm of his hand pressed against its surface. I knew by the way he leaned that he was still weak. His eyes were closed, and he was concentrating, a startled look in his face.

"What is it?" I asked, holding my breath.

"It's Will . . ."

I gasped, my pulse quickening. "They found him!"

I ran to the door and threw it open.

"Alexandra, no . . . wait!" Donovan yelled. I felt his grip on my shoulder, but I couldn't stop.

"I have to go. What if Will saw him? He might be able to identify Brightman!" I cried, running for the stairs. I was eager to reach Jones and force him to take me to him.

"Alexandra, stop! You have to listen to me! Something is wrong . . ." I heard Donovan shout, stopping me short at the bottom of the stairs.

My heart in my throat, I searched the living room for Jones but didn't see him. When I saw movement in the kitchen, I yelled to him.

"Jones? Did they find . . ." I began to ask, then stopped abruptly when someone emerged in the kitchen doorway.

Will glared up at me, the wine bottle dangling from his fingers as he fought to catch his breath. His uniform was muddied and torn, his face and hair caked with layers of dirt and sweat. He set the bottle aside when he saw me. His face was frantic.

"Will!" I cried, running to him.

He embraced me, holding me tightly against him. I closed my eyes and let relief wash over me. Will was trembling. He let out a jagged breath.

"I was so scared." I breathed against his shoulder. "I thought you were hurt somewhere or dying."

Will rubbed my cheek with his thumb and held me tighter. "I'm okay. Everything is okay now."

"Alexandra, no!" Donovan yelled from behind me. "Get away from him!"

The panic in his voice startled me, and I opened my eyes. Over Will's shoulder I caught a glimpse of black in the corner of the room. Blinking back my tears of relief, I looked again. It was a boot. Confused, I stepped away from Will. I peered around him as he stood, tense.

Jones was lying on the floor, his head propped against the back wall. He was unconscious, his legs sprawled out in front of him. I jumped back from Will with a gasp. He put his hands up to quiet me before I could speak.

"I had to get to you . . . He was trying to stop me," he panted.

"What did you do to him?" I asked, backing away.

"I just knocked him out. He'll be fine. He doesn't understand . . ."

"Wait a minute," my heart sank into my stomach as I had a revelation. "If he didn't let you in, then how . . .?"

"Alexandra, come this way," Donovan called. "Slowly, towards me."

Backing up to the cabinets, I took a few small steps closer to Donovan and the front door. I kept my eyes on Will.

"When the locksmith came this morning, I . . . I had him make an extra key."

"Why? Why would you do that?" I stammered, edging closer to Donovan, my mind screaming.

Will reached out to me, pleading. "I had a feeling I would need it, and I was right. Alex, just listen to me for a minute. I have to tell you the truth. You don't understand . . ."

Looking down at the hand Will extended toward me, I noticed for the first time that they were streaked with glossy red. I felt wetness on my cheek where he'd touched me, and I reached up to it. When I pulled my hand away, my trembling fingers were tinted with moist crimson.

I gawked at Will and took another step back, panic thundering into my chest. The wild look in Will's eyes sent my mind racing in a thousand different directions.

"What did you do?" I cried. "What did you DO?"

I jumped when the crackle of a radio erupted from Jones' belt in the corner. Conley's muffled voice filled the channel. Will flinched, glancing behind him. Then he focused his intense stare back on me, his eyes locking on mine.

"Chief, this is Conley." The radio squawked. "Come in, Chief. Over."

"Go ahead for Chief," Sully's voice answered.

"I have a ten-twenty on Brightman," Conley continued. "He's dead, sir. A witness saw someone in uniform matching Galia's description leaving his hotel room about forty-five minutes ago. Said he took off on foot through the woods."

I looked in horror at Will. He shook his head, holding my eyes.

"Ten-four, Conley. I'm on my way to the homestead now. Put out an APB on the deputy and then check to see if he's at the station or his house. Radio me when you have a twenty," Sully ordered.

"Ten-four, Chief."

When the radio clicked off, I backed up further. Will closed the gap with one hefty step. The intensity in his eyes made the hair on my neck stand on end. The wildness there made him a stranger.

"You killed him," I whispered, stepping back again. "You killed Brightman. There's blood on your hands."

"Alex, listen to me . . ." he stepped closer.

"Keep coming this way, Alexandra," Donovan instructed. "Slowly. That's right. You're almost there."

I stepped back again. Will took another step towards me.

"I . . . I couldn't find you in the woods," he stammered, his hand outstretched to me. "So I found the road and hiked it to Brightman's hotel. I thought he had you. When I got inside his room, he was already dead, Alex. I checked for a pulse, but he'd been dead for a while. His throat was slit."

Despite his words, the pieces of the puzzle began to fit together.

"You . . . you were the one with the gun this morning. You told me to run. I never saw anyone else, only you," I choked out. "You're the one who shot at me. You wanted me to run so you could shoot me in the back."

"Alex . . ." Will stepped closer.

I reached for Donovan.

"Keep coming to me," Donovan said, his calm wavering.

Another realization dawned on me, and my breath left me in a rush. "Gram warned me that the killer wanted me to trust him. You wanted me to trust you from the day I got here. You were there that night, just like she said!"

I turned to run, but Will caught my wrist and spun me around. "You have to listen to me!"

"Alexandra, go now!" Donovan screamed, sending the knife set on the counter into Will's arm, forcing him to drop his grip on me.

Darting for the front door, I heard Will charge, close on my heels. I flung the door open in his face, and he slammed into it and stammered backwards. I ran out of the house and down the porch as fast as I could. A shriek ripped from my chest when a crash of thunder crackled above and shook the earth beneath me.

"Alex, stop! Damn it, no! Get back here!" Will screamed from the porch, sprinting after me.

Darting down the driveway barefoot, the pavement was ice cold and rough beneath my feet. The rain poured in sheets, making it hard to see past the nearest streetlight. At the end of the driveway, I hesitated. There was no way I would make it to the station, I realized with dread. So I ran in the direction of the narrow dirt road that would take me to Sully's. It was my only chance.

Fueled by terror and sheer adrenaline, it took only seconds to get to the end of the street. I chanced a look back. I could see Will gaining on me through the rain that fell like glass shards on my face.

"Alex, no! Damn it!"

Sucking in shallow breaths, I ran as fast as my throbbing legs would go. The road was murky and drenched in shadow. My breath hovered like ghosts around my face as I ran. It was hard to see the turns in the road until a flash of lightning illuminated the sky enough for me to see where I was going.

The gravel sliced into my bare feet with every panicked step, but I forced myself forward. I could hear Will behind me, his grinding steps closing the gap between us. I tried to move faster, but my chest burned when I sucked in the bitter air. My mind raced with my feet, trying to make sense of this horrid reality. I thought of Gram and what she said in the cemetery. The pieces all fit. *He was there that night . . .*

Finally, I rounded the last turn in the road and considered running into the dark recesses of the woods and cloaking myself in its blackness, but I was too afraid. I couldn't be trapped in the woods with this man. Not again.

I listened for the strumming, longing to know that Donovan was with me in this nightmare. Nothing but my own panting and the rolling thunder above filled my ears. Panic clouded my thoughts. *Donovan must have used the rest of his energy trying to keep Will from coming after me. Maybe he was still weak. What if he couldn't help me this time? I had to get to Sully.*

I kept running, sure that my feet were grinding into nubs and that I would throw up or pass out at any minute. The sound of Will's frantic steps behind me forced me forward. Finally, the lights from Sully's porch glowed ahead. I found new strength to pick up my pace. With a wail, I charged onto the paved street and turned for Sully's house.

"NO!" Will screamed, a feral roar, behind me.

"Please be home. Please be home," I prayed, my legs wobbling beneath me.

Tears streamed down my face, blending with the raindrops that assaulted my cheeks as I ran down the road. When I got closer to the house, I saw Sully's truck in the driveway. I choked back a sob and pushed faster, my heart threatening to shatter under the pressure. I could no longer hear Will's footsteps behind me, but I knew he was there. Maybe I had pulled ahead.

"Uncle Sully!" I forced out a scream as I raced up the driveway and up the steps to the house.

I struggled with the front door, a panicked scream escaping from my throat when my wet hands could not turn the knob. Wiping them on my pants, I fumbled with the knob again. When it finally turned, I bolted into the house. I scanned the living room. Sully was nowhere in sight.

"Uncle Sully!" I screamed again.

Sully appeared, startled, in the kitchen doorway. He was wiping his hands on a towel and froze at the sight of me.

"Alex?"

"It's Will, Uncle Sully . . . he's right behind me! He killed Mom," I sobbed. "It was him. He's the one!"

Sully looked bewildered as he processed the information that I tried to relay to him in my frenzy. Then he dropped the towel suddenly, removing his gun from its holster. He aimed it past me towards the door.

My breath caught in my throat. I turned to see Will in the entryway, gun raised and pointed at Sully. A crash of thunder fractured the sudden silence.

"Stop right there, Deputy," Sully warned. He kept his gun on Will as he looked at me. "Get behind me, Alex.

I started to move toward Sully, trembling, praying that he could finally put an end to this.

"No!" Will screamed, and I stopped mid-step. "Alex, you have to listen to me. Sully killed your mom. That's what I was trying to tell you!"

"What the hell are you talking about? Kiddo, come to me slowly. It's okay. I'm not going to let him hurt you anymore," Sully encouraged. "I should have known . . . I'm so sorry, Alex."

I took a few more steps forward, keeping my back to Will and locking eyes with Sully who stretched out his hand to me.

"Alex, it's true. I got the phone call after I left Brightman's apartment. My buddy from the NYPD called me back . . . the one I told you about," Will pleaded. "He got a hit on the VIN number from that vehicle that fit the description of what you saw. Turns out the red Bronco was registered to Sullivan Wiley. He bought it in Hendersonville two days before the accident."

I watched as Sully's eyes narrowed in anger. Mine grew wide, the shock of Will's words sinking in. My breath caught in my throat, and I turned.

"What?" I croaked, unable to find my voice. I looked back at Sully who was glaring at Will, unblinking. "What is he talking about, Uncle Sully?"

"Lies," Sully said. "He's trying to get you to trust him. None of this is true."

"It's over, Sully. Tell her the truth." Will sneered. "Tell her why you did it. She deserves that much, don't you think?"

"Don't listen to him, Alex. He's trying to confuse you. Come here, Kiddo," Sully whispered, still reaching for me.

I stared in terror from one to the other.

"It couldn't have been you," I said to Sully. "You were in Iraq . . ."

"See, I checked on that too," Will yelled when I took another step towards Sully. "And according to Camp Bucca records, SSgt Wiley was released from military service for behavioral concerns less than a week before the accident. He was discharged, Alex. They sent him home."

"That's a lie!" Sully barked, and I froze in place. "Everything he is saying is a lie! Did he tell you about his son? Did he tell you the truth? Or did he give you his version of it like he gives everyone else?"

"You son of a bitch!" Will hissed, stepping closer, gun aimed at Sully's head.

Sully stared directly at me. "I bet he told you that his son accidentally shot himself, didn't he?"

"Enough!" Will screamed.

"He didn't want you to know the truth," Sully continued, "that he got drunk and shot his own son!"

I whirled around to Will. His eyes told me that it was true, his face twisting into a portrait of pain and hatred. Lightning illuminated the doorway behind him throwing his eerie, deformed shadow onto the floor. Then just as quickly, it was sucked back out into the dark night. The power flickered and threatened to go out.

"It was dark in the house. I'd been on a stakeout all night. There was drinking after, yes. I thought someone had followed me home. He was supposed to be in bed! It was an accident!" Will seethed between clenched teeth.

"See? He's been lying to you this whole time, Alex, just like he's lying now! He's a master at getting people to trust him. He's had me fooled for years. I should have known. He got fired from the NYPD for being a lousy drunk! No one else would hire him, so he came back home. I took pity on the bastard. I had no idea, Alex . . ." Sully wailed.

I glared at Will. Finally, I had my chance to ask the question that burned into my soul like an incurable fever.

"Why, Will? Why my family? Were we just an accident too? Were you drunk when you hit us? Did you have to kill them to cover your tracks?" I asked, looking him dead in the eyes.

Will's face sank. He shook his head.

"No, Alex, think about it," he said. "Sully's the one who cut the brake cables in my car. He knew you'd be driving it. He grabbed the keys when my back was turned. He was the one in your house . . . He had the damned key! He was in the woods tonight . . . He was wearing a mask when he attacked me. We were struggling for the gun when he shot at you!"

"You knew I'd be driving too," I countered. "It was your car, your suggestion. You had a key to my house too!"

My mind reeled as I considered all the possibilities. I felt dizzy. Like the room, my very life was spinning out of control.

"I didn't get the key until today. I told you that!" Will yelled at me, the frustration on his face was convincing.

"His arm, Alex!" Will shouted. "Tell him to show you his arm! The man who attacked me last night had a bandage on his left forearm, just above the wrist. I saw it when we were struggling over the gun, before I escaped into the woods. Tell him to show you his arm!"

I turned to Sully, eyes wide, and waited. My heart beat in sync with the pounding of the rain on the old cabin roof. His face was unreadable.

"I never told Will about the scratch." I swallowed hard. "He couldn't know."

Sully laughed, a loud booming cackle. "He would know if he were the one you scratched! Tell him to show you HIS arm."

I turned back to Will. He looked me in the eyes, their intensity saying a thousand words all at once. He kept one hand on the gun aimed at Sully and hiked up the sleeve of his uniform with his free hand. There was no bandage there. He switched gun hands and hiked up the sleeve on the other arm. There was nothing. No bandage, not a scratch.

I turned to Sully and stepped away from him. My eyes stayed glued to his face, gauging his reaction.

He shrugged. "That doesn't mean anything. He could have been working with Brightman. Think about it. They were working together. Why else would he kill him?"

"Show her your arm, Sully," Will demanded.

"Just show me your arm. If that's true, then you can just show me," I said waiting, my life hanging on his next move.

Sully hesitated, staring from me to Will.

"I'll show you, Alex, but I don't dare take my sights off of him. He'll attack the first chance he gets. Come on over here, and pull up my sleeves. Go ahead. I have nothing to hide."

I glared at him, considering.

"Don't do it," Will begged. "You have to run, Alex. Run for the back door while I have you covered. You don't have to believe either of us right now. Just run."

"So you can shoot her in the back like you tried to do last night? Enough of this!" Sully roared just as a deafening crack of thunder erupted from the street. With a flash the house was plunged into total darkness.

"Alexandra, get down! Now!" Donovan screamed above the crack of thunder.

"Donovan!" I cried, hitting the floor as a second explosion echoed in my ears. A blood curdling shriek rose up from my throat when I realized it was a gunshot. Then all was silent except for the pounding of the relentless rain.

For a wild moment, I lay frozen to the floor, trying to contain my breath so I could hear movement around me. I waited for my eyes to adjust, but they found no trace of light to adjust to. Utterly blind in the overwhelming dark, I struggled to hear the strumming, but it was no use. The thunder and rain masked the diminished rhythm.

"This way, Alexandra!" Donovan's strained voice came from my left.

Turning my body in that direction, I began to crawl on my stomach towards his voice. It was too quiet. Something was very wrong. I realized with paralyzing horror that I was trapped in the house with the person who killed my parents. One of the men I loved had been shot and was most likely dead. The other wanted me just as dead.

I scurried soundlessly across the floor towards Donovan's voice. Using my fingers to dig into the plush carpet, I pulled myself forward inch by inch.

"Sshh, sshh, stop. Don't move," Donovan whispered from beside me.

The sound of footsteps, slow and heavy, moved across the carpeted floor beside me. The footsteps paused. I held my breath. I didn't know where in the room I was. The darkness that engulfed me was both my saving grace and my condemner. My only hope was that the murderer was as blinded as I was. The footsteps continued across the room in deliberate, slow steps away from me.

"Okay, Alexandra," Donovan panted. "Come this way. Come towards me . . . That's it. Keep moving."

Continuing to claw my way soundlessly forward, I heard movement behind me. It was the sound of fabric being dragged across carpet. A faint moan. I looked in the direction of the sound as a flash of lightning illuminated the scene before me for a few fleeting seconds.

I was near the kitchen now. A tall figure at the other end of the room, their features drenched in shadow, dragged a body towards the door. The figure turned toward me as the room was again plunged into darkness.

When the thunder rolled, I scurried into the kitchen. When the thunder faded into the distance, I froze and listened. Footsteps, slow and deliberate, moved toward me.

"That's it. Keep coming this way. Slowly . . ." Donovan's voice was strained and desperate, but he remained calm. I clung to his voice.

Clawing towards him, I was careful not to make a sound against the less forgiving, hardwood kitchen floor. When the footsteps came again, I froze. He was listening for me. I waited until he continued his approach to move forward again.

Another flash of lightning revealed that I was deep inside the kitchen. A wave of relief washed over me when I realized that Donovan was leading me to the back door. I waited for the accompanying roll of thunder before I scurried across the floor again, this time aiming for the back door.

Feeling along the cabinets, I kept the image of the kitchen where I'd spent so many childhood nights, at the forefront of my mind. I tried to remember the feeling of safety that had always surrounded me here.

Thunder growled to life outside, so I crawled along faster. After a few steps my hands stumbled across the loose floorboard. It pinched my palm as it squeaked. I froze again, my hand still on the board as the thunder came to a stop. I'd forgotten all about the loose floorboard.

I didn't dare move my hand for fear that the board would squeak again. Not knowing what to do, I listened to the footsteps grow steadily closer.

"Alexandra . . . keep moving. You're almost there," Donovan beckoned.

My mind screamed that I couldn't move. I prayed that Donovan would somehow hear. The footsteps continued closer. In a panic, I grabbed at the floorboard with my free hand, trying to force it still so I could remove the other. To my shock the board lifted into my hand, my other hand falling into the recess in the floor.

For a second I didn't move. I listened to see if I'd been heard. The footsteps paused for a minute, and I remained still until they continued on their path toward me, but the steps were no faster. Maybe they hadn't heard me.

I was about to pull my hand from the floor when I felt something soft beneath my fingertips. Grabbing onto fabric, I pulled it from below the floor. The buttery cloth was slick between my fingers. Flattening it out on the floor, I ran my finger along its edges. One fat bulk of fabric was surrounded by five narrower ones. It was a leather glove, I realized with cold dread. And it was slick with moisture.

Shaking, I dared to dip my hand into the hole in the floor again even as the footsteps came steadily nearer. In a craze, I felt around until my fingers came into contact with cool metal. I grabbed the object and pulled it from the hole with frenzied curiosity. I had to know what it was, if it was what I was afraid it was.

It too was moist. I clutched at the metal object with one hand and felt along its edges with the fingertips of my other hand. The sharp, pointy edge on one end led to a rough, curved coil on the other, sending me into an elevated plane of panic and shock. Lightning flashed into the room in succession, making me feel as though I were caught in an old, horror-movie projection.

My worst fears were confirmed when I looked down at the sinister knife in my hands. Covered in drying blood, the snake-shaped handle twisted in my grip. I dropped it with a clang to the floor and covered my mouth with my bloodied hands. I looked up in time to see Sully glare at me from the kitchen doorway. Then the room was thrown into darkness once again.

"Sully . . . NO." I choked out the words.

"My God," Donovan gasped in horror beside me. "I led you right to him!"

I couldn't breathe. None of this could be real. It had to be another nightmare. I had to wake up. Footsteps charged at me from the doorway.

"Run, Alexandra!" Donovan screamed.

Getting to my feet, I bolted for the back door. An explosion of white heat erupted behind me, and I ducked as the cabinet beside me burst into splinters of oak finish. With a scream I reached the back door as a flash of lightning illuminated the kitchen.

I struggled with the knob as behind me drawer after kitchen drawer burst open. Their contents hurled themselves into Sully's face as he struggled to get to me, gun raised. When he took aim, Donovan screamed, and a cabinet door flung open, knocking the gun from Sully's hand.

Twisting the knob, I tugged hysterically. The door would not open. I realized with helpless dismay that the deadbolt was locked. Plunged into darkness again, I felt frantically around the knob and prayed that the key was in the lock.

"No!" I screamed when my fingers found the empty keyhole.

"Duck!" Donovan screamed and I hit the floor just in time to dodge Sully's grasping hands.

His fingers clutched for me in the darkness and tugged at my hair. I yanked free, sliding across the floor to the other corner. Sully growled in frustration, the now familiar sound making the hairs on my neck stand on edge.

I backed myself as far into the corner as I could. When I heard panting next to me in the darkness, I knew that Donovan was near, but weak.

"You can't hide forever, Kiddo." Sully's voice was that of a stranger. "You know, it's a shame that it had to end this way. It was nice having you back. Just like old times."

I held my breath in the corner, keeping my eyes focused on Sully's voice in front of me. The thunder rolled in the distance as the storm began to pass. What light broke through the windows was only enough to cause a faint flicker before it vanished and the house was black once again.

"But, just like old times, you ran off with another man. After everything I did for you. Like mother like daughter," he spat. "You made me do it. The both of you . . . made me kill my own brothers. First Gary, now Will. I told you he was no good for you, but that didn't matter to you, did it?"

Sully's footsteps sounded on the kitchen floor beside me, kicking strewn utensils aside as he paced.

"I thought you'd be different, Alex, but I could tell right away you were just like her. Do you know the things I did for her?" Sully ranted.

None of it made sense. My mind whirled, trying to discern his words and the sheer hatred in his tone.

"I took care of her after she had you. I made her part of my family. I helped her buy that damned house. That was supposed to be OUR home!" Sully shouted. I bit down on my tongue to suppress a scream.

"I only enlisted in the Army to be able to provide for her . . . for the three of us. That wasn't good enough for her though, was it?"

I remained still, listening, trying to figure out what to do. *Someone heard the gunshots . . . The police were coming*, I told myself. Sully's footsteps came to a halt. A series of strange clicks sounded in the room, followed by a slow, steady hiss.

"She couldn't wait for me to finish one damned tour!" Sully continued, the rage building in his voice as he began to pace again.

". . . and Gary. He was only supposed to stay with Gram while I was away. I should have known that he would take everything I cared about, everything I worked for. He always had to have everything, while I had NOTHING!"

Sully paced away from me. I sucked in a ragged breath. My body from shock. I couldn't stop it. *It was Sully*, I told myself over and over in my mind. *Sully killed my mother. Sully, the man I'd loved like a father.*

"It's . . . okay, Alexandra. We'll find . . . another way out of this. Have to get you . . . to the front door . . ." Donovan strained beside me. I felt his warmth on my hand, but it quickly vanished.

"When you came back, I was almost glad that I couldn't get to you that night," Sully chuckled. "I actually thought we could start over, that we could have a second chance. You look so much like her. I thought maybe . . ."

"This way!" Donovan called out to me. I crawled cautiously towards his voice.

Drowning Sully out, I tried not to be distracted by his crazed words, but I couldn't help it. I'd waited my whole life to discover the truth, to finally know the reasons why.

"Good, keep coming," Donovan whispered as I crept closer.

"You had eyes for Will from the get go," Sully hissed. "A whore just like your mother."

I stammered and almost lost my balance.

"Don't . . . listen to him, Alexandra," Donovan urged. "Just . . . listen . . . to my voice. Keep moving."

I forced my body forward though I trembled, paralyzed with shock and fear and growing rage. As I felt along the wall, my fingers found the doorway into the living room. Something caught my attention before I could make it to the safety of the carpet. I smelled something. A foul, pungent odor filled the room and burned my eyes. Suddenly the hissing made sense. Sully had turned on the gas burners on the stove. The room was filling with flammable vapor.

I contemplated making a run for the door, but was unsure if I could make it without stumbling in the dark. As I readied myself to make the charge, the electricity flickered, filling the house with sputtering light.

Then it came back on.

Turning slowly, I stared in horror at Sully's twisted face just feet away. A sinister smile curled his lips, and for a few tormenting moments, our eyes locked on one another.

"Chief? Chief, this is Conley. Come in, Chief," Conley's voice erupted from Sully's belt.

Sully's eyes remained locked on mine as he reached for his radio.

"Go ahead," he answered.

"We got a call that there were gunshots heard coming from your house. Is everything alright, sir? Over."

Sully smirked and cleared his throat. "No! It's Galia! He attacked us. I tried to stop him, but I was too late. He killed Alex. Oh, God . . . hurry! I smell gas!"

My stomach heaved. I knew he was going to kill me. No one would ever know that he killed my mother, Gary, Brightman, Will . . . and me. I glanced behind me to the front door. Will laid in a pool of blood in the entryway. I wanted to run to him, but I knew I wouldn't make it. Turning back to Sully, I met the hatred in his cold stare. He would catch me no matter where I tried to run. There was nothing I could do.

"Hang in there, Chief. We're on the way."

Sully dropped the radio to the floor. "Looks like your luck has finally run out."

"Alexandra, the knife . . . do you see it?" Donovan whispered from beside me.

I looked to the floor. There, beside where the radio came to a clanking rest was the snake-handled knife. I nodded as Sully took a step towards me, and I took an unsteady step back.

"The lights . . . I have to take them out. When I say so, grab the knife. Do not hesitate . . . use it!" Donovan instructed.

"What?" I cried as Sully charged at me.

With loud pops, shards of glass shattered from every light bulb in the living room. They erupted in succession, causing Sully to hesitate. Again, the house was plunged into total darkness.

"Now, Alexandra!" Donovan screamed, and I dove in the direction of the knife, my hands flailing.

I heard Sully stumble behind me with an enraged howl. Then he charged at me again. My frantic fingers connected with the radio. I knew the knife was to the left of it. My fingers groped desperately as a hand clamped down on my sore ankle and dug into my skin. Screaming, I kicked as hard as I could with my other leg. Though I connected with bone and flesh, Sully's grip only tightened. He dragged me towards him.

"I don't know how you keep doing it, but you're not going to get away from me this time," he growled. "I tried to warn you, to get you to leave. I even tried to make Will look guilty, to get you to see that I was the one who could protect you. I killed Brightman for you! But it wasn't enough for you, was it? I showed you mercy, and you still ran off with him. No more . . . it's over."

I continued to kick as hard as I could, digging my fingernails into the wood of the floor. Overpowering hands gripped my shoulders and flung me onto my back. I pushed and struggled, beating against the iron hands that pinned me and wrapped around my throat.

"Donovan . . .helggg . . ." I gargled as Sully's hands crushed my larynx.

I couldn't breathe. Every ounce of air was wrung from my lungs. My body went numb. Though my heart raced in my ears, I felt tired, like I could slip away and finally bring this nightmare to a close. Sully won, and I was dead. A part of me longed for it, welcomed it even.

Suddenly, Sully's body was flung back. The crushing grip on my throat slipped away as his fingers groped for me. Gasping for air, I heard the muffled grunts above me as my body began to tingle and come back to life.

"The . . . knife!" Donovan strained.

Shaking the fog from my head and still coughing, I groped along the floor, but my fingers were numb. I moved my hands back and forth until I finally connected with the cold metal handle. With a heaving breath I wrapped my fingers around the coiled knife. While Donovan and Sully struggled above, I could feel Sully's menacing fingers straining for me, reaching again for my throat.

"I . . . can't hold him," Donovan shrieked as he lost his grip on Sully. "Now, Alexandra!"

Sully lunged at me again. With a wild cry, I thrust the knife forward. I felt it tear into flesh and come to rest against solid bone before I let my hands drop to the floor. Sully's anguished howl reminded me of the night of the accident, of Gary's final dying shriek. Sully stumbled backwards. I shot to my feet.

Lights flashed through the windows. The wailing of sirens descended on the house. I looked up and saw Sully hunched over, the knife embedded in his gut. He looked down in shock, and then wrapping his hands around the wound, he staggered out of the kitchen. I watched, my body trembling, as he stumbled into the living room.

The sirens grew louder, and the house flickered red and blue. I followed behind Sully, not daring to take my eyes off of him. Then I noticed with a start that Will was looking at me from where he lay on the floor. He struggled to move. I started to run to him, but stopped cold when Sully began to laugh. His deep, menacing chuckle turned my blood to ice in my veins.

When Sully reached the entryway, he turned and smiled, blood trickling from the corners of his mouth. He held up a chrome lighter and slowly flipped the cap back with his thumb.

"Oh, God, no," I whispered, remembering the fumes that still filled the house.

Sully flicked the igniter. He laughed as the flame grew in his hand. I watched him toss the lighter towards me and turn to run. The world became slow and fuzzy all around me as I watched the flame dance and flicker in the air as it flew towards me.

I bolted for the front door, but it was as if my legs were sinking into deeper sand with every step. As I neared the front of the living room, I saw Sully reach the front door only to be pulled back by frantic hands. Will clutched onto his calf from where he lay, bloodied, in the entryway. He pulled Sully back towards him with a cry.

"Looks like we both have an appointment in HELL!" Will gurgled.

Sully shrieked above the sirens that roared down the street.

Behind me, I heard the clank of the lighter as it hit the kitchen floor. I stopped running. I knew I wouldn't make it. A calm washed over me then as I accepted my fate. I turned to face the erupting flames.

There, in the flesh before me, was Donovan. He was clearer to me than any tangible thing I'd ever laid eyes on. His blue eyes burned into mine, his face a mask of pure love and serenity. He held out his arms to me as the house trembled and filled with gruesome orange light. Tears fell from my eyes as I ran to him.

He caught me in his arms and wrapped them around me. His warm body pressed up against mine, solid flesh on flesh. I looked into his face at last as he wiped my tears and drew me closer.

Explosive heat and destruction erupted around us, and we fell to the floor. I felt nothing but the warmth of his skin against mine. Amid the roar of detonation and the wail of sirens around us, I heard only the strumming against me, slow and steady. I could feel only Donovan's body surrounding me while the world blew apart around us.

As I began to lose consciousness, I blinked up again. My gaze locked with Donovan's as he looked down on me with concern and unwavering focus. The house around us fractured, consumed by bright hot flame and roaring destruction. I saw none of it. The last things I saw, before I closed my eyes one final time, was Donovan's strong arms embracing me and the two great, luminously feathered wings that shielded me from harm.

Fourteen

When I opened my eyes again, I squinted against the radiant light that surrounded me. It enveloped me like a soft, downy quilt. There was no sky, no earth, only warm brightness. There was no worry, fear, or sadness anymore. For the first time since my family's accident, I felt completely at peace.

Time was suspended, or it simply failed to exist at all. The horror of the past hours melted away. Nothing mattered except for this place, this contentment. I wanted nothing more than to lose myself in the tranquility of it, to sink back into it and let it embrace me forever.

"Alexandra," a voice called to me. There was no mistaking the rich velvet of it.

I looked up to the hand that offered itself to me, and I reached for it. When our hands met, flesh against flesh, I felt a jolt of warmth rush through me. He lifted me to my feet from where I lay cradled by the serene, radiant glow. Staring into his blue eyes, I lifted a hand to touch his face. He cradled my palm there.

"Is this real?" I whispered, amazed at the smoothness of my own voice.

Donovan smiled. "It's more real than anything you've ever known."

I took in the atmosphere surrounding us. Warm light danced from all around. There was neither a beginning nor an end to it. We were alone, yet I could feel the presence of many. My heart warmed with their endless, bounding love.

Like a rite of passage, I could sense the multitude that waited to congratulate me on the other side of forever. I couldn't see them, but I knew they congregated in the distance amidst the brilliant light.

"Am I dead?" I asked.

Donovan smiled and kissed my palm. "No, you're not dead."

"Where are we? Is this where you come from? It's beautiful . . . beyond words."

"It has never been as beautiful as it is right now," he said, holding my eyes with his.

I was confused. This had to be heaven. I had to be dead. If it meant I could stay here with Donovan forever, I was at peace with that.

"I have to be dead. It's okay . . ."

Donovan shook his head. "You're not dead, Alexandra. You still have so much life to live. You've not yet fulfilled your life's purpose."

"Did you save me?"

I remembered the explosion, though it felt so very long ago. The fire had engulfed the small cabin. I remembered seeing Donovan, as clearly as I saw the orange flames and splintered ash.

"You saved yourself. You believed, Alexandra. In your purpose, in me . . . in Him." Donovan motioned to the space surrounding us. "Even as the world was crumbling around you, you believed that I was with you. And more than ever, I was. You did that."

I tried to remember the terrifying details of those final moments, but it was hard to conjure the horrific images in this place which emanated only tranquility. Then I remembered the grotesque way in which Sully's face had contorted with hatred as he attacked me, and it all came back to me. I remembered how it felt to pierce through his flesh with his own knife. I remembered being frozen with fear and dread as the lighter flew into the air, dooming us all.

More so, I remembered the calm that washed over me in the split seconds before the house exploded into flames. I remembered thinking that no matter what happened, I felt overwhelmingly thankful. I'd been more blessed in life than most. I was able to see and feel tangible evidence of the most incredible love of all. I was able to see, hear and feel a love like no other. A love that had sent a Guardian to protect me and the life I was meant to live.

In those last violent moments I was able to look death in the eye unafraid, because if it was time, if I'd served my purpose, I could accept it because I knew the kind of love that awaited me on the other side. When I turned to see Donovan waiting for me, arms open, I let go of everything else. All the doubt and fear that had plagued my entire life vanished.

"I saw you, like I can see you now," I smiled.

"I told you that you would when you were ready."

My smile faded. "It was Sully . . . the whole time. I don't understand why."

"Some things you will never understand." Donovan squeezed my hand. "Sully was sick. He was torn between the truth and his love for you, and the jealousy and hate that skewed his perception. I should have seen it. I am so sorry I failed you. I let your love for him blind me.

"You have never failed me," I whispered. "I did love him . . . I still do. I can't believe he killed them."

The tranquility in my heart began to fade.

"My mom . . . she always said that she loved him as a brother. And Gary. How could he murder his own flesh and blood?"

"Some people are so blinded to the good, to the beauty of the world, that they overlook the gifts that are meant for them because they become consumed with want of another's. That's what happened to Sully. It happens to so many others who can't see past their own pain. They let evil in because it's all they choose to know."

Donovan sighed and ran a hand through my hair. "Sometimes it's easier to see the darkness around you than it is to look up to the light."

"And some people try to hide from the darkness. They run from it . . ."

Donovan nodded. "You're talking about Will."

"Is he dead?" I asked, my voice barely a whisper.

"Yes, Alexandra," he said, wiping the tear that fell into my cheek. "He's dead. I'm so sorry."

"You knew he was going to die, didn't you? That's why you didn't want me to get too close . . ."

"I sensed it. I didn't know how or why, but I knew his time was short. That's why I wanted you far away from him," Donovan sighed. "But he gave his life to protect you, and for that I will be eternally grateful."

"Is he . . . here? Is he okay?" I could not hold back my sobs.

Donovan held me close. "He is here. I can feel his presence just beyond us. You can feel it too, Alexandra, if you search with your heart and not with your eyes."

I closed my eyes, releasing a row of crystalline tears. Feeling out beyond my grief, I reached out with all of my heart to the space beyond us. Overwhelming love and joy met me.

"He sends his love to you," Donovan whispered into my ear.

In my mind, in my heart, I spotted Will. He stood off in the illuminated distance and turned to me with a smile. I never saw such happiness in his eyes. They were alive with elation, as if lit from within.

"I see him!" I gasped, my sobs turning into those of joy.

As I watched, Will bent down. He wrapped his arms around a small child who walked beside him through the warm light. He lifted him high and then held him close. The boy laughed and smiled as he hugged his father around the neck. Will turned to me once more and winked. Then with one last reassuring nod, he disappeared into the expanse of incandescent ivory.

"He's okay," I whispered.

"Will is not the only one who's okay," Donovan whispered again in my ear. "Someone else wants you to know that."

My breath caught as another figure came into view. She walked towards me smiling, her golden hair shimmered in the dancing light.

"Mom?" I cried out.

My mother waved to me from where she stood in the distance. Her warm smile filled my heart. She held a hand to hers.

"Mom! I love you so much . . ." I cried out, laughing with unrestrained joy and tears.

While I watched with my mind, my mother waved to me again. Then she grasped the hand of a second figure who joined her. Gary turned to me and smiled, offering me a grateful bow. They waved to me once more. Then together they walked off into the vast warmth.

"Mom, don't go! I miss you so much!" I cried.

I felt Donovan's arms tighten around me.

"She will be right here waiting for you. It will be as if you were never apart. She'll be waiting for you. Alexandra. We all will be." His voice broke with those last words. I opened my eyes and stared into his face. Something was wrong.

"What do you mean?"

When Donovan didn't answer, I took a step away from him. His arms fell.

"You said, 'we.'" What do you mean?"

The sorrow on his face deepened and he had to collect himself before answering. "My purpose has been fulfilled, Alexandra. I . . ."

"No!" I was suddenly furious. The brightness around me dimmed as if reflecting my despair.

"You can't leave me. You said you weren't going anywhere. I need you!"

Donovan lowered his head. "It's time for me to go, Alexandra. It's time for me to join the others. You don't need me anymore. If I stay, I'll only distract you from living a normal, happy life. Everything you need is with you in your heart. Your mother,

Gary, Will . . . me. You're going to live a long and wonderful life. I've served my purpose in it."

I shook my head, trying to understand. "Is this because you couldn't sense Sully? That was my fault, you said!"

"No, Alexandra . . ."

"Is it because you interfered to save me? Take it back! Damn it, take it back. I want to stay here with you. It's okay if you didn't save me. My purpose is to be here with you, and with Mom and Gary. Damn it, you can't leave me too." I was hysterical, my voice raising to a fevered pitch. "You have been with me my whole life. My purpose is to be with you!"

Donovan grabbed me and pulled me close to him. I beat my hands against his chest and cried. He held me close until the fight went out of me and I gave in to despair, sinking into his arms. I heard a sob escape his throat, though he tried to stifle it.

For the first time, the sound of him did not soothe me. It filled my ears with a faint, almost inaudible rhythm. The strumming had slowed to almost nothing. I feared this would be the last time I would hear it. He had been with me my whole life. I realized as my heart broke and the tears ran out that a lifetime had not been enough.

"I'm not strong enough to be without you," I whimpered.

"You have never been as strong as you are now. You believed when your whole world was falling down around you. It's time for you to take your life back now. There is so much joy and happiness left for you to discover. Keep believing, and miracles will happen for you."

I wiped my eyes and looked into his face. I committed every rugged detail of it to my memory. "I have no one left."

"There is nothing that is lost that cannot be restored," Donovan smiled weakly.

In the distance I heard a soft voice. At first the voice was too faint to make out. I turned to look into the expanse of light around me. The voice got clearer as it called my name, beckoning for me to go back. It was a familiar voice, full of love and concern. I turned back to Donovan.

"Go, Alexandra . . ." he whispered, taking a step back.

I was torn between my desires to run towards the familiar voice and to stay with Donovan for as long as possible. The voice grew louder, and I turned towards it again. When I looked back, Donovan was walking into the luminous depth behind me. He turned to me and smiled, the tears in his eyes tearing at me.

"Wait . . ." I called to him.

"Go," he whispered.

"Alex . . . Alex, wake up," the voice beckoned to me, and I hesitated, my eyes locked on Donovan.

"I have always loved you, Donovan," I said, wishing I had said it sooner.

"For me, my time with you has been no longer than a few precious days, but I will love you for eternity, Alexandra," Donovan whispered.

"Thank you again, for my life."

"No," he said gently, "thank you for mine."

With those final words, he walked away. The brightness engulfed him as I stood there unmoving, willing my heart to beat on.

"Alex!" the voice pleaded. "Come back to me!"

Turning to the familiar voice, I took a deep breath. Then I walked away from the brightness towards it.

Fifteen

"Alex, wake up, dear. You have to wake up."

When I opened my eyes, I found myself once again blinking against the brightness of my surroundings. This time, however, my eyes were assaulted by the unnatural glare of fluorescent lighting. As my eyes adjusted, I took in the marbled ceiling tiles and whitewashed walls. I was in a hospital room.

"Alex, honey!"

I turned toward the familiar voice, grimacing at the pounding in my temple. The pain was forgotten the instant I came face to face with the woman sitting beside my bed. My eyes widened, and I sat up and took in the familiarity on her face.

"Gram?" I whispered, my throat raw.

The elderly woman giggled with relief and patted my hand. "Thank God, you are alright. I was so worried . . . You're so banged up."

I looked down at myself, to the numerous bandages and bruises and to the I.V. stuck in my arm. I felt like hell, but as I moved my arms and legs, I noted that nothing seemed broken. I turned my attention back to Gram.

"You called me Alex. You recognize me?"

"Yes, dear, everything is so much clearer to me now."

The small woman gathered me up in her fragile arms. Gram squeezed me and clung to me. We both wept as we embraced one another.

"Gram, I'm so sorry about Sully. I . . ." I tried to explain as I pulled away. How could I explain to her what had happened?

"Ssshhh, hush now. None of this was your fault. Do you understand me?" Gram insisted, wiping her tears with a tissue she clutched in her hand. "If my mind would have been worth anything at all, I could have stopped him. This is my fault, Alex."

I wiped my own tears with the back of my hand. "What are you talking about, Gram? You said something like this before in the cemetery. You tried to warn me. Do you remember?"

"I don't know what happened. So much of these last years have been so fuzzy," Gram whispered.

"Sullivan wasn't giving your grandmother her medication. He didn't want her to remember what she saw that night. He knew that if he kept her confused, no one would have given her a second thought if she did say anything."

Nadine stood in the open doorway, a bouquet of white lilies in her hands. She came into the room and set the flowers on the table just inside the door. Then she had a seat on a chair in the corner of the room.

"She's as good as gold now though," Nadine laughed. "Bugged the mess out of the nurses at the home until they finally agreed to let her come visit. You'd think she was never lost. It's just a miracle."

I looked from Nadine back to Gram. The spark was back in Gram's eyes. She was now exactly how I remembered her growing up. I hugged her tightly, then held her out at arm's length.

"What did you see that night, Gram? The night of the accident. . . . Do you remember?"

As she recalled that night, Gram looked off into the distance, seeing something I could not.

"It was just before I got the call that there'd been an accident. I wasn't expecting Gary to be home until quite late. He liked to stay with you and your mom for as long as possible, you know. He insisted that he still live with me after the wedding, until his brother got back from his tour," Gram smiled, and I waited for her to continue. "I was in bed reading when I heard movement downstairs. I thought maybe Gary had come home early. I wanted to ask him how your recital went. He was so excited for you when he left."

I patted her hand and held back my tears as she went on.

"When I walked into the kitchen . . . Sullivan was standing by the back door. I was in shock. It took me a minute to realize it was him. He'd been in Iraq for almost a year, but suddenly there he was, standing in the kitchen. He had the strangest look on his face when he saw me. Like he'd gotten caught with a hand in the cookie jar." Gram turned to me, her voice lowering. "Then I noticed that his shirt was covered in blood. I . . . I asked him if he had been hurt. I was about to ask him what he was doing there, but he ran out the back door before I could. That's when I got the phone call."

Gram looked away. "Everything happened so quickly after that. I started to question if I'd really seen him at all. When he showed up a couple of days later, he acted like he hadn't seen me in months. He said he'd just left Iraq. I was so confused. Alex, I'm sorry. I . . . I should have said something."

"No, Gram. None of this is your fault. He deceived us all," I said. "I'm just so grateful that you're okay. I should have come home years ago. I should have helped take care for you."

We embraced again and cried together, over Sully, over our lost time together, over everything. I finally had my Gram back. After all of these years, she was back. After a long moment, Gram took hold of my shoulders and looked me in the face.

"We have one another now, and that's all that matters. I can't believe just how beautiful and strong a woman you've turned out to be. I've missed you so much, my darling girl."

I smiled at her. "I can't believe I have you back."

Sadness washed over me when I thought about the love I lost. As happy as I was to have Gram back, how could I go on without Donovan? Was he really gone?

"Well, well. You're awake," a male voice called from the doorway.

I turned to see a tall, middle-aged doctor smiling at me.

"I must say, young lady, you have us all pretty stumped," he said, coming into the room to check my pupils with his ophthalmoscope. "You are very lucky to be alive. You survived a major explosion with just some moderate bruising and a few scratches."

"I just wish I wasn't the only one," I whispered.

"I am very sorry for your loss." The doctor nodded sympathetically. "Some officers from the Hendersonville police department stopped by to ask you some questions. I asked them to come back in the morning. I figured you'd need some time. I would like to hold you overnight for observations. I suspect that you'll check out just fine and be able to go home in the morning."

"That's great, Doctor," Gram said.

I didn't know if it was good news or not. Donovan was my home. What would it be like to go back to the house without him, or Sully, or Will? I wondered if I should go back to Chicago. There was too much to consider, too much I didn't want to think about. I longed more than anything to just close my eyes and be back in that glorious light with Donovan, where things made sense and I was at peace.

"I'm afraid visiting hours are over for tonight. We need to let this young lady get some rest," the doctor mandated, and Gram looked at me, worried.

"It's okay, Gram. I'll be fine. I'm just tired and sore."

"Okay," Gram said, standing. "I'll make sure someone gets me here as soon as possible in the morning. I'll annoy the mess out of them again if I have to."

I held onto Gram's hand and gave it a squeeze. "I love you so much, Gram."

Gram smiled down at me and sighed happily. "I love you too, precious girl. Now get some rest," she said. Then she leaned down and kissed my forehead before leaving the room.

"Your vitals are looking good. How does the rest of you feel?" The doctor looked down on me with practiced concern.

"Like I've been through an explosion," I said.

The doctor collected his clipboard and patted my foot on his way out. "I'll send the nurse in to give you something for the pain. I'll have her give you something to help you sleep too."

"I've been asleep for like eighteen hours already," I argued. "Is that really necessary?"

The doctor paused at the door and turned to look at me.

"You've been through a lot. Your body and mind need to rest," he said, giving me another reassuring smile before he left the room.

I sat there a moment, not sure which emotion was going to take hold of me first: sorrow, bitterness, despair. *Gratitude. That's what I should be feeling*, I thought. I was alive against all odds. Gram was alive, lucid, back from the recesses of her mind. I was thankful for all of that. I wished it was enough.

"It's okay to be upset," a quiet voice spoke from the corner of the room. "It's okay to be angry."

I jumped, startled, turning in the direction of the voice.

"Nadine," I breathed, relaxing. "I forgot you were here."

"I'm sorry, honey," she said as she stood and walked over to me. "I didn't mean to startle you."

I collected myself and tried to look happy. "It's okay. I guess I'm still in shock."

"I know, child," she said, taking hold of my hand. "It's okay to be upset. You've lost a whole lot in a matter of a few hours. At least, you think you have."

I sat up and looked at her. "What does that mean?"

Nadine had a seat on the edge of my bed. "Well, Sullivan was not the uncle that you thought he was. He was a sick, sick man. Even though you can't lose something that you never really had, it's okay to mourn who you thought he was."

"Something I never really had . . ." I repeated, my eyes welling with tears.

"You're feeling a greater loss right now, aren't you?" Nadine interrupted.

Tears ran down my face as I looked up into her sympathetic face. "Yes."

Nadine smiled and squeezed my hand.

"The greatest gifts we get in life are also the hardest to let go of," she said. "Sometimes we mourn them so completely that we consume ourselves with what we've lost and overlook what we are given in their place."

I wiped my face with my bruised hand. "How do you know so much?"

"It's important to remember that some gifts," Nadine smiled and pointed to the heavens, "can never truly be lost."

I stared at Nadine, at her warm smile and bright eyes. "How . . .?"

"How are we doing in here?" A stout nurse interrupted as she walked in with a pitcher of water and a cup. She set them down beside the white lilies on the table and turned to me.

"Oh, well . . ." I stammered, "my head aches a little, but other than that I'm okay."

"The doctor said you were having some pain," the nurse said cheerily, retrieving a syringe from her scrubs pocket. "I'm just going to give you a pain reliever and a moderate dose of relaxant. It should knock you right out. The doctor wants you to get lots of rest."

The nurse inserted the syringe into the IV and smiled casually at me. I looked at Nadine and then back to the nurse.

"I'm sorry, I know visiting hours are over. My friend was just about to leave," I said, motioning to Nadine.

The nurse looked confused. She lowered her eyes at me and then turned and looked behind her. She seemed to search the room for someone, but saw no one. She looked back to me concerned.

"Hmm, I think you need to rest that head of yours," she said with a smirk. "I'll be back to check on you shortly."

The nurse walked to the door, then turned to scrutinize me once more before leaving the room. In shock, I turned to Nadine. She smiled back, knowingly.

"She couldn't see you!"

Nadine shook her head. "No, child. She doesn't have your gift."

I sat up straighter. "You're a . . . a."

"A Guardian? Of course I am," she giggled. "Why, I've been looking after your sweet Gram since she was barely older than you are now."

I couldn't breathe, I couldn't think.

"Boy, did she give me a run for my money too," Nadine continued. "Living with a murderer for the last decade and a half."

My mind raced. I thought of every time I'd been with Nadine. I thought about when we first met at Sully's house. I realized that Sully never introduced us, had never directly spoken to Nadine. At church, Nadine sat next to me. She never spoke with anyone else, just me. I realized with astonishment that no one had ever addressed Nadine except for me.

"Does . . . Gram know?" I stammered.

Nadine smiled and patted my hand. "Oh, I suspect she knows on some level. That woman has strong faith, always has."

"But . . . I can see you with no problem?"

"That's because it's easier for you to believe that I'd be looking after your Gram. Your mind accepts it easily . . . even if you didn't recognize me for what I am."

"How many more like you are out there?" I asked, still stunned.

"He sends us wherever we are needed, some straight from the heavens themselves. Others are everyday people just like you or any random man on the street. We can all be called upon to be protectors at any time, at any given moment. He can use anyone, and any circumstance."

"Right, then when they aren't needed anymore, they're torn away," I whispered, unable to keep the anger from my voice.

Nadine shook her head. "You're letting yourself be blinded by your loss. Don't let yourself miss the blessing in store for you."

"I know, I have Gram back. She's well and in good health. I should be more grateful." I lowered my head.

"Your Gram has her granddaughter back as well as her mind, which is why she is no longer in need of me," Nadine sighed.

"So, you're just going to leave her? Just like that?" I cried. "That's what you do . . ."

"No, child," Nadine answered, looking deep into my eyes, "I'm going home to prepare for when she gets there."

My breath caught in my throat, but Nadine smiled at me. "Now, don't you go fretting just yet. Gram's got quite a few more years to spend with you first. That, my child, is her blessing. I pray you don't miss yours."

I shook my head in frustration, the medication quickly fogging my mind.

"I don't know what that is," I sighed, defeated and weary.

Nadine gave my hand one last pat. "You will. When you decide to open your mind, to look past your loss, you will see it. Don't let yourself be so blinded by what you have lost that you don't see what you have to gain. Remember, all things are possible. Now, lay yourself down and get some rest. Things will be clearer in the morning."

I slipped down into the covers, the muscle relaxant making my limbs foreign to my body. I felt heavy, like I could sink into the mattress and through to the floor. The ache in my head eased. It became hard to hold my eyes open. There were still so many questions, so much I didn't understand, but my mind was spinning, unable to focus on any one thought. I knew it was useless to resist my exhaustion.

"Thank you, Nadine," I said, knowing my time with her was coming to an end. "Thank you for looking over Gram."

"There's no need to thank me, child." Nadine tucked the covers up over me and then walked to straighten the flowers on the table. "We'll meet again, Alexandra."

"It was you. You were the one who left the flowers at the accident site . . . on their graves."

Nadine turned to me and grinned. "I wanted you to see that your parents are loved. You must always see the beauty among the devastation."

Nadine switched off the light and walked to the door. She turned to me once more.

"You've been given such a gift, Alexandra. Don't miss out on the miracles right in front of you. Take care of our Gram."

I could barely keep my eyes open. I wanted to plead with Nadine to stay. I wanted to understand.

"I'll see you" was all I could muster before Nadine giggled once more and closed the door.

The next morning I awoke to the sunlight on my face. It took me a minute to remember where I was. As the stark white walls took focus, I realized that I'd been knocked out in a dreamless sleep in my hospital room.

"Time to get up," the nurse said. "I'm going to need to check your vitals before they come in to question you."

I sat up, noting that my head felt much better, as did my body. "Question me?"

The nurse walked over to me and wrapped a cuff around my arm. "There are a couple of officers here waiting to take your statement. You're free to get dressed if you'd like. Your grandmother was here bright and early. She left some of your clothes for you."

She motioned to my suitcase, which laid in a chair in the corner.

"Is she still here?" I asked, sitting up.

"She went to get you some breakfast. I don't think she approved of our selection." The nurse grinned and removed my I.V. "I'll give you a few minutes before I send the officers in. I'm sure you want to get it over with as soon as possible, bless your heart."

"Yes, thank you," I said, and the nurse left the room.

Rubbing my arm where the needle had been, I slowly stepped out of the bed. My legs were stiff. It took me a minute to put all of my weight on them. I stared at the lilies on the table and recalled my conversation with Nadine. In the light of day I was still stunned at the revelation that Nadine had been Gram's guardian all along. If I could see her, how many more could I see? How many had I seen walking among the rest of us? I wished I hadn't fallen asleep, that the drugs hadn't been so quick to work. There was so much more I wanted to understand.

Hobbling to the chair, I picked out a comfortable outfit and went into the small bathroom. Instinctively, I looked into the mirror above the sink and waited. I longed to see Donovan's smiling face looking back at me. When I accepted that my own bruised face was the only I would see, I continued to get dressed.

I told the officers everything that happened the night Sully and Will were killed. I told them about my parents' accident, and they confirmed that the car Sully turned into the salvage yard was in fact the same car that ran us off the road that fateful night. I was not surprised that Will was right. I just wished that I'd believed him when he told me.

As the officers finished taking my statement, Gram walked in with another familiar face. Evelyn smiled sympathetically from behind a layer of hot pink lipstick.

"Oh, sweetheart, I am so sorry. I just had no idea. I feel so responsible. I just can't believe it." Evelyn scurried over to me in her six-inch heels and hugged me.

"It's okay. No one had any idea," I said.

"I called Evelyn as soon as I got up this morning. I knew she'd help me convince those goons back at the retirement home to let me escape for the day. You should have seen their tongues wagging out of their faces," Gram laughed.

"It was no problem. You can imagine my surprise to hear her speaking to me like nothing ever happened to her after all these years." Evelyn poked a thumb at Gram.

"You look much better. I think that rest did you a lot of good. I brought you some breakfast." Gram set the brown paper bag and a cup of coffee down on the bedside table.

I had a seat on the bed and opened up the bag, happy to see the bagel sandwich inside. By the time I finished my breakfast and was savoring the last bit of hot coffee on my raw throat, the nurse came back in with a wheel chair.

"You are all set. Your release papers are at the front desk along with a prescription for a mild pain reliever. Remember, no sports or any other activity where you could bang that head for a few weeks."

"I don't know how I'm going to break the news to the roller derby team," I mumbled, earning a cross look from the nurse.

"Well, her sense of humor is back. That's a good sign." Gram chuckled. "Evelyn and I are going to get the car and pull it around. We'll see you out front in a minute."

"Okay, see you in a minute," I said, grabbing my bag.

The nurse motioned me to the wheel chair, and I rolled my eyes. "Is that really necessary? I'm walking just fine right now."

"It's hospital policy. If want to leave, you sit," she answered with a grin.

Grudgingly, I had a seat and let the nurse wheel me into the line at the receptionist's desk. I adjusted in the seat and looked around the waiting room. The lobby was busier than I expected for so early in the morning. Some people sat back with magazines and cups of coffee. Children busied themselves in the corner where several toys and children's books were strategically placed. Most people though, were fixated on the flat-screen TV, which hung on the wall next to me. They were all enthralled with the latest reports about the shooting at Fort Bragg.

I started to look away, not having the heart to hear of any more pain and destruction. Before I did, something caught my eye. Below the television sat a decorative table, meant for hiding the wires of the TV. On top of the table, almost out of place, sat an enormous vase filled with dozens of white lilies. I stared at them, remembering what Nadine said to me the night before. *Remember to see the beauty among the devastation.*

Leaving my bag in the wheelchair, I asked the nurse to hold my place in line. Then I slowly made my way to the television. On the screen was a picture of the outside of a hospital. The white words beneath it read: *Womack Army Medical Center*. I got closer so I could hear what the reporter was saying.

"*. . . sad day for soldiers at Fort Bragg and for the many thankful families who owe the life of their loved one to this man. Today, at oh-twelve-hundred, SFC Donovan Pritchard will be taken off of life support as hundreds gather at Womack Army Medical Center to pay their last respects to the fallen hero.*"

I gasped when I heard the name of the wounded soldier and stumbled faster to the television, not caring that I was blocking others in the waiting room. Stopping just inches from the screen, I watched, eyes wide, as the reporter continued.

"SFC Pritchard was mortally wounded Thursday when a fellow Fort Bragg soldier opened fire on his regiment as they gathered for morning drills. Pritchard contained the gunman even as he was shot numerous times in the torso and legs. His selfless act saved countless lives, and he has been awarded the Soldier's Medal for his heroic act."

My surroundings froze and disintegrated around me as a picture of SFC Pritchard flashed onto the screen. Though he wore a desert-camo uniform, I immediately recognized the intense blue eyes that peered out from below a dusty helmet. I was staring into the face of my Donovan . . . my hero . . . a man.

"SFC Pritchard leaves behind no family, but will be forever remembered and honored among soldiers and family here at Fort Bragg and by a nation who will be forever grateful." The reporter finished and continued to the next story.

I remained in a state of shock, my mind reeling. *Could it really be him?* My Donovan had been with me my whole life. The shooting happened only a few days ago. *How was that possible?* I couldn't make sense of it, couldn't conceive of the possibility that Donovan was alive, at least for now, only hours away. It just couldn't be.

Then all of the conversations of the past days flooded back into my mind. I remembered the things that Donovan said to me:

Time for you is linear. It doesn't exist that way for me . . . For me it is as close as yesterday. Your whole life, for me, has been a handful of days.

I shook my head. It seemed too impossible, but the meaning of Nadine's words from the night before started to make sense.

We can all be called upon to be his angels at any time, to protect his people at any given moment. He can use anyone, and any circumstance . . . Don't miss out on the miracle right in front of you.

Letting out a rush of breath, I frantically searched the wall for a clock. I found one above the receptionist's desk. It was already almost eight a.m. There was no time for doubt. I ran to the front door, the stiffness in my legs forgotten.

"Excuse me, miss, you have to sign these papers!" The receptionist yelled, and I raced back to the counter.

"I have to wheel you out too," the nurse reminded me.

I grabbed the clipboard and scribbled my name and then hopped back into the wheelchair.

"Please, I have to go now!" I urged.

The receptionist glared at me as she looked over the paperwork.

"Where are you in such a rush to?

"To find my blessing," I cried as the nurse wheeled me out the door.

Gram and Evelyn waited out front in Evelyn's car. I got up from the chair and threw myself into the back seat. They turned from the front seat, startled.

"What in the world is going on, dear?" Gram asked.

"I know this is going to sound crazy, but, Evelyn, I need you to take me to Fort Bragg. Like, right now."

"Fort Bragg? That's all the way in Fayetteville. It's a four-hour drive from here. What on earth do you want to go down there for?" Evelyn's voice raised in pitch.

Gram turned in her seat and held out a hand to me. "What is this about, Alex? You can tell me."

I stared deep into Gram's eyes and prayed that she would understand. "Gram, are you feeling okay? Is this too much for you?"

"Gracious dear, I haven't felt this great in over a decade. What's troubling you?"

Tears welled up in my eyes, I didn't know if I could explain.

"I need to go to Womack Hospital. He's about to be taken off of life support. I have to get there before they . . ." The tears flowed down my cheeks, and Gram squeezed my hand. I tried to continue. "Gram, I can't explain it . . . but I know him."

Evelyn gasped. "You mean that poor soldier that stopped that gunman? You know him?"

I stared into Gram's eyes, "I think I'm meant to go there. I have to go right now . . . before it's too late."

Gram stared back at me and nodded. She didn't ask any questions. She just gave my hand a squeeze and turned back to Evelyn. "Evelyn, we're going to Fort Bragg. Let's make it in a jiffy too."

Evelyn looked at Gram in shock and then registered her serious tone. She nodded obediently and put the car into drive with a shrug.

"I always did like the sight of a man in uniform," she smiled, pulling the car onto the main road towards the highway.

Sixteen

I remained silent as I stared out the window, lost in thought. Evelyn and Gram discussed the events of the last years, but I could think only of Donovan. I wrestled with the craziness of what I was doing. It was insane. Could the man lying in that hospital bed really be the same spirit who protected me from harm my entire life? I knew it was him. There was no mistaking those eyes and that kind smile. I didn't know how it was possible, but Donovan would say it didn't mean it wasn't. I had to get to him before it was too late. I had to make it.

It was almost noon by the time we pulled into the checkpoint at Fort Bragg. I let them photocopy my driver's license, and after a thorough search of Evelyn's car, we were allowed on base. I was sure that Evelyn's flirting had much to do with our success.

"They said the hospital is all the way down the road on the left," Evelyn informed us when she climbed back behind the wheel.

As we approached the hospital, I took in the rows of cars parked along the curb and the crowds that walked, candles in hand, down the sidewalk towards the building. Evelyn pulled into the ER driveway, but came to a sudden stop when faced with the bumper-to-bumper traffic there. I looked up to the hospital entrance, to where hundreds of people gathered in the parking lot, some with posters, and all with tears in their eyes.

"What do you want me to do now? I can try to go back up the road to park?" Evelyn asked.

Panicked, I looked at the clock on the dash. It was five minutes to noon. I didn't know what to do.

Gram grabbed my hand. "Go, Alex. If this is what you are meant to do, then don't let anything stop you. Go. Hurry."

Hopping out of the car, I ran as fast as my bruised legs would carry me. I pushed my way past the crowd, stopping short when I reached the security guard at the front door.

He looked down on me with reprimand in his eyes.

"If you're not having an emergency, the hospital is closed to civilians," he spat.

I hesitated, frantically plotting my next move as he stepped toward me. Before he could force me to turn back, a friendly face stepped up from the crowd. Smiling down on me, the man placed his hand on the security guard's shoulder. The guard's fierce look melted. He grinned at me and nodded for me to pass.

"Just this once," the guard conceded.

I stared into the friendly face of the man beside the guard, knowing I was the only one who could see him. He nodded to me, and I ran through the front doors of the hospital.

When I reached the front desk, I had to take a second to catch my breath.

"Where can I direct you?" The unemotional secretary didn't even look at me.

"Donovan Pritchard's room, please," I pleaded.

The secretary turned her attention from the screen in front of her and glared at me, her face a mask on impatience. "Are you family?"

"Not exactly," I said, desperation in my voice. "But I've known him all my life, please. I came as soon as I could."

"No visitors allowed," she mumbled, annoyed.

"You don't understand . . ." I begged.

"I'm sorry, miss, but no vis. . ." the woman began again. Before she could finish, another kind face stepped up behind the secretary. I watched as the woman laid a hand on the secretary's shoulder. The secretary turned back to me, an expression of peace on her face.

"You know, just this once couldn't hurt." She smiled. "Donovan Pritchard is in room 206. Second floor, take a right at the end of the hall."

"Thank you!" I cried, my eyes fixed on the kind eyes of the stranger who grinned and nodded from beside the secretary.

Bolting forward, I took the stairs by twos, gritting my teeth against the pain in my head and the bruises on my body. None of it mattered.

When I reached the top, I forced myself down the long hallway until I found room 206. Gasping, I watched as a handful of doctors and men in uniform left the room. They looked at me, their faces solemn, before walking off.

My heart threatened to crumble in my chest as I reached for the door and stepped inside.

"They just took out all of the tubes," a voice from the corner of the room said to me. "It won't be long now."

For a few seconds all I could do was stand there, listening to the steady beep of the heart rate monitor. When I mustered the courage to walk forward, I looked down on the man who lay in the bed before me. A sob ripped from my throat.

It was him. Donovan lay in front of me, looking even more bruised and battered than I did.

"Did you know him?" the voice asked me.

I tore my eyes away from Donovan to face the man who stood a few feet from the bed. He was dressed in full military dress, his sleeve insignia indicating him as an officer.

"He's been there for me all my life," I whispered, turning back to Donovan.

"He saved my life and the life of my men. It's a damned shame. He deserves to live a long and happy life," the officer said, moving toward the door. "He doesn't have any family still living, so I've been here praying for his recovery every day. I prayed he would have a second chance at life, to find his happiness. It's a damned shame."

"What are his injuries? Is there no chance he'll recover?" I asked, breathless.

"He was shot in the chest numerous times and took one to the leg. They got all the bullets out and were able to rebuild his lung, but he never started breathing on his own again. I guess the fight just wasn't in him. His soul must have had somewhere else it wanted to be. He'll be at peace soon," the officer explained. With a sigh, he shook his head. "You should know, he never let go of the shooter. Even when he lay there gasping for breath, he refused to let go. He saved a lot of lives. You should be very proud. I'll leave you alone."

I barely heard the officer leave as I approached Donovan on the bed. All I could hear above the soft, steady beeping of the heart monitor was my own shaky breath. He looked so helpless and weak. I wasn't used to seeing him so . . . human.

I stared down at him a minute and then reached out with a trembling hand and grasped his. Gasping, I bowed my head, letting the tears flow. For the first time, his hand was ice cold. I looked up and wiped the tears from my cheeks. His perfect face was littered with small cuts, and a large bruise had formed above his right eye. Bending over, I kissed the bruise there and took a deep breath.

"I don't believe you're here," I sobbed, squeezing his hand to me. "I don't understand how any of this is possible, but you taught me something, you know. You taught me to see the beauty in the impossible. Right now, you are the most beautiful thing my eyes have ever seen."

I took a deep breath, collected myself.

"Maybe that's why I'm here, you know? Maybe God wanted me to have this chance to see you . . . like this. To know that you were real." I cried silently, staring into the face that had seen me through my worst nightmares.

The heart rate monitor's rhythm slowed, and I gasped. Donovan's heartbeat was slowing. Before I could panic, I noticed that there was something familiar about the steady, rhythmic sound. I put my hand to my mouth when I realized why.

Leaning over, I laid my head on Donovan's chest. There, beating against my ear was the slow and steady strumming that was distinctly Donovan. The strumming slowed and began to fade as I listened and sobbed uncontrollably against his chest.

"Please, no," I whispered. "Please don't take him. Please don't. Not him too. Please . . . let him live. You sent him to save me, to give me my life back. Now I'm begging you, bring him back to me. I know you can. I know you led me here for a reason. Bring him back to me . . . Please, bring him back."

When I was cried out, I lay there, barely breathing as I listened to the strumming of Donovan's heartbeat against my ear. As I memorized every tone and fluctuation, it faded slowly. Then it stopped.

I lay there unmoving, unable to cry or react, entombed in disbelief. A string of nurses and uniforms entered the room. They stared at me a moment.

"He's gone," one of them whispered to me, placing a gentle hand on my shoulder.

"No," I whispered. "He's not gone. Just give him a minute."

"Miss, I'm sorry. You have to let us take him now."

"No!" I cried. "He's not gone. He's not . . . just wait . . ."

The uniformed officer entered the room and looked down on me from where I lay, head resting on Donovan's chest.

He cleared his throat. "It's obvious that you loved him very much. He was a great man . . . but it's his time. You have to let him go."

I looked up at the officer wearily as other soldiers entered the room.

"He's not gone . . . It's not his time yet." I said. "He told me once that there's nothing that is lost that can't be restored. All things are possible. This is my miracle. He is my miracle. My mind is open, and I can see that now. He's not gone."

While I talked to the officer, one of the soldiers grasped me around the waist and lifted me away from Donovan. I kicked, fighting to get free of him as I cried out.

"He's not gone! Just wait! Just wait . . ."

The soldier shushed me sympathetically as he carried me away. I went limp in his arms. As he carted me toward the door, a beep sounded in the room. The soldier froze. Everyone in the room turned to the monitor.

Another beep. Then another.

The soldier lowered me to the ground, and we all stared in amazement as the monitor began to beep in a steady, constant rhythm.

Breaking free of the soldier, I ran to Donovan and laid my head in his chest. The steady strumming filled my ear with renewed strength. I laid there, letting relief wash over me as the strumming calmed me as it always had.

When a warm hand reached for mine, I shot up. Donovan's cool, blue eyes glared at me in disbelief. His breath was labored but strong.

"Alexandra?" His velvet voice was a hoarse whisper. "Am I still dreaming?"

I kissed his warm hand.

"You're not dreaming," I whispered. "This is real. You . . . me. It's real."

"How?" he asked, his eyes searching mine.

"Someone told me where to find you," I said with a weary smile. "It's not a dream. It's impossible. I don't know how . . . how we could spend a lifetime together while you lay here suspended between life and death for only a few days. I don't know why any of this is happening . . ."

Donovan nodded up at me and smiled, running his fingers through my hair.

"I know why," he whispered. "A lifetime wasn't enough."

Donovan sat up slowly, wincing as he did. He looked into my eyes as the people around us gawked in disbelief, not knowing how to react. He wiped the tears from my cheeks and ran his finger over the features of my face, as if checking to make sure I was real.

"I thought you were a dying man's dream . . . your whole life, our life together. You saved me, Alexandra."

I smiled, the overwhelming joy in my heart reminding me of that peaceful, incandescent place.

"I guess that makes us even," I whispered.

Donovan collected me carefully into his arms. I closed my eyes as he drew me close. When our lips met, the entire world melted away into a warm, luminous glow.

The End

Epilogue

"Come on, Mommy! The paint is going to dry."

We laughed as my daughter and I raced down the driveway, purple hands waving in the spring breeze. I followed her golden tresses as she skipped down the gravel drive. When we reached the mailbox, we paused and stared at it for a minute, scrutinizing.

"I think they should go here," I suggested. The tiny, five year old nodded in approval. Her bright blue eyes focused on the exact spot.

"Okay." I laughed. "On the count of three. One . . . two . . . three!"

My daughter's small hand left a tiny, purple print right next to the small, faded print that I'd left more than twenty years ago. I chose to place my purple-covered hand right atop of the larger fading print, and I held it there for a few seconds. When I removed it, I saw that the hand prints were the exact same size.

"I think it looks perfect," my daughter giggled.

"You know what, Willow? I think you are absolutely right."

The little girl smiled and grabbed my purple hand with hers. We walked back up the driveway, purple hands joined.

"Mommy, tell me the story again."

"Again? You always want to hear it, don't you?" I chuckled as the house came into view.

Donovan watched us from where he sat on the porch swing. He smiled lovingly at his two girls and laughed.

"It is an incredible story, isn't it? I tell you what. Since you did such a great job of helping me decorate the mailbox, I'll tell you the story at bedtime. Right now we have a code purple to take care of," I said, swinging my baby girl by our joined purple hands.

"Hurry up now, you two! I need some help with these cookies!" Gram yelled from the front door.

We looked at each other excitedly before my daughter, with a joyous shout, ran for the kitchen. I stopped a moment and looked at my family gathered on the front porch and remembered a time when I thought I'd lost everything I'd ever wanted. Donovan smiled at me and patted the bench beside him. With a laugh of utter joy and contentment, I ran home.

The series continues with:

Messenger
Book Two

As a prisoner of North Carolina's central prison, Logan Foster thinks he's losing his mind when the woman he killed suddenly appears in his cell to warn him of catastrophic events to come. When he seeks help from psychologist Willow Prichard, she wants to dismiss Logan as delusional, but there is something oddly familiar about his stories of a visiting spirit.

When news spreads of the sudden deaths occurring at a popular marathon series around the country, Logan knows he's the only one who can stop the killer, but who will heed the warning that will save lives when it comes from a man who has taken them?

Available now!

A.L. Crouch

A.L. Crouch, author of the *Guardian* series, graduated with honors from North Carolina State University with a degree in English. She currently teaches high school creative writing in her hometown of Cary, North Carolina. She is a member of the NC Writers' Network and spends her summers off from teaching formulating tales of suspense and the supernatural. When she's not working to raise up young writers or keeping her readers jumping, she is spending time with her husband and two sons exploring the majestic mountains and coasts of North Carolina.

For more information and other titles by A.L. Crouch visit:
www.alcrouch.com

Made in the USA
Columbia, SC
08 December 2023

27980027R10155